As Good As It Got

Also by Isabel Sharpe

WOMEN ON THE EDGE OF A NERVOUS BREAKTHROUGH

As Good As It Got

ISABEL SHARPE

AVON

An Imprint of HarperCollins*Publishers*

HarperCollins books may be purchased for educational, business, or sales promo-
tional use. For information please write: Special Markets Department, HarperCollins
Publishers, 10 East 53rd Street, New York, NY 10022.

FIRST EDITION

Designed by Diahann Sturge

Library of Congress Cataloging-in-Publication Data
Sharpe, Isabel.
  As good as it got / Isabel Sharpe.—1st ed.
    p. cm.
ISBN 978-0-06-114056-3
I. Title.
PS3619.H356645A94   2008
813'.6—dc22   2007043364

08 09 10 11 12   OV/RRD 10 9 8 7 6 5 4 3 2 1

Chapter 1

Back home. Thank goodness. Frowning at the wilting plants in her garden—she'd been gone four days and they embraced the opportunity to humiliate her yet again in front of her green-thumb neighbors—Cindy Matterson jiggled her key in her back door lock until she found the sweet spot and could twist it open.

She stepped inside, experiencing the usual sick sense of loss when her beloved dog, Max—part Corgi and part who knew what—was no longer there to greet her. She dropped her overnight bag and glanced at the answering machine in the phone nook tucked into the back wall. The machine blinked, announcing the welcome-home message her husband always left. Cindy smiled fondly, pressed Play, and mouthed along with his deep serious voice. "Welcome home, honey, hope you had a good trip, I'll be back by seven tonight."

She didn't leave town often, not like he did, traveling the world over for General Electric, but she sometimes went to visit friends, or in this case to visit her parents in Princeton, New Jersey, so they could make her feel inadequate about pretty much every way she'd chosen to live her life. Who could pass that up?

No, she wasn't a history professor like her dad, or an art history professor like Mom. Nor did she have a career the narrow way people defined the word. Spending every minute in full-blown panic trying to keep up was not for her. Someday they'd find out the high rates of cancer and heart disease in this country were caused by people forcing themselves to do more than their bodies and brains were meant to do.

Cindy had made it through high school in Princeton and raised a wonderful daughter, Lucy, now a junior at—where else?—Princeton. She'd have liked more children, but Kevin wanted to stop at one, so they did. All that was plenty of satisfaction for her. Nowadays she read and volunteered here and there. She used to enjoy visiting antique shops, but now didn't feel she could, after Kevin paid an exorbitant fee to the decorator he thought they needed. They probably did. Cindy didn't exactly have an impressive knack.

A glance into the kitchen produced a wince at the build-up of dishes. She'd only been gone three days, and Kevin seemed to have used enough dishes for twice that. Obviously he hadn't worked at the office all weekend, as he too often did. She hadn't bargained on her marriage being quite this lonely, but then life threw all sorts of stuff at you, and you could either become miserable and depressed or deal with it and choose to be happy anyway. Why would anyone pick any other path?

Upstairs, overnight bag in hand again, she entered their lovely spacious bedroom, with the decorator's choice of stain on the hardwood and the decorator's choice of Oriental rugs and knickknacks and wrought iron and everything else.

But she had to admit the room was beautiful. Usually. At that moment, their king-sized bed was unmade and strewn with Kevin's clothes. He couldn't have tidied up even a bit for her homecoming? Usually he was the neater of the two. He must have been in a horrible rush this morning. Not like him at all.

Cindy gathered up a pile of shirts and underwear and dumped them into the quaint wicker and canvas hamper, also decorator-chosen. Sometimes she felt like she lived in some other person's home. Her ideal would have been a rustic cabin in the Rocky Mountains or an ivy-covered stone cottage in the English countryside. Maybe a villa in the south of France, but that part of the world was becoming too chic for someone like her.

Kevin's clothes cleaned up, she pulled at the sheets— Neiman Marcus 604 thread count, the price of which had nearly given her a heart attack, but that's what Kevin grew up with—and the thin cotton blanket and cream-colored quilt, all they needed for summer in Milwaukee.

A lump remained at the foot of the bed after she'd carefully arranged the covers. She frowned and tugged up the various layers again. Still there. Must be one of Kevin's socks, though she hadn't noticed any singles during her earlier sweep. Maybe its mate was on the floor?

She sighed and reached underneath, scrabbling around until her fingers touched something too soft and too satiny to be a sock. Dragged out into the muted gray light of a cloudy day, it proved to be underpants. A thong actually. Black, trimmed with red lace. Not hers.

But how had—

Her brain caught up with her surprise.

Not again.

She sank onto the bed, staring at the panties, hands starting to shake. Was it all going to happen again? No, no, it couldn't. There was some other explanation. Like . . .

Like . . .

Like she couldn't come up with another explanation.

Right now she had some respite through the miracle of denial, but she knew that not too far off the pain and shame would hit—and, since she was a woman, probably guilt too, that once again she hadn't been enough for him. Then she'd have to go through the anger and depression and bargaining stages again, and it was not going to be fun. At all.

However, during this tiny peephole of sanity she could think rationally. Maybe she should call her friend Marjory. The last time Kevin did this, Marjory stood by her, though she'd been furious at Cindy for staying in the marriage. Cindy intended to stay this time too, because she'd sworn in front of God and man and umpteen thousands of intimidating dollars' worth of guests and flowers and food and rented space that she would, until death. This wasn't death, though soon it would feel like it.

Of course he'd promised too, to be faithful, but one broken promise didn't give all-out license to break them all.

Last time, Marjory might have understood on some level and maybe admired her for fighting so hard for her marriage, for enduring those stiff counseling appointments and silent dinners until they'd worked through the worst and were able to move on.

This time Marjory would say Cindy was an idiot for staying. And so would her parents—who still refused to be civil to Kevin after he'd done this the first time, when she and Kevin still lived in Boston, and the second time, when they'd moved to Chicago. And so would probably everyone else she knew, except her grandma Louise, who thought you should stand by your man even when he was in the process of aiming a pistol at your head.

Cindy launched the panties onto the bed as if they'd ignited. What kind of woman left a man's home where she wasn't supposed to be in the first place, and didn't notice she no longer had on underwear? Maybe a woman who didn't usually wear underwear. Or a woman who wanted to be caught. Or . . .

Wild hope arose. Maybe it was a mistake. Maybe Kevin was secretly a cross-dresser, or maybe . . .

No, she didn't think so. The woman probably went everywhere toting a bag full of sex toys and hot lingerie and just—oops!—left some behind.

And here came the anger, rushing at her like the huge boulder in the Indiana Jones movie, only she had nowhere to run to avoid it. And no Max to comfort her. Always when she was feeling low, she'd lie down, on the floor if the low was really low, and he'd curl up next to her or on her tummy. Lying with him, feeling warmed and adored and worried over, was about as good as it got. Though it did bother her sometimes that the good-as-it-got in her life came from being prostrate with a dog.

But without Max now and with all this anger, tears would inevitably come. If she gave in, she'd spend the rest of the afternoon sobbing and furious. Then when Kevin came home, she'd be a puffy-eyed, red-nosed mess and all he'd think was how could he have stood her for so long?

So she wouldn't. Instead . . . she'd practice her tennis, which Kevin wanted her to learn so they could be a cute tennis-playing couple at the country club.

Downstairs, changed into sweats and sneakers, she was inspired to grab a tub of split pea soup—Kevin's favorite—from the freezer, which his mother had made and stored during her last visit, and plunk it into a big soup pot over low flame to thaw and heat. Kevin would love having his favorite soup for dinner.

An hour later, still breathing hard from the energy required to chase down the driveway after all the balls she missed on rebound from the garage, she came back inside, feeling as if a tennis ball had turned to rock and lodged itself inside her chest. She turned on the oven for frozen bakery breadsticks, ran upstairs to shower, and put on a blue cotton "skort," which in her day were called "culottes," and a white polo top.

Back down, bursting with unpleasantly manic energy, she set the stage on their dining table, using wedding china, candles, crystal, and a slightly bedraggled bunch of peonies thrust into a vase too large for them.

There. All the house needed was Kevin.

Fifteen agonizing minutes later his car turned into the driveway. The rock tennis ball in her chest became lead. She made a false start in one direction, then another, then forced herself to be still several feet from the back door where he would come in, and began humming a tune that had been stuck in her head all day, which she couldn't place.

She wished she had a capacity for alcohol, because it seemed like now would be a good time to pour herself a stiff one and toss it back defiantly. However, in her case, espe-

cially on an empty stomach and raw nerves, she'd just unravel and have to be carried to bed.

His key hit the lock. Cindy wasn't going to open the door
for him today. Nor would she throw her arms around him
and welcome him home in her usual fashion. Instead, she
hummed louder.

"Hey, there, look who's back." He smiled, and she hated
him for being able to stand there, tall and still boyish in spite
of the encroaching gray, smiling at her as if he hadn't been
ejaculating into someone else in their bed that morning, and
probably all weekend too. "How was the trip?"

"Very enjoyable." She enunciated carefully so she wouldn't
blubber and so he wouldn't notice that she was upset, which
was a waste of time because when she was calm and happy
she'd never say anything like *Very enjoyable.*

His eyes narrowed; his chin jutted like Max sniffing the
wind to see which kind was blowing.

An ill one. From him doing no good.

"Your parents well?"

"Yes. They send love." Which was ludicrous because they'd
more likely send anthrax if they could get away with it.

He loosened his tie, handsome as the day they met, alumni
weekend at Princeton Day School, when she was a sixteen-
year-old student helping out and he was twenty-one coming
back to his alma mater. She still got a little thrill looking at
him, though obviously these days he had to get his thrills
elsewhere.

"Where's my hug?"

"Your hug." She couldn't do it. "I don't know. Did you
lose it?"

Now he was looking nervous, glancing at her as he set

down his briefcase and plopped on top of it a copy of the day's *New York Times*, which he'd finish reading that night in bed. "C'mon, Cinds, you must have one for me somewhere."

He put his arms around her, and she let herself burrow against his warmth for one-one-thousand, two-one-thousand, and that was it, or she'd start crying.

"You hungry?" She tried to pull away, but he held her so all she could do was lean back and pretend she needed the distance to focus. Nearly forty and her eyes weren't what they used to be, something like that. "I brought out your mom's pea soup. So you'd have something *hot* waiting for you, which I know you like."

The dig was too subtle. He didn't react. "Fabulous. I'm starved."

Then he kissed her, and she actually had to hold back a gag thinking of those lips pressed against some other woman's. Again. She managed to pull away this time, or maybe he'd just released her.

"Ten minutes and soup will be on the table."

"I'll go change. Sorry the house was such a mess when you got back. I was—"

"I understand. You were busy." How she kept acid out of the word *busy*, she didn't know, but she deserved a medal.

"Yeah, it was a crazy weekend."

"I'll just bet." The smile stayed on her face, and she even softened her eyes into what would look like wifely sympathy and affection, nearly choking with the need to scream, *How could you? How could you?* Melodrama of the type he hated most, which he'd only use as proof of her inadequacy. No doubt the woman who'd left underwear upstairs was as cool and sophisticated and brilliant as the other two, not that

Cindy had met either of them. But she knew. Because if he wanted someone just like Cindy, he wouldn't need to stray.

He shot her another glance before turning and walking up the stairs, decorator-covered with a runner and brass rods, which Cindy hated. Ten years they'd been in this house, moving from Chicago for this fabulous new job he'd been lusting after for so long. And now there was more lusting of the other kind. Because Kevin couldn't get enough sex or good-enough sex or whatever it was he missed from her. She wasn't sure. Sometimes during counseling sessions she'd felt as if she were trying to understand the feelings of a block of wood.

Ten minutes later, jacket off, business suit exchanged for gray sweats and a faded blue Orlando Magic T-shirt he'd gotten on a family trip to Florida, Kevin Matterson was ready for dinner.

And so was his lovely wife, Cindy.

She put the deep cream soup bowl in front of Kevin, then got her own and sat down to watch. He would dip his spoon in cautiously, skim the surface, testing for temperature against his lips. If it was too hot, he'd make a pained face and drink water, avoiding her eyes. If it was too cold, he'd eat, but without comment or relish. If it was just right, her wee baby bear would smile at her and say that it was good.

He smiled at her tonight, and dipped his spoon again. "Delicious."

She watched him over the silver bread basket, a gift from some aunt of his, which held the still-warm breadsticks. She was too nervous to do more than stir her soup around.

On his fifth spoonful, a bit of red lace surfaced in his bowl. She would have expected him to take longer to reach paydirt, but there it was. And now the whole goop-coated thing came into view, dangling forlornly on the end of his spoon.

"What the hell is this?"

"Looks like panties." She managed a calm mouthful of soup, but it tasted like plaster. Or how she imagined plaster would taste, since she wasn't in the habit of eating it. Her heart was thudding so painfully she was afraid it was the beginning of a heart attack. But she wouldn't give him and Ms. Sexy Sophistication the gift of her death.

"What are panties doing in my soup?"

She couldn't believe he had the nerve to be indignant. Unless he thought they were hers. Or unless . . . there was some other explanation?

Hope again. Beautiful hope, a shining ball of it, rising up from the pit of her raging stomach. Would she never learn?

"That's strange. There were panties in our bed when I got home too. Maybe aliens are planting women's underwear throughout the city? Or maybe they're a gift from above. Isn't there a song about that? Panties from heaven?"

Okay, she was starting to sound a little hysterical. But really, she was entitled.

By now Kevin had put two and two together and come up with a rose is a rose is a stinking cheater. His face had gone wooden, and her fear and dread joined forces to squeeze the hope ball until it imploded and sank back into the gloom of her guts.

"Cindy, I had no idea . . . I didn't realize . . ." He was looking very ill now, and she realized with certainty that for the rest of her life she would never want to eat split pea soup again.

"Last time was supposed to be the last one, Kevin. Is this like old rock stars who have seven farewell tours? Or is this really the end? The grand finale? The last hurrah?" She gestured to the dripping mess in his soup. "Your swan thong?"

The line was so clever she almost giggled. She wasn't much of a punster, not like her father, but that one was pretty good. Or would have been if she wasn't sounding even more hysterical now.

Kevin put his head in his hands and gave her a good view of the slight thinning on his crown, which she wasn't sure he'd discovered yet.

"God, Cindy. This wasn't supposed to happen."

"No, of course not. Why would you want me to find out?"

He lifted his face and the expression on it scared her. He wasn't looking contrite, or angry, or stubbornly unaffected, not like the other times. He looked . . . anguished.

"You would have found out." He nearly whispered the words, but just when she was going to say *What?* her brain managed to sort them out.

"What do you mean?"

"I was going to tell you."

She snorted her disbelief, and then what he was saying hit her another way, and the bright ball rose again. "You mean it's over?"

"No." Anguish again, and a tear, then another one. His, not hers. Her shock made it very hard to take in what they were talking about.

Kevin was crying. Something dark and terrifying sounded a warning, like the shark chords in the movie *Jaws*, as if her subconscious had already lived her life and was letting her know a really bad part was coming up.

"I was going to tell you, Cindy." He spoke gently, as if he were talking to a special needs child. "Because . . . I'm leaving."

She was so stunned that this didn't compute at all. "Leaving."

"Yes." He couldn't look at her, and she couldn't look away from him.

"Leaving . . ." She had become suddenly stupid and nothing made sense. " . . . me? Our marriage?"

"Yes. *Yes*." He was impatient now, anxious to get this little unpleasantness over with.

He couldn't mean it. Twenty-one years of marriage, solid in every way but his affairs, which she'd chosen to put up with. He always came back. He would always come back. It was an unspoken agreement. His breaking that agreement was worse than breaking his vow to be faithful. Way worse. They were married. He had to stay with her until death. That was how it worked.

She stood and started pacing. "Why are you saying you're leaving this time and not the others?"

"Because . . . I love her."

She stopped to stare at him until a harsh laugh broke out, a bitter middle-aged woman's laugh, not hers. Nothing he could say could have been more horrible. Not that this panty-leaver had bigger tits, a tighter ass, straddled him better than a bronc rider—all that Cindy could forgive and understand. But love was reserved for the wife, and sex for the mistress, everyone knew that.

"You *love her*?" She screeched the words, which she thought was pretty understandable given the circumstances, but he wouldn't.

"I knew you'd get this way." His jaw set like cold rock; they were back on familiar ground.

She threw out her arms then brought her hands back to grip her head, fingers bent like claws. "What *should* I do, Kevin? Say, 'There, there, I understand. I'll be gone by morning, don't give me another thought'?"

"You'll be taken care of. By me, financially. And Patty has—"

"You are in love with someone named *Patty*?" Control was gone, she might as well face it. "I *hate* that name."

"She's found a place that will help you—"

"*What?*" Finding out he loved someone else was bad, but the pain of finding out this woman had done research to help Cindy get over the agony *she* caused was so acute, Cindy just stood there, trying to get more words out over little gasps that took the place of breathing.

"It's in Maine. It's a camp. For women who—"

"You plotted with her to send me off to *camp*? Like I'm a child you want out of the *way*?"

"She was trying to help."

"That . . . bitch."

"She's not—"

"*Bitch.*"

"You don't know—"

"All-bitch Patty, special sauce, lettuce, cheese, pick—"

"Stop it." He stood abruptly, gesturing, and knocked over his soup. The thick green liquid flowed, lavalike, over the table, chunks of ham and black and red lace in sharp relief as the rest settled into the thick cotton cloth. "We'll talk about it in the morning, when you're calmer."

"Calmer." She laughed bitterly again, regretting the panty

trick, regretting her fury, regretting everything but her daughter and her marriage to this wonderful handsome man who was her whole adult existence. "I'm supposed to take the ruin of my life calmly? Go away quietly to the camp your mistress picked out, so you and she can screw in our bed? In our house? In—"

"I'm staying at her place tonight." He walked out of the room and then upstairs. She stood in the dining room, staring at the split-pea-coated panties on her beautiful table, which had belonged to his grandma Matterson. He was supposed to back down at the sight of the thong. He was supposed to apologize. He was supposed to get rid of the woman, or promise to be discreet going forward, swear it was just sex and that he was always faithful to Cindy in his heart, where it mattered.

She crumpled back into her chair, the humid hammy smell of the soup making her want to throw up.

He wasn't supposed to want to leave.

Chapter 2

Inching. No, centimetering. No, millimetering. Ann pulled her silver Mercedes—one of the few things she'd been able to keep from her old life—ahead until it practically climbed onto the back of the Honda Civic in front of her, wishing every car on the Mass Pike except hers would be sucked into the belly of a spaceship and taken to a far distant planet.

Another inch forward. An idiot in an SUV—or was that redundant?—drove past on the shoulder. She gave him the surreptitious finger. Special place in hell for people who thought the rules were for someone else.

The traffic shifted again. Following the barrier of the Civic, she made it an entire half foot that time. Whoa, she'd better slow down. At this rate she might get home sometime this century. "Home" being a temporary concept, her childhood home in Framingham, which hadn't been hers since she graduated from Brown and moved out two decades ago. She'd just had the substantial nonpleasure of having to sell her real adult home, along with nearly everything in it, to settle surprise debts her late husband had apparently been sure he could pay off before she found out.

Best laid plans . . .

The guy in the car next to her started honking his horn over and over, loud, futile ear-splitting blasts. She understood his frustration, even as she rolled up her window and sent him a glare. Four lanes packed with cars in front and behind as far as she could see, engines idling with suppressed energy, gallons of fossil fuel needlessly burning. Too many people. Just too damn many people. Why didn't everyone stop having so many kids? Couldn't they see what was happening around them?

On either side of the cars channeled along their asphalt conveyor belt, sunlit trees stood swaying in the warm July breeze, unaffected by timetables or commuter duties, delays or frustrations. Above them, endless sky and the type of puffy peaceful clouds Paul had called "Simpson clouds" because they looked like those that parted during the cartoon's opening theme song.

Right now Ann wanted to invoke another cartoon and have her Mercedes sprout helicopter blades so she could rise, Jetson-like, above the claustrophobia and sail blissfully onward.

What had she been thinking not to insist her interview be held that morning so she could avoid rush hour? She hadn't been thinking. She'd been so grateful to have a shot at a job, she would have gone to an interview at 3:00 A.M. In her underwear. On the moon.

For the first time in her life she was in the terrifying and humbling—God, she hated being humble—position of needing money. Badly. No, desperately. No, frantically. The first time she'd ever been in the position of lacking a definitive answer to the question, "What happens next?"

She knew hers was a risky field. But she and Paul had plenty of money, or so she thought, ha ha ha. He'd retired early from real estate and was making even more for them investing, or so he said, ha ha ha. She'd done well in the tough field of Information Technology sales, and was proud of adding not only to their comfortable lifestyle, but also to their promisingly affluent retirement.

Ha ha ha.

Oh, they had such plans. A chalet in Aspen. A farmhouse in Tuscany. She'd trusted Paul's financial savvy. Didn't blink when he said he'd invested this much in this or that much in that. Didn't notice when he stopped talking about his work. Didn't see or rather ignored the signs that something was wrong. No, really wrong. No, fatally wrong.

Her cell rang. Fighting the familiar painful pressure of tears, she fished in her purse, wishing she'd stopped at Starbucks for an iced café mocha. Today's bullshit excuse for an interview had wrung her out, now this traffic . . .

She blinked at her cell display. "Hi, Ma."

"I heard about the ghastly traffic on the radio, thought I'd call. You stuck in it?"

"Up to my eyeballs."

Her mom made tsk-tsk noises and Ann smiled, probably her first sincere one all day. Forty-three years old and Mom's sympathy still helped make everything feel better. "How did your interview go?"

"Terrible. The guy picked my brains for two hours on sales

and marketing strategies, then told me, gee, they weren't quite ready to hire. He just wanted ideas. Complete waste of time."

Another inch. The yellow Scion behind her bounced to a stop, apparently just avoiding her rear bumper.

Ann's personal hell would be like this. An eternal traffic jam, freedom and space just out of reach, no way of getting where she needed to go.

Ha. Forget hell, her life had become that now. She glanced at her gas gauge, hovering on empty. She should have filled up on her way in.

"Your old friend Betsy Spalding just called. I gave her your cell number, hope that was okay."

"Wow. I haven't spoken to her in years."

"She heard about Paul."

"Right." Ann's pleasure died in the kick to her stomach. By now she should be used to it. People found out. People couldn't wait to tell each other. Did you hear? Ann's husband killed himself. *Gasp. No. Really?* Lost all their money and then some. She got fired and he couldn't take the guilt. Put a metal wastebasket over his head so the bullet wouldn't make such a mess. Neighbor walking by heard the shot and called 911. *Gasp. No. Really?*

Along with the horror of news that bad, the dark pleasure, and a certain pride that the tragedy happened to someone they could claim connection to, the frisson of anticipation that they'd be the next one passing the tidbit along in the guise of deepest pain and sympathy. *Did you hear?*

"Betsy runs a camp in Maine for women who are 'suddenly single,' as she put it."

"Oh for God's sake." The kick turned her stomach sour and sick. "She's going to try to sell me?"

"I think she wants to *offer* you the chance to go. Apparently it's a great place for support and for—"

"Right. I'm so broke I'm living with my parents, but I'd be glad to fork out money for some touchy-feely estrogen camp." She closed her eyes, loathing the bitchy bitterness she couldn't seem to control anymore. Her mother sighed, that bone-weary sigh she reserved for trying to make her children understand how much of an endless trial they were. As usual, it worked.

"Just talk to her, Ann. They have scholarships. It might be good for you to have a change of—"

"Ma. I need to find a job." Her voice cracked and she nearly caused an accident blindly edging her Mercedes forward when the Civic in front of her hadn't yet edged. "I don't have time for—"

"You have all the time you want right now. Your Dad and I think the camp would be good for you. You're holding too much in."

"I'm—" Ann's throat muscles contracted so tightly her throat felt like it had caught fire. "Ma . . . "

"Think about it, okay? She'll probably call you right away. She said she would."

"I bet." Ann rolled her eyes. Ambulance chaser. "Thanks for the warning."

"Not warning, heads-up. I want you to listen and think it over seriously. Your dad and I are worried about you."

"I'm fine, Ma. I'm always fine. You know that about me." She clicked off the phone and tossed it onto the passenger seat, breathing hard, open-mouthed, to try and release tension. An ambulance wailed by on the shoulder, followed by a police car. Ann shuddered and lost the fight to one tear in each eye. Up there where the jam started, someone's life might just have changed in one unexpected instant they'd wish they could take back for the rest of their lives.

Soon someone else getting dinner or reading or watching TV or driving home from work might pick up his or her phone with no thought to it being anyone but a child, or a friend, or a telemarketer. *I'm sorry to have to tell you, there's been an accident . . .*

Sometimes it seemed ludicrous that so many other people's lives were going on normally, that their days and nights continued in smooth uninterrupted patterns. Her life had been like that once, though there were days now when it seemed she'd always been coping with this anger and guilt and grief and upheaval. Given Paul's suicide and the surprise disclosure of their financial ruin, at times she felt those bad days held more of the truth. The perfection of their charmed life had existed mostly in her mind. How could she not have noticed how bad his depression was getting, how far he'd withdrawn from her and from everyone? Why hadn't she—

"Jesus, Ann." She'd promised herself no more going down this road. Six months later, it was ridiculous. No, pointless. No, damaging.

Her phone rang again, an unfamiliar number. "Hello?"

"Ann? This is Betsy Spalding. A voice from your past." A voice gentler and lower than Ann remembered. As if in the years since Betsy had been a high school bimbo cheerleader, she'd found great inner peace. Or had a lobotomy. Or was more likely affecting that annoying sorry-for-your-loss hushed monotone people felt obliged to speak to Ann with. Ann equaled loss for most people these days. Her mental state, her financial state . . . just call her the empty part of the glass.

The Civic moved an entire half car length, which was exciting enough for her to speak pleasantly, even though she was in the mood to tell Betsy where she could put her camp. "Hi, Betsy. Mom just called, said she'd spoken to you."

"Yes, it was good to talk to her."

Ann let the silence hang. Betsy called, she could get around to her sales pitch all by herself.

"So . . . how *are* you?" Said with that emphasis on *are*, which communicated that Betsy *knew*. Oh, how she knew. And how dreadfully sorry and yadda yadda.

"Ducky." The word flew out like a hurled dagger. "You?"

"I'm . . . fine. Thanks."

Ann lifted her hand from the wheel and let it drop back. "Actually, since you knew me, I've turned into a bitch. Sorry."

"Stress is an inevitable reaction to what you've been through."

"Right." Ann rolled her eyes. And here came the wind-up for the pitch.

"I don't know if your mom told you about the camp I run." Bingo. "She mentioned it."

"For women in your situation."

Ann snorted. Who the hell was in her situation? How many women had been fired because of one lousy year missing quota following five years overshooting it, and then had their husbands blow half their heads off instead of facing that they'd ruined the family? Possibly others, but others weren't her, which meant one, as far as she was concerned.

One woman, currently sitting in traffic hell, nearly out of gas, money, and patience, and no chance of escaping anytime soon. "What do you mean, in my situation?"

"Women who've lost the men in their lives. Who feel cut adrift from the life they knew, from dedicated sources of emotional and financial support. Whose occasional feelings of hopelessness alternate with a manic determination to fix everything, cycling back into hopelessness when the task seems too great. Who have unrealistic expectations of rescue mixed with periods of brutal awareness that there's no rescue at hand."

Ann's mouth opened for a retort, then snapped shut. Another half car length opened up in front of her and she filled it. Okay. So there were other women in her situation.

"Um . . . yeah." She cleared the huskiness from her throat and reached for who-cares irony. No way was she going to break down on the Mass Pike, either her car or her emotions. She might be low on fuel and strength, but she had enough of both to make it. "That's about the size of it."

"Camp Kinsonu has helped hundreds of women. We have a session starting in early August. We're privately subsidized so I can offer you a free ride. Think of it as a starting push on your road back to sanity and peace."

"Um . . . thank you. That is really nice of you. But I need to find a job now. I need to get my life back on track *now*." Her voice cracked again, and she didn't add that sitting around in the woods with miserable women sounded about as much fun as she'd have sitting around here. No, less. A lot less.

"Think about it. Each session is only two weeks, so you won't lose much time. We fill up quickly, but I can hold your spot for another couple of weeks."

Her spot? Ann grimaced. There was no such thing as her spot. Right now she just wanted to get Betsy off the phone, get home, and have an economy-sized martini and a couple of glasses of wine with dinner, enough to take the edge off for a few precious hours. "Okay, thanks for calling."

"I'll send you a brochure. Give me your address?"

Ann twisted the phone away so Betsy wouldn't hear her exhaling annoyance. Then she caught herself starting to give the number of the house she and Paul had bought in Wayland ten years earlier, and had to start over with her parents' address. Someday maybe this would all sink in. She wished it would hurry the hell up so she could stop having to feel this much.

Betsy cheerfully promised to get the brochure in the mail the next day. Incredibly, the traffic started a slow, earnest roll forward. Relief eased some of the tension in Ann's chest. She thanked Betsy sincerely and hung up, making a mental note to ditch the brochure without opening it. Her foot left the brake and pushed down on the gas. Finally. Time to move forward.

Her engine faltered, sputtered, made one last valiant effort to run on fumes . . . and died.

Chapter 3

Martha took in a deep breath over nine counts, filling first her belly, then her rib cage, then higher into her chest. She held that for a count of three, then blew out a sustained exhalation for fifteen counts until her lungs were as empty as possible. When her body prodded her for more oxygen, she repeated the process. And again. And again.

She was sitting on her couch in front of the blaring TV, feet tucked under her, favorite shawl drawn tightly around her shoulders. This one had purple, yellow, and black stripes, and thin coins tied into the fringe, which tinkled when she moved. Eldon had bought the shawl on a trip to Mexico her senior year in college, when they were dating openly. He'd said the shawl reminded him of her—colorful and musical.

Most of the world didn't see colorful and musical in Martha. Most of the world saw fat and flaky and not very attractive, which was why losing Eldon would be like losing part of herself.

The commercial for Coke ended with a flourish of marketing eagerness, and the local news came back on. She had to remind herself to keep her relaxation exercise going.

Five and a half weeks ago Eldon Cresswell, Vermont's favorite state senator, widely considered a shoo-in as the next governor, had been the subject of daily news stories for an endless, agonizing week while he lay first in a stroke-induced coma, then in the limbo horror of waking and sleeping cycles without real consciousness.

As of yesterday he'd spent a full month in that state, referred to noneuphemistically as "persistent vegetative." Sooner or later this milestone would go public, since patients who failed to wake during the first thirty days had a much lower chance of ever doing so, though recovery wasn't unheard of.

Nine counts in, three held, fifteen out. More than almost anything, Martha wanted to rush to the hospital to be with him. A deep part of her believed that if Eldon could only hear her voice, he'd wake up. But there was one thing she wanted more than to speak to him, and that was to avoid their love being discovered by the press and having Eldon's good name dragged through the mud by people who wouldn't understand. Now was the worst possible time to bring on the scandal they'd managed to avoid for nearly twenty years.

After his night nurse must have mentioned the daily calls from Eldon's "sister" to his wife, of course Bianca put a stop to them. Now, Martha had to rely on VTTV's perky blond anchor, Kathy Ashcroft, for news, like everyone else in the state.

Kathy finished a story on a black bear cub found playing with a kitten in someone's back yard, and turned to a new camera angle, smile fading theatrically. Behind her, Eldon's publicity photo appeared, which made Martha jerk involuntarily, even though she was braced for the sight. She hated that picture. Eldon at his most political, his most polished. The picture that represented every reason he'd married Bianca Souterman instead of Martha Danvers.

Kathy Ashcroft, vainly trying to suppress her perkiness, speculated that Senator Cresswell's wife Bianca, beloved by Vermonters—who compared her to the late Jackie O—would take over his seat in the state senate, but that there had been no official word from the governor's mansion. VTTV was going live, to Bob Silkwood, standing by with the senator's wife and three children at their lovely home in—

Martha grabbed the remote and zapped the set to dark. She didn't need to see the senator's wife and three children at their lovely home to know how the segment would go. Bianca, beautiful and impeccably dressed as always, would show courage, dignity, and enough sorrow to convey her grief, but not enough to spoil her makeup. The children would be somber and achingly attractive. Hearts would break all over the state, watching the brave family cope with such devastating loss.

Martha got to wallow in the devastation all by herself, in eye-swelling, face-contorting, all-out grief, over and over again. Eldon could be replaced in the political world. No doubt his frigid wife would make a fine senator in Montpelier. She'd meet someone else whose needs suited hers and would live happily ever after, as she had always been destined to live. But no one could replace Eldon for Martha. He'd been her true love, best friend, sometimes her only friend, her entire adult life.

A soft knock sounded. She tamped down the burst of

adrenaline—when would she stop hoping it was him?—unfolded her legs and ambled numbly toward the door.

It was Ricky, his skinny six-year-old body swallowed up by worn hand-me-downs from one of his brothers—or both of his brothers. "I brought up your mail."

He handed her the bundle, eyes down, shoulders hunched. A streak of dusty gray swooped across one pale cheek. She was glad to see him. She needed to focus on something other than the void inside her. "Thanks, Ricky. You want to come in? I think I have a bag of Snickers bars that needs eating. You know, before they go bad."

He looked up at that, and in spite of the beginnings of a smile, she could see he'd been crying. Either his selfish parents had been fighting again or his brothers had ganged up on him. "I'll help. Overripe Snickers are terrible."

Same joke every time, and they both still enjoyed it. Sometimes she wanted to petition to adopt him on the grounds that his parents were idiots. She'd been considering talking to Eldon about what they could do for Ricky the day before Eldon's stroke. She knew the answer was "Nothing," but at least she'd felt good acting as if rescue were possible, and felt good planning to talk to Eldon.

She always felt good around Eldon, even when she was just watching him on TV or standing anonymously in the crowd at one of his public appearances. He had the kind of powerful personality that made people believe he could fix everything and everyone. It didn't seem possible she'd never feel good with him again, so she'd believe instead that he was going to wake up. All she'd have to do was wait. After twenty years of making do with the bits and pieces he could give her out of his manic schedule, sometimes no more than his special wave on TV, seen by thousands, meant only for her, Martha understood how to wait.

She ushered Ricky in, happy that her spare, too-brown, three-room apartment could be her constant gift to him, a place he could feel safe and cheerful. She took the pile of mail from his grubby fingers, paused over one handwritten envelope with no return address, and set it aside on top of her TV to open when he left. The rest, the usual bills and junk, she'd toss onto her bed when she passed the doorway.

"So, now. The Snickers." She led him into the kitchen, shawl jingling, and reached into the cabinet—cheap wood stained to look like cherry—where she kept her stash of comfort. "Miniatures today. Peanut Snickers, Almond Snickers, and Snickers Cruncher. Two of each?"

"How about three."

"Two to start." She counted out six bon-bon-sized candy bars for each of them.

"Got any news?" His voice barely sounded through caramel, nuts, and chocolate. "You know, important stuff?"

"What do you think?"

He shrugged, but when he looked up again, his eyes were bright and hopeful.

"Well." She couldn't help smiling. "I did hear something."

He swallowed eagerly. "Yeah?"

"I heard . . . that the Snickers orchards had a par-*tic*-ularly good growing season this year. Which was a relief after the *disaster* that nearly happened last year."

He giggled. "What disaster?"

"You don't know? Well . . . " She opened her eyes wide, spread out her shawl, and let her mind reach out to the collective unconscious in search of plot possibilities, relieved not to have to think about her troubles for this short while. "It involved the evil witches and wizards of the Twilight Magic Candy Company, and their head wizard, named Baldezaar, who had a part-*tic*-ularly nasty and aggressive sweet tooth . . ."

For the next several minutes, she spun out the story, careful to add one of the drawn-out gory battles Ricky loved, but also swirling in descriptions of a sweeter nature. She ended, of course, on a moral high note, with the evil witches and wizards all but banished and the candy season saved.

Another knock on the door, this one loud and insistent, accompanied by a shout. "Ricky, you in there?"

"*Dad.*" Ricky hopped off the chair and ran to the front door.

Martha turned the corner to see Jim Spangler, skinny like his son, barely out of his own childhood at twenty-four or -five at most, squatting down, arms open to receive the little body, which stopped a foot away.

"You and Mom done fighting?" This from Ricky in a sulky superior tone.

"Yeah." His father touched his son's shoulder, uncomfortably guilty. "Sorry, little man. Your mom and I get pissed sometimes."

"No *kidding.*"

Martha moved forward. She wanted to tell this boy-father about spiritual centeredness, about deep breathing and positive karma, about learning to control angry impulses, about treating people you love with respect and compassion. But all he'd see would be a fat, middle-aged woman lecturing. Her words would bounce off him and scatter on the floor, sound waves from a tree falling alone in the forest.

"Ricky was upset."

Jim barely glanced at her. "Yeah. I know. You don't have to come down here, Ricky. You can—"

"Martha told me another really cool story, Dad. This one was about wizards and witches and candy trees and—"

"That's great. You want to go get ice cream with me?"

"Sure! Yeah! Okay!" He gave his father a high five and followed him toward the stairs, turning to wave at Martha.

She closed the door on his happy face disappearing down the building steps. Ricky wasn't her problem to solve. He loved his parents, even if his dad was an immature horse's butt and his mother was a self-absorbed brat. He'd grow up and be who he was going to be no matter what Martha did. What did she think, that thirty years down the road he'd be accepting a Nobel prize, saying he'd have been a failure without Martha Danvers's Snickers stories?

A few steps into her apartment, breathing too high and too rapid, which would only lead to pain and panic, she stopped and forced her inhale-exhale down low and slow. All day long, over and over, the same cycle. Ahead of her, stretching out as far as she dared let herself imagine, more of the same desperate emptiness. Unless Eldon woke up.

The flash of white on the dull metal top of her TV caught her eye as she moved past. The envelope. She peered at the postmark, from Maine, and tore it open eagerly.

Once upon a time a good man loved a good woman so deeply, he faked a stroke in order to escape the punishment of public life and the chains that bound him to a heartless and icy female. No longer could he stand living the lie. As soon as he was free, on the

wild, beautiful island he'd bought for them in Maine,
he wrote to her, begging her to join him so they could
put their years of isolation behind them forever . . .

Instead, a brochure. *Camp Kinsonu for Women. Stronger Every Day, Stronger Every Way.* And a note.

Hello, Martha. A donor who wishes to remain anonymous has secured a place for you at Camp Kinsonu for the early August session, starting on the 4th. Please look over the enclosed and let us know as soon as possible if you will be attending. We look forward to being able to share with you the healing process that has helped so many other suddenly single women.

Sincerely,
Betsy Spalding

Martha went over the note three times, heart rate shooting up higher with each successive reading.

There was only one person besides her who knew she was suddenly single, not counting the Cold One. And only one person she knew well who had the kind of money to send her to a place like this. And only one person who would care enough to want to help her through this pain. A person the media claimed was unable to speak and think for himself for the last month.

Eldon Cresswell. Her Eldon.

Chapter 4

C indy stood back and surveyed the room that would be hers for the next two weeks, already in love with the ale-colored knotty pine walls and exposed beams. The bed was twin, good quality and comfortable, though she'd brought her own pillow from home, because she never slept well on other people's pillows. Next to the bed stood blue-shaded white lamps that complemented the blue and white bedspreads. Watercolors enlivened the walls, seaside land-scapes mostly, and cute braided rag rugs softened the floors.

The staff had put a basket on the table by her bed with home-baked cookies, an apple, and some hard fruit candies. On the tastefully battered dresser, a bouquet of white fuzzy flowers had been arranged in a gray-blue pottery vase etched with ferns. Nice touches that gave the impression of luxury without detracting from the casual charm of the place.

She was going to love it here. The air smelled so sweet, and the hushed lapping of the ocean would make her sleep, she was sure of it. She hadn't done so well sleeping over the last few weeks, not with Kevin off all the time with his new girlfriend and with no Max to comfort her. She'd told Marjory about his latest, and then told her parents. Predictably, they insisted she file for divorce immediately. She didn't see the point. He'd be back soon enough and they could go on. She probably shouldn't have told Mom and Dad this time. Why give them more fuel for their belief that Cindy failed at everything she tried?

In the meantime, she had a nice distraction up here, which Marjory and Mom and Dad all agreed would be good for her, and eventually convinced her as well. Even though she hated that it was Mistress Patty who had found Camp Kinsonu, she was glad to be here now. Compared to moping around at home, this felt like freedom.

In a file next to her bed lay the sheaf of papers she'd gotten at registration in the lodge. The camp director, Betsy Spalding, who had to be the nicest lady on earth, greeted each woman with a huge long hug. Cindy felt sort of stupid hugging someone she'd never met, but three seconds in Betsy's strong arms left her feeling that this woman knew everything about her, understood it all, and would help her get through every shred of pain or die trying.

That probably sounded over the top, but it's exactly what she felt.

Now, sitting on the firm mattress, Cindy leafed through the file. One paper invited her to a bonfire talk and sing-along that night, and another laid out her schedule with all the activities she'd chosen. Archery, hiking, art class—she hadn't painted since she was a girl!—tennis, so she could play with Kevin and not embarrass herself . . . and one mandatory class she hadn't signed up for. Baking. Ugh. The only thing she knew how to bake was burned lumps of cement and raw lumps of goo, but Betsy said campers could only change the classes they picked themselves, so Cindy was stuck with that, and with group therapy and the special trip to one of the islands in the bay the last day, which sounded fine.

As for the rest, she couldn't wait to get started. Her mom had gone to a camp in Maine when she was a girl, and this seemed so much like her stories. Except Mom's camp didn't have massages and other fancy spa stuff. Cindy could get all that pampering back home. When things weren't going well, she liked to keep moving.

She put the file aside, clenched her fists and beat a light rhythm on her thighs. Tum-da-da-tum. Tum-da-da-tum.

The cabin would hold four women. Maybe the others would be here soon. She jumped up and strode through the small common area, comfortably furnished with navy and olive couches lightened with floral throw pillows, and a wooden lobster trap covered by a clear acrylic top for a coffee table. An attractive arrangement of shells had been glued to one wall, and on the opposite wall a pretty cloth showing different types of local wildflowers hung between windows that faced the sea.

Out the door, across the screened-in front porch whose sturdy wooden chairs looked perfect for reading in, she followed the path past the largest building, the lodge, also shingled with dark green shutters, where she'd registered and was told that meetings and some activities would be held, up through spare clumps of birches and firs toward the parking lot, where she thought some of the others might be arriving.

She was in luck! a car had just pulled in, a silver Mercedes with Massachusetts plates. She stood by the edge of the grassy lot until the car stopped, then moved toward it, brimming with excitement. Maybe she'd make a new friend. Maybe this woman would be one of the other three in her cabin.

A dark head showed above the car's roof, then the shoulders of a sage-colored suit jacket that looked like linen. Cindy kept walking, conscious of her denim wraparound skirt, her simple cotton shirt, and her pink sneakers with ruffled white ankle socks, which she wore in somewhat joking defiance of fashion rules.

The woman turned. She was beautiful, with the kind of dewy skin that didn't show age, a nose that didn't dare bump asymmetrically, and a strong chin that wouldn't tolerate any sagging under it. Right now she was breathing the beautiful clear sea air as if it were a delicious gift.

"Hi there." Cindy drew closer, hand outstretched, drinking in the style and beauty of the new arrival the same way the new arrival was drinking in the pure air. But then this kind of woman wouldn't be thrilled to meet someone like Cindy. "I'm Cindy."

They shook, the woman's lackluster grip taking Cindy by surprise. She looked forceful enough to complete a triathalon, then come back to start her real workout.

"I'm Ann."

"Ann Redding?" Cindy clapped her hands together. "You're in my cabin!"

The woman's eyes flicked briefly over Cindy's outfit, resting for an extra beat on the ruffled ankle socks. "Really?"

"Oh, don't worry. Not everyone here will be as dowdy as I am. And besides, you know what they say . . . socks don't make the woman." She smiled widely, expecting the startled look on Ann's face. Women like Ann expected women like Cindy not to know how they came across. Cindy liked to surprise them with direct acknowledgment. "I'm a good roommate, I'm quiet, and I don't snore. There are other women here you can—"

"Roommate?" Ann said the word as if it was something foul she ate.

"Cabin-mate. We have our own bedrooms." And then as Ann sagged into relief, Cindy couldn't help adding, "But the walls are practically cardboard, so there's not much privacy. Need help with your cases?"

"No thanks."

"You sure?"

"I'm fine on my own."

"Hey, none of us is fine on our own or we wouldn't be here." She said it breezily, and laughed at her own joke. Ann didn't join in. Ann must have been through much worse man-stuff than Cindy had.

Another car moved into the driveway. Cindy said a cheery good-bye and left Ann in her cherished aloneness to struggle with her heavy-looking suitcases over the bumpy grassy terrain, instead of accepting help from a potential friend. Whatever.

This car looked more promising. A Hyundai, with a few small rust spots. Maybe this person would be gladder to see Cindy. If her name turned out to be Martha or Dinah, then she'd be in their cabin too.

The car pulled in cautiously, then the driver switched off the engine, which seemed fairly huffy about being switched off because it jolted and knocked a few times before accepting its fate.

Cindy waited, craning her neck to see. The driver's door squawked open. A spiky brown head of hair emerged, followed by a large slow-moving body wrapped in a faded purple, yellow, and black shawl that jingled.

"Hi there." Cindy waved and moved closer, holding out her hand for a shake.

The woman had striking features. Light eyes that bulged slightly, long lashes that pointed down over them, a small sharp nose, and a cupid's bow mouth. Her skin was very pale and fine-pored, but she had a natural blush that kept her from looking corpselike. Her age was hard to guess, with the fat smoothing out any wrinkles. She looked sad, and a little freaked out, and didn't respond to Cindy's greeting or offer to shake hands.

"I'm Cindy." She found herself speaking clearly and gently, in case the woman was mentally challenged or deaf, or not a native English speaker.

The woman nodded and looked back into her car as if it might offer her the chance to escape. "I'm Martha. Danvers."

"Oh, Martha! How great! You're in my cabin."

Martha looked startled instead of pleased. Maybe Cindy's enthusiasm seemed over the top, but when you came to a strange place at a difficult time in your life, the people sharing your cabin were sort of like family, or would become that way. At least, that's how she looked at it.

Apparently, Martha didn't.

"Do you want me to help you with your suitcases?"

Martha took in what appeared to be the largest breath

Cindy had ever seen anyone take in. Then she blew it out for what seemed equally like forever. Cindy waited. Slapped at a mosquito on her arm. Scratched another bite on her leg . . .

"I only have one. One suitcase."

Whew! Cindy had started to think she wasn't going to answer at all. "Oh, good for you. I really envy people who know how to pack light. I didn't know what to bring, so I ended up bringing everything."

Martha's mouth turned up wryly. "So did I."

On cue, a sea gull shrieked laughter out on the bay. Cindy cringed. "Oh. Well, I'm really silly about shopping. Nothing ever seems to look right, and instead of wiping everything out and building a sensible coordinating wardrobe, I just keep buying pieces here and there and hoping I come up with something." She gestured disparagingly at her comfortable clothes. "So far no good, huh."

Martha didn't answer. She must be in a lot of pain too. Cindy wasn't exactly having the time of her life either, but at least she could be pleasant.

"Where are you from, Martha?"

"Vermont."

"Oh?"

A nod. End of that story, apparently.

Okay, so this wasn't going to work. Maybe when Martha had settled in more, she'd be friendlier. Cindy hoped so. She hadn't come here to feel as lonely as she did at home with Max gone. And Martha looked so sad and lost, Cindy wanted friendship for her sake too.

"Registration is in that big building right there." She pointed. "I'd be happy to help you with your—"

"Please." Martha held up a ringless hand. Cindy still wore

her wedding band, though she had considered taking it off in case some of the women here objected that she still considered herself firmly attached. It was just that she hadn't taken the ring off since Kevin slipped it on her finger twenty-one years ago, on June 30. "I'd like to be alone."

"Oh. Sure." Cindy backed away, wanting to ask why the hell Martha and Ann had come to a camp crowded with women if they wanted to be alone? "No problem. Just offering. I'll see you later, I guess."

Martha didn't answer. She moved around to the back of her car, opened her trunk and just stood there, staring inside. Cindy's heart broke. This woman's husband must have left her for real.

"You know . . ." She walked over to Martha, put her hand on the woman's shoulder, felt her flinch and moved it off quickly. "This is really hard for all of us. We're all in this together, for the next two weeks. I just think if you—"

"Thank you. I'm okay."

Cindy felt a twinge of annoyance at the curt dismissal and had to stop herself from saying *Fine* in an injured tone and making this into more than it needed to be.

Martha hauled her suitcase out of her trunk, slammed the lid and lumbered toward the registration building. Halfway there, she stopped, stood frozen for several beats, then turned and plunged down the path toward the shore, leaving her suitcase, which hesitated, then slowly toppled over onto its side.

Oh gosh. Cindy moved quickly toward the administrative cabin, then broke into a jog, then a run, passing Ann, who was still trying to drag her suitcases over the gravelly path. Someone should know Martha was on her way down to the sea, in case she was crying or, God forbid, tried to kill her-self. Someone with experience in how to handle women in pain. So far Cindy had struck out twice, and a third time might mean an end to Martha's inning.

Whoever their fourth roommate, Dinah, was, Cindy hoped she'd turn out to be more of a friend than Martha and Ann were ever likely to be.

Martha stumbled on an exposed root then walked faster and faster through a small clearing, past a large shingled build-ing with a wooden sign that read REGISTRATION, and under it, a red sign on white cotton, WELCOME, with the W like a sea gull in flight, until the path dead-ended perpendicular to another path along the rocky edge. A woman was coming toward her from the right along the oceanside path, wearing some cute shorts/top combo straight from an L.L.Bean cata-log, calling a greeting and smiling.

Martha whirled in the other direction and strode toward an area where the pines grew larger and the alders reached shoulder height. Ahead on the path she saw another woman, this one shapely and fit, blond hair long and thick, wear-ing tight jeans and layered tops. Martha hesitated, feeling like a video game character escaping predators, and plunged through a growth of alders, their leaves catching and pulling the fringe of her shawl, creepy fingers holding her back.

Eldon. She missed Eldon. She didn't want to be here, she wanted to be home waiting for him to wake up and come to her. Why had she enrolled?

Because Eldon had chosen this place for her and she had to keep reminding herself that he'd have wanted to take care of her. He could still wake up. And having come so close to death, he'd rethink his life and his priorities. She and Eldon had found that rarest of treasures: true love, the kind that never died, never wavered. Its power would bring them back together. She had to remember that and believe.

One final push and she was on the other side, breathing fast, sweat breaking out on her forehead. In front of her the bay spread blue and inviting, space and peace and freedom. She felt as if a dark box that had been holding her inside was suddenly opened up to let in light and air.

Once upon a time there was a woman named Martha, who was so full of pain that she walked to the end of the earth, following the setting sun. At the end of the earth lay a clear blue beckoning ocean. Though she didn't know how to swim, Martha took off her clothes and plunged into the water. She found magically that she could swim, and she set out toward the sun, hoping to fling herself into the clean yellow fire. Eventually, though, she became exhausted and was forced instead to welcome the long slow drop under the sea. But the gods, who had been watching her long journey, took pity and turned her into a mermaid, who still haunts the sea with her eerie sad songs.

The drop to sea level from the shore was about ten feet, but in front of her a flat-topped outcropping sloped gently down. She moved forward onto the craggy rock, buckled and cracked and scarred, colored with white veins of quartz and green scabs of lichen. Not to mention generous contributions by the gulls—crab and mussel shells from their dinners and postdigestive offerings. She scanned the shore on either side. No one.

Thank God. She needed time to recenter. To rid herself of the conviction that it had been a mistake to come to this camp. Eldon wouldn't make that kind of mistake. As his journey would teach him about his life, so this one could teach her about hers.

She sank down on the flattest surface she could find and pulled her legs under her, straightened her spine, closed her eyes and went inside herself.

The call of a sea gull made one eye open. It swooped down and settled on a rock sticking out of the green-blue water, shamelessly photogenic.

Again she closed her eyes, starting the familiar relaxation patterns, the familiar retreat inside . . .

A boat engine, at first a distant drone, became suddenly louder, and she saw that the small craft had come out from behind one of the three islands in the bay. Two men were in it, one tiny shape standing in the stern, one even tinier sitting in front. Her heart pounded hopefully. Eldon, coming to meet her. The boat drew closer on its way west, and she realized the man in the front was of course not Eldon, but a dog. She imagined it, eyes narrowed, fur and ears streaming back, loving the speed and the salt spray and the company of its master. Life would be much simpler as a dog.

She blocked the sight again and let her mind reach beyond the present space, beyond consciousness, to the place where she was at complete peace, where no thought disturbed her, the place of total relaxation where inadvertent joy filled her like a golden—

"Hey there."

A male voice, unexpected, jerked her somewhat painfully back into full consciousness and she opened her eyes. He was young, probably early to mid-thirties, and very handsome, coming toward her on the rock in sure, bare feet, which would explain why she hadn't heard him.

"You okay?" He stood looking down at her, tousled hair falling nearly to his eyebrows in front, shorter on the back and sides. His eyes were light—not quite blue, she couldn't tell what color exactly. A tiny gold hoop glinted in one ear. His nose was lightly sunburned. He wore a blue T-shirt and faded ripped jeans, and looked like a rumpled pop star. She could imagine throngs of women throwing their underpants at him.

"I was meditating."

"Oh, yeah, okay." He sat down beside her, long legs stretched along the rock in front of him, leaning back on his palms, oblivious to the concept of meditation requiring silence and, in her case, privacy. She felt a prickle of irritation. "Meditation is cool. I spent some time in a temple in Thailand. Did a lot of self-exploration, a lot of chanting, a whole lot of meditation. Very cool people, those monks. Very cool. They've got their heads on straight. A lot straighter than most people in this country, chasing the dollar all day long. That's a wearying bullshit race."

Martha had no idea what to say to him. Men didn't come up to her and start talking. *Go away* seemed extreme, but it was on the tip of her tongue. "Right."

"What's your name? I'm Patrick. I work here at camp. Just started this summer, actually."

"I'm Martha."

"Yeah, right, Martha Danvers." He grinned as if she was a celebrity he'd been wanting to meet all his life. "Nice to meet you."

She wasn't sure if it was mutual, but she murmured something polite.

"That's a great shawl. Is that a prayer shawl? I know besides the Jewish faith, there's a Christian feminist ministry that uses shawls to—"

"It was a gift."

"Yeah, okay. All right. It's really fine." He lifted his hands from the rock, examined his palms, brushed them off and settled them down again, staring out into the bay. "It's so beautiful here, isn't it? You ever been to the Maine coast before?"

"No." She and Eldon had wanted to schedule a weekend away for the two of them farther south, near Kennebunkport, but it never worked out. She'd been trying not to remember her disappointment, and was further irritated when Patrick brought it up.

"So what prompted you to come down here by yourself, Martha Danvers? You haven't registered yet. They're expecting you."

"No. I haven't." She wondered if the tall gangly woman, Cindy, had gone running to tell them Martha had disappeared into the woods. "I wasn't sure if I wanted to stay."

"Why not?" He turned to her in amazement, and she saw that his eyes were gray and dark-lashed, and very beautiful. Too beautiful for a man.

"I don't belong here."

He smiled, but sadly, and she saw the faint lines in his forehead now. Mid-thirties. "Everyone belongs here if they've lost someone. You lost someone. Why would you think you didn't belong?"

She wasn't going to tell him about the beautiful stylish women or the hope she hadn't lost the promise of Eldon. He had no right to that part of her. Instead she shrugged.

"Give it a chance." He was leaning closer now, and she registered that he smelled like some kind of wood, or grass, something natural and fragrant. "You don't take any risks, you'll never end up anywhere but dead and forgotten."

She inhaled sharply and struggled to her feet, nearly over-balancing on the uneven surface. "I'm not a risk-taker. I don't like to—"

"Hey, whoa." He rose and put a strong hand on her arm as if to keep her from toppling down the rock face, though she'd already regained her balance. "No one's going to push you to do anything if you don't want to. There are a lot of really good classes and resources, but if you want to sit here and meditate for two weeks, you can do that too."

"I can do that at home."

"Not like this." He gestured out at the view, islands glowing yellow-green in the sun just starting to lose its brilliance to the late afternoon. "And you'd be cheating the rest of the women."

"How do you figure that?" She spoke more sharply than she meant to.

His hand was still on her arm, and standing close to him like this she could see he was quite tall, taller than Eldon, well over six feet. "You can call me crazy, but I'm really good at reading people."

She leaned away. He had a magnetic intensity about him, and this close it was nearly unbearable. "I should—"

"I can see something special inside you, Martha Danvers." He was nearly whispering, and it made his words way too intimate for her comfort. A flush rose in her cheeks. "Even standing up on the shore, watching you sitting here alone, off in your own world. You have a light inside you, a spiritual guiding light. Don't keep that to yourself. There are women here who can benefit from what you have to offer."

She snorted to shake off the stupid part of her that such utter crap appealed to. "I'm a private person. I like to be alone."

"Sure. Okay. That's fine. But you can still give them something they really need." His thumb moved against the skin of her wrist; she couldn't tell if he knew he was doing it. "I guess I'm asking you to give them a chance at your healing power."

This was absolutely too much. She turned an incredulous stare on him, and was surprised to find his face open, completely sincere. Either he was a really good liar or he absolutely believed what he was saying. A surprise flash of pleasure lit inside her. "I . . . I don't—"

"Come up with me. I'll take you to registration. You can meet Betsy, who is like the Earth Mother of camp. I think you'll really hit it off with her. In fact, I can see you someday as her assistant here, when you come through the other side of your pain. Most of the Kinsonu staff were once campers. I can see you being just that type of person the women here will need."

"Yeah. Um. Yeah, okay." She let him guide her up the path, his hand at her back until the way was too narrow for them side by side.

What just happened? She thought Eldon was a smooth talker, but this guy should run for God. She'd never met anyone who could spout so much tempting bullshit with such seductive sincerity. Not that she met too many people outside her job at the DOT. No one, really.

* * *

Betsy welcomed her to Camp Kinsonu in the plain plank lodge with a long hug, as if they'd been best friends their whole lives and Betsy had lived every second of Martha's pain with her. Martha wasn't wild about strangers touching her, and in the last ten minutes she'd had two to deal with.

"Welcome. We are *so* glad to have you with us." She was younger than Martha expected an Earth Mother to be, probably forty, slender, lovely, with flawless skin and teeth, a short mannish blond haircut and a direct blue stare that went on a little too long when she was speaking. She was dressed in a plain white shirt and baggy khaki shorts, and radiated solid, sincere warmth. "You're in Cabin Four. Here's a folder with your choices for electives this session, plus your assigned class, the scheduled group and support activities, and information on your cabin's trip the last day. You are welcome to change the electives, but we do ask that you give us twenty-four hours notice, and that if you skip a session, you let the instructor or someone know where you are. We don't want to intrude on privacy, at the same time, we are morally if not legally liable for the health and happiness of our guests."

Martha nodded dumbly. Mild panic started crawling up her spine. She couldn't do this. "I'm not sure I'll be . . . I don't think I can—"

"You're going to do fine."

"I can't stay here." She forgot to monitor her breath, and if flew up into her chest and heaved there like a bird fighting a net.

"Martha." Betsy laid a firm hand on her shoulder, which told her in no uncertain terms that she was, in fact, going to stay. If that wasn't enough, the light in Betsy's blue eyes shone with utter faith. "If you can find the strength to keep going after your loss, you can certainly handle Camp Kinsonu."

Martha nodded, fighting for control and calm. She'd stay. Not for Betsy, not for Patrick, but because she couldn't bring herself to disappoint Eldon.

Chapter 5

Ann stepped onto Cabin Four's screened-in porch and greedily inhaled the soft night air. She would have loved to say she'd come out to become one with the natural world, but she was actually escaping. Behind her in the common area, she could still hear Dinah prattling. If anyone could make jingly-shawl woman and horsey-cheerful woman bearable, it was Dinah. Blond, mid-fifties, barely over five feet, and stacked like a stripper, verbiage exited her mouth with such speed and relentless constancy that Ann was nearly as impressed as she was irritated. Or would have been if Dinah had anything of the slightest interest to say. She'd be the perfect power-saving option in households that kept the TV on all day for noise.

The joke made her think of Paul, and how much he'd have loved it, how much he'd have enjoyed poking fun at this place with her, and that made her throat ache and the familiar panic of disconnect start up again. Why had she thought coming to this place was a good idea? Exchanging the stress and misery of her life for the stress and misery of dozens of other women's lives thrown on top for good measure? She wasn't a team player. One of the reasons her marriage to Paul worked so well was that they were both loners. Both reviled the kind of rah-rah let's-go emotion that bonded other people so artificially. She suspected she'd been fired partly for her lack of that attitude. If a challenge or opportunity arose, she went for a solution or score by herself. Who else could she trust?

Paul. She laughed sickeningly. *Oh, yes, please, someone turn up the irony, we're all getting too cozy here.*

A self-pitying tear tried to enter her eye, and she scowled until it retreated. She was tired. The drive up had been hell, temperatures murderously near ninety in Massachusetts and traffic up the wazoo on I-95. She'd cranked up the A/C in the Mercedes, blasted Cindy Lauper's *She's So Unusual*, the Beatle's *Rubber Soul*, and Joni Mitchell's *Blue* albums, singing along in her ragged voice, which made valiant leaps toward pitches rather than landing on them. Needless to say, she'd done a lot of stage managing when it came to high school and college musicals.

But she'd made it, with only one stop in New Hampshire for lunch at a mom and pop restaurant that should have been awarded a spot in the Food Hall of Shame.

And by the way, if she'd known there wasn't going to be booze here at Camp Kitchy-koo, she would also have stopped at the New Hampshire state liquor store and stocked up. What kind of cocktail social was held without cocktails? Calling club soda with lime a cocktail was like calling chop suey Chinese food. Her chicken divan at dinner had sat up and begged to be washed down with a glass or two or three of sauvignon blanc or pinot noir.

But no.

One thing about this place, though . . . one thing . . . She'd stepped reluctantly out of her climate controlled car on arrival, expecting another oven blast of summer. And ohhh, the air. Nothing she'd ever remembered breathing had seemed so clear and sweet and pure. Her tight lungs practically jumped out of her body to get enough of it down.

Maybe nothing else would come from her sentence here, but at least she'd finally remembered how to breathe.

A few female bodies exited cabins around her, then a few more, heading for the shore, some somber and silent, some chatting, only one laughing. Fish schools, lemmings, a she-wolf pack, hooooooowl! Bonfire tonight, with inspirational speakers and sing-along. Girly Girl Scout heaven. Maybe later they could play truth or dare. No, try on makeup. No, share sad stories and cry.

Okay. She was being snarky, and should take the time to feel ashamed, but she'd rather get in her car and find the nearest bar. A shot of whiskey for penance, followed by a second, then, as expected numerically, a third. Or a couple of martinis, to take the edge off this damn tension she was never quite without. Unfortunately, in this part of the world the nearest watering hole was probably an hour away and closed up for the night at eight.

Behind her, the noise that was Dinah preceded Martha and Ann out of the cabin. The Amazing Babbler was still talking about every stick of furniture in her houses, from what seemed like dozens of marriages, what it looked like, where it stood, where it had come from, and how much it cost. Even Cindy looked haggard. Martha seemed to have the ability to tune shit like that out. Maybe she could teach Ann the technique, to save her from being jailed for Dinahcide.

"You coming with us, Ann?" Cindy interrupted the chatter, anxiously peering at Ann's face in the growing darkness.

Some women naturally assumed the role of mother hen; Cindy was one of those. But Ann didn't need a mother. She had one back home in Framingham. A mother who had a big hand in persuading her daughter into this mess in the first place. You could grow up and become as rich and powerful as the Queen of England—or J. K. Rowling—but when your mother was around, you were still just a kid.

"Sure. I'll come." What the hell else was there to do? She wasn't going to sit in that depressingly cute cabin by herself and boohoo how she felt so cut off from everything familiar and secure. "But if they sing 'Kumbayah,' I'm outta here."

Martha smirked along with Cindy's giggle, but the comment launched Dinah off on a tale about her summer camp experience and how she'd been chosen to sing the solo on parents' day in front of the whole camp, and how she'd been stung by a bee minutes before this incredible honor was to have taken place, and how . . .

This fascinating tale took them down the narrow bumpy path to the wooden steps to the small sandy cove where a bonfire already blazed. Around it sat roughly thirty women, all ages and shapes and sizes, all in emotional agony.

No, she'd been wrong. Not "Kumbayah." "We Shall Overcome." She felt it in her bones.

The mismatched quartet from Cabin Four picked a spot on the ocean side of the fire, and sat waiting for the program to begin while Dinah entertained them into stupor with her views on the best way to clean beach tar from one's feet and how many of the oceanside plants were edible if you knew where to look, which of course she did.

Breezes mixed the scent of burning wood with the already wonderful fragrance of tide and pine. If she closed her eyes, Ann could imagine her and Paul here, sharing a bottle of something-or-other, watching the stars, maybe making love on the sand in the firelight.

Except they wouldn't. Bugs, sand, and sticks would stop them. They were creatures of comfort in all things, now that she thought about it. And definitely bed people when it came to sex.

She sighed. Too soon now, but she'd like to think she'd be able to have decent sex again one day. No, good sex. No, great sex. Paul had withdrawn from her physically in the last few years as well.

Betsy stood and held up both her hands, palms facing, elbows at ninety degrees. She had barely aged since Ann last saw her at their tenth high school reunion, but she'd changed nonetheless. Gotten stronger somehow, exchanged the ditz for a more centered presence, though obviously she'd retained her cheerleading instincts. She'd hugged Ann for so long at the registration table that Ann nearly had to shove her away before she had an anxiety attack. Yes, okay, she was grieving, could everyone please keep emotional triggers far, far away?

The get-to-know-you chatter dissipated and died, replaced by an expectant silence that went on until Ann rolled her eyes. Was this the evening's program, "Staring at Betsy"? Were they supposed to guess what she was? Frozen orchestra conductor? Woman holding invisible yarn for winding?

Betsy inhaled suddenly and began clapping, a slow, powerful, rhythmic clap. After a dozen or so seconds someone else joined, then another, then another, and then everyone was clap-clap-clapping along. Everyone except Ann, who clearly had missed the point; unless it was summoning some demon god of coastal Maine. Or the Grateful Dead, late for their performance.

Cindy nudged her and she gave in. Clap . . . clap . . . clap. Whee.

The clapping accelerated all around the fire, under its own strange force, faster and faster, until palms must have been burning and until speed shattered the rhythm into staccato applause and laughter.

Then gradual silence, except for the lap of waves and occasional cracking sparks from the fire, while they all again stared at Betsy.

Okay, Ann admitted it. She wanted to know what would happen next. Maybe their fearless leader would strip and then they'd all get naked and go leaping around the beach. Ann had a dim memory of rumors involving just that on Betsy's junior prom night.

Betsy opened her mouth, then closed it on a tone, "Hmmmm."

It took only a few seconds this time, "Hmmmm," someone joined in, then everyone did. Almost everyone. This one was easier because Ann could keep her mouth closed and no one could tell if she were hmmming or not.

Slowly, Betsy raised her arm. The *hmmms* rose obediently in pitch. Her arm lowered. So did the *hmmms*, struggling discordantly at the bottom, then settling into unison. U-up? Do-o-own. U-u-up? Do-o-wn, do-o-own, lower, lower, until laughter infiltrated the growling Buddhist monk sound. How low could they go?

Betsy shot her arm straight up over her head and a huge shriek rose from the women—Harpies on the Hunt—then wild laughter and more applause.

Ann laughed too. People were sheep. Even she had felt it, yeah, okay, the surge of community and power. Baaa.

But when they started passing out Kool-Aid, she was gone.

A log crumbled and a shower of sparks flew up, drawing attention to the astonishing display of stars beginning to crowd the sky. A man's form distracted Ann from the light show. A nice man's form, tall, solid, and strong, striding forward with an armful of wood and a poker to tend the fire. His hair was blond, longish, nicely tousled, the glint of an earring in his right ear. He had that sexy who-cares look about him that people in Ann's tightly directed social circle lacked and that drew her, though she couldn't always separate the disdain from the envy. Something of a wild boy.

As if he sensed her staring, he met her eyes through the ragged leaping edges of the flames. Ohhh, and how poetic to see a wild boy through fire, as if he were broadcasting his maleness directly from hell.

Around her women had started chanting and waving their arms, for whatever mysterious reason Betsy deemed necessary, a surreal background to the fiery exchange of Her gaze and His. He smiled and threw on another log. Ann looked away, but not before excitement she hadn't felt in a long, long time had stirred. No, shaken. No, gotten up and danced.

Silly sheep-woman. Paul was barely cold and already she was getting hot? What good would that do? Better to concentrate on chanting and waving her arms.

. . . What was she saying?

Luckily, before she'd have to suffer that indignity, the chanting stopped and Betsy let silence settle again.

"Welcome, women. I welcome you to Camp Kinsonu. In the Passamaquoddy language Kinsonu means, 'She is strong.' You've all come from places of pain. In the next two weeks we'll help you, whether you want to begin your healing process physically or mentally or spiritually, or all three. We're here to set you on your path to recovery.

"We can't work miracles . . . only you can travel the long journey through your own grief. But we'll provide bedrock to stand on while you take that difficult turn away from the past toward a happier future.

"And now . . . " She smiled at the blond guy. "I'd like to introduce some of the people you'll be meeting here at camp, starting with Patrick, my assistant. In case any of you are offended by, or excited by, seeing a gorgeous young man among vulnerable women, I can assure you that unless you look like Brad Pitt, you are safe from him."

Gay? Ann stared while a murmur ran around the group, most likely part relief, part disappointment. She never would have guessed in a million years.

"Hi, ladies." He stood next to Betsy, smiling, confident, body posture loose but still commanding, his face glowing in the firelight.

Him?

"Let me tell you a little about myself. I come from a pretty bad place, an abusive childhood in Iowa, teenage addictions, a couple of young-adult brushes with the law. Not healthy. Five years ago I was beaten and left for dead in Miami by someone I owed money to. I recovered over the next year, working harder than I'd ever worked at anything, physically, emotionally, spiritually, with the help of a dedicated physical therapist who never gave up on me, no matter what. I loved him." The smooth voice thickened. "He gave me my life back. Then AIDS took his."

Another murmur through the crowd. Sympathy, understanding.

Ann frowned. Gay? *Seriously?*

"I had to leave, put as much distance as possible between myself and memories of him. I went to Thailand, lived with monks, stripped my life down to essentials. I spent five months there, learning, growing, finding peace.

"But I wasn't one of them. So I came back to the States, still drifting, but determined not to choose a bad road again. And then one night in L.A., down to my last ten bucks, I was ready to say to hell with it and spend it all on booze. I took a step toward the bar, and I swear this is true—a flyer for City University flew up and hit me in the face. The admissions people saw something in me and took a chance with a full scholarship. I worked my ass off and got my degree in psychology. I've been accepted to the University of Minnesota master's program this fall, and I hope to go on to get my Ph.D.

"If I could turn my life around from addiction, self-destruction, loss, physical wounds, hopelessness, and poverty, I guarantee all of you can turn your lives around too. Welcome to Camp Kinsonu. If there's anything I can do to help you while you're here . . . " His eyes flicked to Ann's briefly, then away. " . . . you let me know. Thanks."

An awed silence, then warm applause that lasted well beyond a polite interval. The breeze blew. The fire crackled. The waves lapped at the shore, farther and farther away as the tide went out. More staff members were introduced. The cook, the massage therapist, the kayaking instructor, the art teacher. Each told matter-of-fact stories of pain that had led them to this place and inspired them to stay on to help others.

Ann fidgeted through it all, uncomfortable with people tossing off casual stories of suffering and redemption. She looked around at the stricken faces of her fellow Kinsonuites, traces of tears glistening on cheeks. Okay. Maybe she was just an unfeeling bitch.

Patrick the Wild Boy had scored the most dramatic tale. That much pain. That much alone time. That many risks, to travel to the other side of the world and immerse himself in a culture he didn't belong to. Her whole adult life she'd stayed comfortably rooted in her culture, in her social class, in the world she'd created. And so had Paul.

"Now, here's Pamela to lead us in a few songs before bed," Betsy announced. "I'm sure you're all exhausted. This air is good for sleeping, but if you have trouble, come to the main cabin. Our nurse on duty has warm milk, holistic and herbal remedies, and over-the-counter tablets that can help for the first nights if you need them. Okay, Pamela."

Pamela hauled out her guitar and tuned, strumming and smiling. She had gorgeous thick auburn hair and straight white teeth, and Ann caught herself reflexively peeking at Patrick, the way she used to peek at Ethan Rosner in tenth grade history to see if he was checking out Betsy's tight sweater when she got up to give an oral report.

Ethan always was. But gay Patrick was looking at Ann. Or maybe just in her direction. But with enough interest to make her pivot her head straight toward guitar-totin' Pamela. Honestly. She needed to get a clue. No, a grip. No, medication.

"This one you all might remember from some years back. A female power anthem made famous in 1972 by a lady from down under."

Oh God. Oh no.

"Her name was Helen Reddy . . . "

Please help me. She swung around to her cabin-mates. Cindy was watching Pamela with shining eyes. Dinah was whispering to her glassy-eyed neighbor. Martha was staring at her hands.

Ann turned in the other direction and encountered Patrick again, who was grinning openly now.

She made a face and mouthed, *Help!*

He grinned wider. A connection. She couldn't help the thrill.

Pamela strummed and struck up some rousing chords. "I am woman. Hear me roar!"

The women did. Roared like lionesses, like prisoners freed, like the oppressed finally rid of their tormentors. And then they all joined in, fumbling words when they didn't know or had forgotten them, joining in one long glorious yell for each chorus, "Yes, I am wise . . . "

Cindy poked Ann, jerked her head insistently toward Pamela and pointed to Ann's mouth. "Sing," she shouted.

Ann shook her head. Glanced again at grinning Patrick of the Flames, and wished for Paul and safety and order and calm.

I am woman . . .

Chapter 6

Ann dragged her eyelids open, registered pine walls and the most god-awful clanging drifting over from her ghastly dream into waking reality. Her brain gradually worked out where she was and that the horrendous noise—some kind of bell—would be her signal to get up every morning for the next two weeks.

She closed her eyes again, not even wanting to know what time it was. Wait, she knew what time it was. Too early o'clock. Twice already that morning the roar of motors out on the bay had woken her. Lobstermen. Very picturesque. Better at anchor.

The dream lingered—she'd been in bed with Paul. They'd made love and he was still on top of her, his skin warm and slightly damp from the exertion. She'd been smiling up at him, so happy that everyone had been wrong about him dying. Even better, he'd been smiling too, really smiling, not the soulless baring of teeth with eyes a million miles away that she'd tried too many times to explain away as stress or fatigue. She'd been about to tell him how much she missed him while he was dead, when his eyes rolled up and he slumped off her, leaden and still, his head horribly half gone, but bloodless, like a doll's china head fractured. Someone else had screamed while she tried to call 911, but her fingers wouldn't work; she kept punching the wrong numbers. Then sirens, Paul's body gone, and the terrible clanging of the church bell announcing his funeral.

Which turned out to be Camp Kinsonu's bell, announcing hers.

Why was she here? She still wasn't sure.

Her cabin-mates were up already, at least one or two of them, creaking boards, running water, thunking jars and combs back into place on pine shelves, Dinah prattling about God knew what.

In Ann's heaven, no one would be allowed to speak before caffeine happened.

Up nearly to sitting, she gave in and fell half back, propped on her elbows, eyes open to a reluctant squint, mouth open to a long yawn. Early mornings and Ann had long been worst enemies. On weekends she'd lie in, sometimes for an hour—usually two or three hours after Paul had gotten up to run, then to sip his cappuccino reading the *New York Times*—soaking in the glorious knowledge that her body had been able to get as much sleep as it craved and would not be forced to move until absolutely necessary. She and Paul had decided not to have children, and lazy mornings were one of the perks. Sometimes she'd regretted the decision. Now she was doubly glad they'd made it. Hard enough hauling her own pain around without coping with kids who missed

Daddy. Maybe that made her horribly selfish, but she didn't see how grief left room for any other way to be.

"Ann?" A timid knock at her door.

"Yuh." She dragged the syllable out and got herself all the way up to sitting, blinking painfully.

"It's Cindy. Just wanted to make sure you heard the bell."

"Damn hard to miss."

"Oh. Well. We'll see you at breakfast?"

"Right." Breakfast. Christ. Maybe she should skip it. Except they probably took roll and came after no-shows with a doctor. No, with antidepressants. No, a straitjacket.

Cindy's footsteps mercifully receded. Ann let herself flop back, staring at the random pattern of brown knots in the pine ceiling.

Okay. She was here, she might as well deal with it. On the count of five . . . four . . . three . . . two . . . one and a half . . .

She sat up, swung her legs over the edge of the bed, feet resting on cool wood. Up. At 'em. Yee-haw.

The green shades sprang open at the first tug, eager to let in light. She pushed the window wider and bent to inhale piney morning air through the screen. At least today would bring a change from the deadening nonroutine of the last several months. Another deep breath, the sight of a sea gull soaring, and her head started clearing. Somewhat. Nice not being hung over too.

Well. That was all the perky bright side she had in her.

Showered in the tiny tinny stall, dressed in jeans and a coral sweater, made-up minimally, because why bother, she made her way to the "dining room," a largish building next to the lodge, with a wide screened-in wraparound porch, red-checker-clothed picnic tables arranged around the perimeter, about half full of women, with more arriving. Inside, the breakfast buffet, eggs, muffins, pancakes, bacon and sausage, all of which looked hot, fresh, and utterly nauseating to her churning stomach.

She picked up a tray and a plate—china, not plastic—real silverware, a thick soft paper napkin, and bypassed the hot food, nodding to the smiling plump woman standing behind the chafing dishes.

"Eggs? Bacon?"

"No. Thanks." She dropped a piece of wheat bread into a toaster that could hold six slices, picked up tiny tubs of butter and Maine wild blueberry honey, and waited.

A petite blonde jostled by her, chattering with a friend, then turned with an apology and a warm smile Ann couldn't seem to return. At work she had no problem meeting people or talking to strangers. Hell, it was her job, and she was damn good at it, or had been until this past year. But here . . . who was she? A widow, defined only by her pain and by her loss. She didn't want people to know that person. She had nothing to offer as that person. Hell, she didn't even want to *be* that person.

She watched women fill their plates, feeling more isolated than she did in her familiar surroundings in Massachusetts, which were all now torturously notable for being without Paul.

So? No one was keeping her here. She could climb into her car and drive home again. Back to her parents' house. Back to sleeping late, eating their food, watching their shows, drinking their liquor, scouring want ads and alumni directories for graduates of Brown with careers in information technology or sales who might help her get a job.

Crap.

Toast popped and harvested, she headed for her primary fuel source: coffee. In mugs that held half what her gargantuan one did at home, the mug Paul bought after he accidentally swept her favorite off her computer table to its doom. He'd been as crestfallen as a boy, eager to make it right. One of the few circumstances in which his cynicism cracked and showed vulnerability. Too bad he hadn't broken more of her favorite things in the year before he died. Maybe she could have gotten through . . .

Enough.

Feeling like the new kid in middle school, she ventured out onto the porch of widows, divorcées and dumpees chattering over their breakfasts as if they were already old friends. Anxiety stirred up her already stirred-up stomach. Where to sit? She didn't want to talk to any of these people.

"Ann!" Cindy beckoned cheerily from a corner table. She was smiling, showing her big teeth, short dark hair reminiscent of Cindy Williams in the *Laverne and Shirley* TV show, orange lace showing at the vee of a large navy sweater that had probably belonged to her husband. Next to her sat Martha, wrapped in the same weird musical shawl from yesterday, staring out at the sea as if she longed to hurl herself into it. Across from them—the inevitable. Dinah, bleached hair puffy and immobile, wearing one of those white jogging suits old people wore in Florida.

Ann lifted her mug to acknowledge Cindy and trudged over. Her club, apparently, her tribe. Accidental friends at best. Real friends knew better than to expect her to talk at breakfast.

As it turned out, of course, since Dinah was presiding, no

words were required from anyone else. Ann sat and sipped her coffee, which was excellent, made a halfhearted attempt to eat her toast, gave up and got more coffee.

Coffee was her friend. No, her love. No, her salvation.

"You're not eating." Cindy frowned at Ann's plate and gestured to her own, which held more than Martha's, though Martha was twice her size. "This food is incredible. I'll probably gain twenty pounds in the next two weeks."

"Probably."

Cindy's face fell. Ann considered apologizing, then settled on pretending not to notice.

The sooner people figured out she was a bitch, the sooner they'd leave her alone.

"Group therapy this morning." Dinah picked up a piece of toast, negotiating it carefully around über-manicured nails, and started spreading jelly. The toast wobbled, then took a dive—jelly side down—onto her shelf of a chest, clad under the white jogging suit in tight yellow material that brought spandex to mind. "Aw, cheez-whiz. I swear it's like my boobs are magnetized. I'm always doing this. This one time I was out to dinner when I was dating Frank, my second husband, and I was eating this huge rack of ribs . . . "

Ann tuned her out, took the last tepid sip of her second cup. Group therapy. She wanted to go about as much as she'd wanted to go to Paul's memorial service. The night before that ghastly event she'd lain awake for hours, shaking. She knew grief was pain; she'd found out quickly it was also deep physical stress.

The next day at the Presbyterian church his parents went to, she was stunned by the turnout. Not because she thought Paul and his family had no friends or support system, but because the crowd of sad faces had brought home shockingly that the tragedy hadn't just happened to her.

"Good morning."

She tensed—as if she wasn't already tense enough—at the sound of Patrick's voice.

"Good morning!" Cindy and Dinah chorused the greeting, faces turned eagerly toward him. Even Martha took her gaze off the sea. Ann didn't move.

He scooted onto the bench next to her; his thigh touched hers briefly. "How's everyone?"

Cindy and Dinah assured him they were fine. Martha nodded and turned back to the ocean, wistfully resting her chins on her plump hand.

"How's Ann?" His low voice seemed too intimate.

"Dandy." She didn't look at him. His presence threatened to drag her out of the familiar black depths of her mood, and that irritated her.

"Dandy, huh." From the corner of her eye she saw him glance at his watch. "I've got time, you want to take a walk?"

Boom. Just like that, her composure up and ran off with the milkman. She turned, unprepared for how beautiful he was even in broad daylight where flaws tended to show, his gray eyes probing and concerned, blond hair boyishly mussed over his forehead, skin smooth and relatively unlined. No ravages from his brutal past.

"I . . . don't think—" Exactly. She wasn't capable of thought at all. "—so, but thanks."

"Do you good. Fresh air and a chance to talk to someone who gets it."

"Gets it?" Her scorn battled an unexpected twinge of

longing to escape this box of estrogen for the simple, sensible, calming company of a man.

"Get what you're feeling. I do, you know. I've been there. Once I—"

"Patrick?" Betsy's voice, calling from across the room.

"Yeah." He kept his eyes on Ann's a beat longer, then turned to grin at Betsy's approach. "What's doing, boss?"

"You're needed in Cabin Three, are you able to go? Good morning, everyone." Betsy stood solidly planted, arms loosely at her side, beaming at her flock, blue eyes serene, blond curls a flawlessly symmetrical halo. "I hope you all slept well."

Assorted murmurings of assent, all lies. Whenever Ann had been awake, she'd heard at least one body thrashing and sighing in the dark.

"I'm good to go. See ya later." Patrick got up with easy grace, laid his hand on Ann's shoulder and bent his head down close. "You'll be okay?"

"Yes-s-s." She spoke impatiently, but his concern gave her an unexpected lift.

"Good." He squeezed her shoulder, bowed to the other women, and left with Betsy.

"Ann!" Cindy's eyes were completely round. "Did he just ask you *out?*"

Ann scoffed, her shoulder still feeling the pressure of his hand. "I'm sure he has instructions to scope out the worst basket cases and offer his manly chest to cry on."

"Ha!" Dinah had resumed dabbing at the jelly staining her yolk-and-white outfit. "He's not manly. Remember? He's that *other* way."

"Right." Ann scooted disgustedly away from her. Zero

tolerance for homophobia aside, she didn't care to share her theory that Patrick was as immune to women as James Bond.

"You going?" Dinah looked up from her monster bosom. "See you in therapy."

"I don't know if I want to go." Cindy laughed anxiously. Her hands fluttered up and pressed tightly against her cheeks, as if she were afraid of losing them. "I've never been to therapy with strangers. I think I'll hate it."

Join the club.

"Aw, it's nothing, sweetie." Dinah waved away Cindy's concern. "I've been in tons of therapy with my husbands, you know, to work on the marriages. All you have to do is talk. Just open your mouth and blab about whatever enters your head."

"Which comes naturally to you."

"Oh yes." Dinah nodded happily, Ann's sarcasm having whizzed harmlessly over her head. "The last time I went, with Stanley, my third husband, we were having this sexual issue, where he—"

"See you there." Ann stood abruptly. Words could not express how little she wanted to hear about Stanley's sexual issue.

She threw away the nibbled toast and put her tray on the conveyor belt that moved dirty goods into the kitchen. Kinsonu in a nutshell: soiled women on a conveyor belt, into the camp to be washed and made presentable for reuse. Too bad the deep scratches and cracks of the past couldn't be repaired as perfectly.

Outside, she stepped onto the fresh, fragrant grass, mown from its normal meadow length, and walked back to Cabin Four, sunlight already warming the morning, dappling the ground through the birches, sending out the gift of Christmas-tree whiffs among the firs.

Okay. She'd stay. She'd even work on her attitude. At least through group therapy this morning. If that didn't push her over the edge, nothing would.

Fifteen minutes later, teeth brushed, stomach still painful from too much coffee and not enough food, in spite of a dose of extra-strength antacids, she was sitting in yet another cabin on a comfortable upholstered chair arranged in a circle with other comfortable upholstered chairs on which sat chattery Dinah, jingly Martha, horsey Cindy, and their fair and noble leader, Betsy, erstwhile cheerleading slut.

Against three of the surrounding walls, between the windows, stood colorfully jammed natural-finish bookcases, topped with brass urns, lamps, and small vases of clustered berries, bright red against rich green leaves. On the fourth wall, a brick fireplace with an assortment of shells—scallop, mussel, sea urchin, and bleached sand dollar—arranged in an abstract mosaic on the chimney. Through the windows opposite, Ann could see the sparkling blue bay and peaceful green islands, which gave her the same imprisoned feeling as being in school on the first warm day of spring.

"Welcome, ladies." Betsy bowed her head in greeting. "How was breakfast? Everyone get enough to eat?"

Yesses and nods all around, Cindy patting her stomach contentedly.

"Glad to hear it. Now, you four are being hit with this session first thing on Monday, our first full day. That makes it hard, I know. It's easier when you have an activity or two to help foster trust and to relax a little before we start with the soul-baring. But schedules are schedules and someone had to be first, right?"

She waited for an answer to the rhetorical question.

"Yes." Cindy turned uncertainly to her cabin-mates, as if needing assurance that she'd said the right thing.

"Absolutely. "I don't mind going first, like I said, I'm used to therapy and don't think it's a big deal, so I'm completely comfortable with coming here." Dinah spoke with her attention on arranging her necklaces. "Not a problem for me at all."

Betsy's gaze moved to Martha, who mumbled, "Sure."

"You bet." Ann used her best salesman-hearty tone.

"Good." Betsy looked proud, as if they'd all completed stage one of group therapy: Able to Respond to Simple Questions. "Now, to loosen our minds and our bodies, we'll start with a brief yoga session."

She got up, indicating they should rise with her. "Anyone know the sun salute?"

Martha's hand was the only one to rise.

"I've heard of it!" Dinah fixed her empty eyes on Betsy. "One time I was in New York, in Central Park with Dan, my first husband, and there was this guy doing yoga. We stopped to talk to him and he told us he was doing exactly that, the sun salute, how about that! I never took yoga, but a lot of my friends took it. They said it was very enjoyable how calm it made you. I guess that's why you're doing it for us here, isn't it."

"Right. That's it exactly. Now . . . " Betsy neatly slipped the words in just as Dinah opened her mouth to continue. "We start with Tall Mountain."

She lined them up in front of the windows facing the sea

and led them through the poses, sometimes demonstrating, sometimes coaching, urging them several times to "let the breath move them," whatever that meant. Ann pushed her body through the routine, proud of her strength and flexibility. To her right, Dinah murmured to herself, straining into the poses. Cindy puffed and grunted, unable to straighten her legs, balance a lunge, or hold herself in a plank without her butt rising skyward.

Ann smirked and turned to her left. If Cindy was having such trouble, Martha would be a disaster.

Ann was wrong. Martha's large body moved effortlessly through the routine. She held the positions, breathed deeply, bent and flexed farther and better even than Ann could. More than that, she seemed transformed. Her eyes were open, wide and untroubled, staring at nothing. A small smile curved her lips. The perpetual crease between her eyebrows had smoothed. She seemed powerful and peaceful, Betsy-like, but even more so.

"Eyes forward, please."

Ann moved them forward, wanting to stick her tongue out at Betsy. What difference did it make if she looked forward or sideways or around in circles? But, new attitude in place, she completed the poses, not expertly like Martha, but obediently, in the correct order, keeping her eyes on the sea and the sky.

Ten minutes later, the sun having been saluted to Betsy's satisfaction, they moved again to the chairs, Dinah muttering, Cindy with a hand to her lower back. Ann settled in, prepared for whatever lay ahead. Her stomach still sloshed and gurgled, but she had to admit she felt calmer, and her breath seemed to go more deeply into her body. Better and better.

"Now . . . " Betsy picked up four clipboards gripping single sheets of paper, and a bunch of pens. "Our next exercise will be harder. We'll do this at each session. I'd like you each to write a letter to the man you lost."

The women moved uneasily, Ann suppressing a twinge of irritation. What kind of stamps would get Paul's letter where it needed to go?

"A letter?" Cindy frowned. "To Kevin?"

Betsy smiled placidly. "Not for him to read. Just for you. And for me, if you'll let me. It's how we start the process of excavating our feelings. Once they're out in the open, we can sort them out, interpret them, and help them lose power while we allow ourselves to heal."

Ann felt her pleasant expression harden and had to work not to roll her eyes. *Hold it steady.* Excavating, sorting, interpreting, healing. She could do all those things. She even accepted her clipboard with a smile, though she had no idea what the hell to say to Paul. *Having a lovely time, wish you were here?*

A glance around the room showed Cindy looking nervous, but eager to please her teacher, by golly. Dinah was nodding, fiddling with one of the big cheap rings on her fingers, yeah, yeah, she'd done this all before and would be happy to tell them all about it at great length. Martha . . . well, who could tell. She sat impassively again, a lump on a chair, removed from yoga like a patient taken off life support.

"Here you go." Betsy handed out clipboards and pens to the others. Cindy and Dinah began scratching away immediately. Ann met Martha's eyes, shrugged and smiled. See? She could even be friendly.

Except Martha looked away—and there went friendliness.

So Ann stared at the paper, three holes in the left side, blue lines to write on, pink defining the margin. Cursive lessons and grade school essays, *indent the first line, pen please, no pencils, this is sixth grade not elementary school.*

She resisted a sudden urge to crumple the paper and bounce it off Betsy's serene head, or shred it into tiny confetti pieces and hurl them into the air to flutter down like snow.

No, *good* attitude. Good.

"Ann?" Betsy's voice was honey, molasses, maple syrup—slidy and sweet. "Are you having trouble?"

"No." She gave a tight smile and glanced at Martha, who'd found it in her to write something and was busily scribbling away. The traitor. "No."

"It's a difficult exercise, I know. If you need help, I can—"

"I'm *not* having trouble." Silence while three heads lifted from their bent positions over the clipboards to stare at the problem pupil. Tsk-tsk. Every class had one.

Crap. "Sorry."

"It's okay, Ann." Corn syrup, treacle, caramel. "We're all angry, we're all scared, we're all sad. We have to remember that this is not a time that defines us, just a bump on the road of life which we have to get over before we can move on."

Ann stayed stone still in her chair while figurative vinegar and baking soda made a science project volcano in her stomach. She was not going to be able to listen to this shit for two weeks without saying something much, much worse than she already had. Especially without alcohol to make the pain go away.

She picked up her pen, scratched out a few sentences, her throat barbed, breath high and shallow. Dear Paul, bullshit bullshit bullshit, love, Ann.

Done.

"Everyone finished?" Betsy rose from her chair and collected the papers from Cindy and Dinah. "Martha?"

Martha handed hers over, looking as if she'd rather be eaten by mice. Then, miraculously, she flicked a glance at Ann, which might very possibly have contained an acknowledgment of their shared misery. Very possibly. Regardless, it helped in some weird way, and made Ann able to hand her paper over. *Enjoy, Betsy!* Work your diagnostic magic and come back with a pronouncement. Ann Redding: grieving widow with severe anger issues.

Like she couldn't have figured that out herself.

But okay. Positive karma. Yoga. Sun salute. Upward facing mountain, whatever whatever.

"So. Now we talk. Tell me your stories. Tell me why you are here." Betsy opened her arms wide to the group, expectant smile making her eyes crinkly and warm. "Who wants to go first?"

Apparently no one.

"Okay. Tell you what, I'll go first. I'm Betsy. I grew up in Framingham, Massachusetts. I was a bit of a wild child, as Ann can tell you, since we went to grade school together. I got pregnant young, married young, divorced young. My son wanted to be a musician and was very talented. He was also gay. At seventeen he was killed riding in a car with drunk friends." She spoke calmly, quietly, didn't react to the gasps in the room. "To say it changed my life was an understatement."

Ann clenched her fists. She *hated* this. It was just like the bonfire, only much worse. No doubt Betsy told that story to different groups of strangers every two weeks, rotating in bunches of four, over and over, until the words "he was killed" could be uttered from a clear throat, their meaning lost, part of a performance. Ann didn't ever want to get to that point. Ever.

"I fell apart, hit bottom, and then put my life back together. I got a degree in psychology so I could use my experience to help others. But I found it too painful to try to help parents grieving the loss of their children, so instead I made Camp Kinsonu about coming to a place of peace for suddenly single women." She bowed her head, smiling peacefully. "This camp, this vocation, this calling, have given me such strength and direction. I can't have Justin back, but I have this, his last valuable gift to me."

And . . . curtain! Applause applause, the crowd goes wild! Ladies and gentlemen, we have ourselves a hit.

Ann wanted to jump up, run out the door and keep running until her body gave out. Talking of pain was so artificial here in this warm, attractive room, among women she cared nothing about, who cared nothing about her. These people didn't deserve her feelings about Paul, about his life or his death.

"Who's next?" Betsy made eye contact with each woman except Martha, whose green and gold swirling patterned skirt had apparently hypnotized her.

"I'll go." Dinah raised her hand, adjusted herself in her chair as if preparing for the long haul—which in her case, she undoubtedly was. "I got married young too, to Dan, who I divorced three years later when he developed this weird thing about not letting me talk to any other men. Then I met Frank, and married him, but he was a trucker and never home, and I hated that, so I divorced him too. Then I met Stanley, who was so sweet to me. He was older than me, like eight or nine years, but he got sick. And he died. But honestly, I haven't told a lot of people this, but I don't think that would have lasted either. I'd already started to look around."

Ann had to instruct her face muscles to relax from a look of utter incredulity. Disposable husbands. What a concept. Like being married to a Handi Wipe.

"See, I always seem to pick guys that turn weird after a few years. I know it's not me, because I'm the same, you know? When I'm in love, I'm in love, and it doesn't turn off or shut down at all. At least not until they change into totally different people.

"So I guess I'll wait a while and try again. Husband number four is out there somewhere. I'm an optimist, you know, I figure I'll get it right one of these days, find a guy who really loves me and will stay in love with me instead of whatever . . . you know . . . not. Someone who really wants to communicate, which is so important in a relationship, and to keep communicating. None of my husbands could really communicate."

"Like any of them got the chance?" That was it. Good attitude and Ann were no longer associating.

Dinah flashed a blank questioning look over toward Ann, which pissed her off more.

"I'm sure Stanley's death was hard on you . . . " Betsy smoothed the moment over.

"Oh." Dinah looked faintly surprised at the prompt, as if she'd forgotten about that detail. "Yes. It was. Devastating."

Ann's stomach volcano erupted. "Didn't sound devastating to me."

Oh, and all eyes were on her now, startled, uncomfortable,

anxious. She'd done a splendid job at this her first therapy session.

"You're angry at Dinah for not seeming more upset." Betsy's unruffled tone was particularly enraging.

"No. I'm not angry. Why would I be angry?" She was so angry she couldn't keep her voice from shaking. "It's her business."

Her business to toss off husbands like outfits she wasn't in the mood, for while Ann would give a whole hell of a lot for the chance to do things differently.

"Ann, would you like to talk about your—"

"No." She breathed furiously to keep tears back. " No, I wouldn't."

Betsy gave her a measuring glance that made Ann want to punch her white even teeth out. "Who would like to go next?"

"Oh, well, I will." Cindy half put up her hand, then tugged it down. "My husband and I have been married more than twenty years, mostly happy ones, except for . . . well, Kevin has affairs. He's had three. I'm here this time because he *claims* to be in love with this last one."

She rolled her eyes as if this were immensely ridiculous.

"And you don't think he is?"

"Of course not."

"Why is that?"

Cindy stared at Betsy as if she was the one needing counseling. "Well . . . I mean, she's just a mistress."

Martha looked up then, fixed her eyes on Cindy, and Ann had the surreal impression she wanted to punch Cindy's horse teeth in. Maybe they should do dental damage together. Wasn't that what therapy was for? Letting out your aggression?

"He said he wants a divorce." She laughed and shook her head—in case they hadn't gotten the hilarity the first time. "So I'm here waiting until he gets over his middle-aged crisis and comes back to me."

Ann's eyes narrowed. Was this woman for real? If Paul had ever screwed another woman, he'd be unable to do it again. Ever. With anyone. Even himself.

"I do want to say . . ." Cindy glanced apologetically around the group. "I feel sort of bad. I mean I'm not really here on false pretenses, because he did *say* he was leaving me, but it's not like I've really lost him. And all of you . . . well, I do really feel sorry for you."

Sorry for them? Ann couldn't have heard right. She couldn't.

"What makes you say that, Cindy?" Gentleness dripped from Betsy's tone, and a hint of her own sympathy.

"Well, I mean . . ." Cindy started to look anxious and guilty. "You've all lost people. And I . . . haven't. Not really."

"Oh come on." Ann was ready to hurl herself across the room and strangle Ms. Smug Sorry for Your Losses. "Get real, honey, that man is gone."

Cindy turned to her, dark eyes wide. "I know you think I'm wrong, but I'm not. He'll get tired of her, of whatsername— Patty—and he'll come back to me and things will go on the way they've always gone on."

"With him *cheating* on you?" Ann was beyond surprise, beyond shock. What the hell was wrong with people?

Betsy nodded encouragingly. "Would you like to respond to that, Cindy?"

Cindy looked surprised. "Well, I mean the cheating part isn't great, but he can't help that, I guess. It's just that . . . well, he's my husband. Why wouldn't I want him back? Don't you all want yours back? I count myself lucky I can still have mine."

Ann could only stare. She'd heard some pretty stupid thoughtless comments since Paul died, but that had to take it. "What the hell did you just say?"

"Oh, God." Cindy looked frightened, which she bloody well should. "I don't know. What?"

"Let's first go back to the part where you lie down and beg life to beat you senseless then brag about how good you have it."

"What . . . what do you mean?" Cindy looked wildly to Betsy for help.

"And then let's finish with the part where you rub our noses in our own life's shit." Ann was on a roll now. There was no holding her back. Soon the police would arrive and she'd be hauled away for using excessive words with intent to maim.

"Why are you so mad at me?"

"How can you have so little idea?"

"I think Cindy asked a fair question." Betsy poured her voice balm over the tension in the room. "Would you like to answer, Ann?"

"What do you think?"

Silence except for Cindy's sniffles, while they all undoubtedly wished Ann would drop dead as fervently as she wished they would.

"Okay. We'll move on. Thank you for sharing with us, Cindy." Betsy focused her kind eyes on her next victim. "Martha?"

Martha shook her head quickly, mouth bunched. "I don't want to talk about my situation."

Terrific. Ann had probably just put an end to Cabin Four's group therapy experiences. She should feel wretched, but she was still too pissed.

"That's fine. Well, our hour is nearly up. I hope Martha and Ann can tell us their stories next time we meet. Remember, if you want individual counseling, you can call on me any time, and if I'm not free, Patrick can help out. He's a good listener and we work closely together.

"Now." She clapped her hands together and beamed at them. "A few more sun salutes and it's on to your next activity."

The women lined up, facing the sea. Ann went through the foreign motions again, her breath refusing to come easily, muscles stiff and uncooperative. Afterward, she barged out of the building ahead of the other women, out into the sweet Maine air, feeling as if to match her mood she should be breathing coal dust in a mine. This place was absurd, the women were stupid and ridiculous, and she didn't even have Paul to help her mock them.

Coming here was a mistake. How the hell was she supposed to get better if after the first hour of the first day she already felt ten times worse?

Chapter 7

Dear Kevin,

At first I thought this exercise sounded stupid, but I find I like writing to you, because I can imagine you at your desk in your office upstairs reading this, and if I try harder, I can imagine that I'm actually talking to you. I miss doing that. It's funny knowing you probably won't see this letter. Or maybe someday I'll show it to you, if Betsy lets me have it back. Betsy is the camp leader. I've always heard talk about this or that person being "centered," and never understood the term. Before I met Betsy I thought it meant people who didn't tip over easily, ha ha ha. She's the way I imagine a mother superior in a convent would be, not that I ever had a shot at entering a convent to know for sure. Not once I laid eyes on you.

Anyway, people are nice for the most part. I have three cabin-mates: Dinah, who has been married three times, can you imagine? I don't see how anyone can fall in love that many times. Then there's Martha, who doesn't say very much at all. I can't figure out if she has a fascinating internal life or if she's just weird. And then finally there's Ann, who I think you'd like. In fact, I think you probably should stay away from her, because she's probably exactly your type, ha ha ha.

I'm taking tennis so you and I can play at the country club without me embarrassing you. I'm also taking archery because it makes me think of my mom and her camp. Archery was one of her favorite sports. There's no swimming because the water is too cold, but there is kayaking. Also all kinds of spa treatments, but I want to keep this place special for things I can't do at home.

Oh, and guess what? They put me in a baking class! I can see you rolling your eyes from here. Talk about something I can't do at home!

It's beautiful here. I haven't been able to sleep, but that means I've been able to do lots of star-gazing. You wouldn't believe how many stars you can see away from city lights. Though I suppose you've seen them somewhere on all your travels. The shooting stars are clear as day, sometimes crossing half the sky in a sudden streak. It's disappointing knowing they're lumps of rock heating up through the atmosphere and not real stars. Sometimes I think too much knowledge is a bad thing.

The weather has been gorgeous and the air smells

better than just about anything I've ever smelled,
except you when you're dressed up to go out. I think
we should take a long weekend here sometime soon,
after we patch things up.
   I'll be home in a couple of weeks!

Your loving wife,
Cindy

Cindy walked a little apprehensively up the narrow trail toward Betsy's private cabin, set a short way up the gentle slope above the lodge, its dark green door flanked by uncertain roses on one side and an apologetic lilac on the other. Cindy caught herself being surprised, as if Betsy should have been able to look the plants right in the petals and inspire them to grow and thrive. Maybe the Maine coast wasn't the best place for every kind of blooming.

She'd been summoned right after her pottery class this afternoon, which had gone much better than her tennis lesson after group therapy. Cindy had managed to give the patient, earnest tennis instructor a bloody nose with a mis-hit ball. Nearby players rushed to offer tissues dug out of pockets, but Cindy had been rooted to the spot by shame, like the time she broke her mother's vase when the heavy wet crystal slipped out of her hands and shattered in the sink. She hadn't been able to move then either, even with blood flowing from a cut on her forearm. When her mom came in and found Cindy crying, she'd been exasperated. Why the fuss? It wasn't the first time Cindy had been clumsy, and God knew it wouldn't be the last.

Laura had been awfully nice too, about having her nose bloodied, as if it happened all the time, which Cindy was pretty sure it didn't. Unable to shake off the horror, she'd gotten through the rest of class by lobbing careful shots against the backboard, which didn't have a nose. Tennis might bring her and Kevin closer, but at this rate it wouldn't do much for her emotional, spiritual, or physical progress at camp.

Lunch, a delicious vegetable soup—and how nice not to mind hot soup in August—restored her. She'd spent her pottery class blissfully producing a thick wobbly bowl that even a kindergarten mom would hesitate to display. But what fun. A lot of the other women had obviously worked the wheel before, but Cindy was determined not to feel inadequate so she didn't. The activity was just the outlet she needed after group therapy and tennis turned out to be difficult. Bloodied nose in one, bloodied spirit in another. She was getting tired of people acting as if she were too stupid to know her own husband.

After pottery class, Patrick had come into the art room, and his eyes picked her out from among the others, which gave her a silly thrill. He was so handsome, it was hard not to react, even knowing he wouldn't react back, not to her or any of the women, even one as beautiful and classy as Ann. He was the kind of man Cindy would probably have had a crush on in grade school, her bad boy type, until she got smart and chose someone solid and . . . well "dependable" was a poor concept in retrospect, but that's how she'd felt about Kevin at the time. Her parents adored him at first, thrilled that Cindy had finally gotten something right. Then the cheating started.

Anyway, Patrick led her out of class into the late morning sunlight and stared intently with those gorgeous gray eyes and told her she had a nonemergency phone call from Lucy, her daughter. She was grateful he'd said nonemergency, because immediately on hearing that Lucy called, she started imagining Kevin having a heart attack while humping his girlfriend. Or worse, suffering cardiac arrest on his way to ask Cindy to come back to him.

Anyone wanting to reach guests at Camp Kinsonu had to call the main number and go through the formidable though admirably centered Betsy. Conversation with the men they were here to get over was absolutely forbidden. That had tickled Cindy, imagining Kevin being told he couldn't speak with her. Kevin wanted what he wanted when he wanted it, which was why his wanting her so many years back had been so thrilling, after so many years of feeling wanted by practically no one. When told he couldn't talk to her, he would jump the next flight to Bangor and show up in person to haul her back. Gave her goose bumps just thinking about it. However, it would take more than a few days for Kevin to realize his mistake with Patty. Next week, probably, he'd be here.

She knocked on the door, and after Betsy's welcoming "Come in," opened it and couldn't help exclaiming because Betsy's cabin was exactly the kind of place she wanted, only she hadn't known until she saw it. Sailing posters, plants, bookshelves, rugs—and the best part, a window seat covered by a cream cushion, with green and blue throw pillows that evoked the sea and matched the navy rug with blue-green flowers on the pine floor. A wood stove took command of the opposite corner, black as nighttime in these woods. She couldn't imagine anything more wonderful than sitting on those cushions, reading with a view of the sea, fire crackling in the stove, maybe a fragrant loaf of cinnamon bread in the oven and a cup of tea at hand, maybe a new Max beside her.

She also couldn't imagine Kevin here. He'd be claustrophobic, antsy, wanting to be out doing and meeting and making things happen. So her cabin would have to stay in her daydreams.

"Hi, Cindy." Betsy sat behind a simple blond wood desk with rounded corners, peering over a pair of black half-glasses perched midway along her nose. The effect was scholarly and chic at the same time, and Cindy almost rued her own perfect vision, which would prevent her getting a pair. "How was your class this afternoon?"

"Oh, wonderful. Though . . . " She grimaced comically. "The pottery world won't be lining up outside my door anytime soon."

"It's the process that matters, Cindy. Not the end." Betsy's eyes held her over the half-glasses, light from the window flashing the lenses opaque. Her gaze seemed to pour inside Cindy, bolster her up, assure her she could make it through with flying colors until Kevin came back. "If your child did something badly the first time, what would you say? 'The world will never line up outside your door, honey'?"

"Oh. No. Of course not." She laughed uncertainly, not expecting to have to defend a comment she'd meant as a joke, and gestured around her. "I adore your cabin. It's just the type of place I wish I lived in."

"Why don't you?"

Cindy blinked. "I'm sorry?"

"Why don't you find a place like this?"

"I . . . well, because . . . I live in Milwaukee. My husband's job took us there."

"I see." Betsy said this as if she couldn't see at all, which was sort of a funny coincidence since she was taking off her glasses while she said it. Cindy fidgeted, feeling as if she should start apologizing for where she lived. Betsy had that effect on her. "One should always live somewhere that feeds the soul."

"Right." Cindy nodded. "Yes. One should. Always."

She was going to say, *I'll get right on that*, but it would sound sarcastic and rude. She didn't mean to be rude, but after being required to defend her life over one lame joke and one compliment to Betsy's taste, at this point she'd just like to know what Lucy wanted.

"Your daughter called." Betsy leaned on her elbows, hands in prayer position, tips of her fingers pressed to her chin. "How do you feel about speaking with her?"

"Oh, I'd like to. Lucy stayed in Princeton for the summer to work for a real estate firm. She probably misses me. Or maybe she has a message from her father." Cindy's voice lifted hopefully, even though she knew it was too soon.

Betsy's eyes narrowed. "Possibly."

"Or maybe she needs advice. Like about cooking. Or men." She'd rushed to deflect the topic of conversation away from Kevin, then realized her reputation as someone to consult about matters of the heart had already been irreparably tarnished. "Or something."

"You don't think she'll upset you or impede your progress here at camp?"

"Oh, no." She shook her head, trying not to wonder what kind of progress could be impeded when she'd barely been here twenty-four hours. "I'm sure it will be fine."

"Then I'm sure it will be too." Betsy broke out her reassuring smile and gestured to a door on Cindy's left, closed with a black iron latch. "The phone is through there. Have a good talk with your daughter. All I ask is that you please check in with me on the way out. If I'm not here, I'll make sure Patrick is."

"Yes. Okay. Thanks." She strode toward the door, eager to sink into a familiar relationship and remind herself the world was still out there to go back to. Not that she was in a hurry to escape, because there was still so much to explore and do here. In fact, even after the disasters today, she sort of hoped Kevin *wouldn't* come back for her until next week. Camp was so fun. She should have gone as a girl, when her mom and dad wanted to send her, instead of moping all summer under their displeasure at her cowardice.

Inside the pretty little bedroom, she dialed the familiar number, hoping her daughter wasn't too busy to talk, and couldn't help the warm swelling in her heart when Lucy answered.

"Hi, sweetheart, it's Mom."

"Mom. Hang on." A rustling, then her daughter's muted voice talking to a coworker, so mature and professional that tears sprang to Cindy's eyes. She and Lucy had spoken only once since Kevin made his little pronouncement about being in love and leaving, and Lucy had been very upset, but more philosophical than Cindy expected. As if she'd seen this coming. As if she was almost relieved finally to have to deal with it instead of having to dread it.

Sometimes Cindy felt as if she lived in a different dimension than most of the people she knew.

"Mom, what the hell is dad doing?"

Cindy's tender maternal tears stopped in a hurry. "What? I . . . don't know, what do you—"

"He moved his bimbo into our house."

Cindy's gasp could probably be heard down by the water. *"What?"*

"She's living there." Her daughter's voice cracked in outrage. "She answered the freaking phone when I called last night."

"But . . . she . . . I mean she can't be."

"Mom." Impatience in Lucy's voice. She'd never been a patient child, not from infancy. Give her something new to try, if she failed the first time, instant hysteria. "I just *told* you she is."

"But I mean . . . " Cindy closed her eyes, feeling as stupid as she sounded. Shocks like this were getting very, very old. She wanted life back the way it was supposed to be. "If she happened to be there when—"

"Living there. Li-ving. Moved in. Given her landlord notice, for all I know."

"But he . . . " She opened her eyes, unable to stand the darkness in her own head, and fixed on a jumbled modern landscape hung over the twin bed across the room. "He never told me—"

"Mom, he never tells you anything. How the hell am I supposed to go home now for vacation before school starts again? How am I supposed to live in that house with them all cozy there together?"

"Oh. Well." Cindy sank onto a hard-backed chair, painted blue, next to the phone table. "I'm sure it's a mistake. I'm sure when I get back from here he'll—"

"Mom, you're out. She's in. You have to understand that." She was nearly crying, heaving breaths to try to stop it, this girl—woman now—who hated showing vulnerability. Like her father. "What am I going to do? Where will I go home to?"

"No, no. It won't come to that. Your home is your home, with me and your father." Cindy shook her head vehemently. "That . . . woman will be out when I get back."

"Mom," Lucy practically shouted. "Get . . . a . . . clue. Your marriage is over."

Cindy inhaled slowly, preparing to be patient. "Sweetheart, it's more complicated than—"

"Complicated my ass, it's simple. He's got Pattycakes, you'll find someone else, but what about *me*? *I* can't just go out and find another set of parents. *I'm* the one who's fucking screwed here."

"Lucy!" Her voice burst out in breathless shock—more shock, God please have mercy—her face hot, a strange buzzing in her ears. "Your language."

"Good, Mom." A hysterical giggle, thick with misery. "My life is falling apart and you're worried about my *language*."

Cindy couldn't do more than work her mouth. Speech seemed out of the question. There was too much to take in. She wanted off the phone, she wanted to bury herself in her bed, pull the covers over her head the way she had as a little girl, waking in the middle of the night with a splitting headache, starved for oxygen. She wanted to wake up now and find the fantasy mother she often dreamed of at her bedside, stroking her hair, telling her she was silly to be afraid of a bad dream, that she was loved more than life itself.

"I'm sorry." Lucy was crying in earnest now, then taking deep breaths, fighting again for control. "I'm sorry, Mom. This is just so *hard*."

"I know." She managed a whisper, guilt deep and dark inside her. She and Kevin had done this to Lucy. Their problems had grown so much bigger than just the two of them. "I promise you, it will all work out. Your father seems to need to . . . explore right now, but it won't last."

"Mom."

"I know him, honey. Better than you do. Just trust me on this. Okay?"

A sniffle. A sob. Quieter then, her breath slowing. Cindy's smile spread. Reassuring her daughter made her feel calmer too. Everything would be okay.

"Thanks, Mom. I gotta get back to work."

"I understand. And you're welcome. Now don't worry. Promise me you won't."

"Okay, Mom. I'll try." She hung up before her mother's *I love you* could make it over the line.

I love you. Cindy sat motionless until the phone startled her with its *bomp-bomp-bomp* chastisement. She put the receiver carefully back in place, feeling like she was in a post-earthquake landscape, waiting for the aftershocks.

Lucy had to be mistaken. Kevin wouldn't install his mistress in her house. Especially without asking her. Even he wasn't that bad. It was a mistake. That was all.

She felt her insides unlock and allowed herself a breath and another smile. A mistake. That was all.

A light tap at the door made her sigh. Betsy was the warmest, sweetest person she'd ever met, but Cindy couldn't bear to talk to her right now. Betsy would want to know what the conversation had been about. She'd give Cindy that concerned look and ask her all kinds of probing questions that would make Cindy sound like an idiot for believing in her husband and in her marriage. Max had faith in her no matter what she said. Maybe she should find out if there were any way she could become a dog and move to a kennel.

"Cindy?"

Cindy lifted her head. The voice was male. "Yes?"

"Can I come in?"

Patrick. What could she say? *Only if you don't make me feel ridiculous.* "Yes. Of course. Come in."

The door opened a few inches and his head appeared around it, as if he were afraid he'd catch her in some embarrassing moment and have to withdraw quickly. "Betsy had to leave for a while. She told me you were on a call from your daughter. It got kinda quiet in here, so I thought I'd check. Make sure you were okay."

She smiled at him, even though her insides still felt cracked and unstable. "I'm fine."

He glanced at her hands, then into her eyes, which were undoubtedly broadcasting her troubled feelings, which made her nervous, so she looked down at her hands, and found them twisted and tight. He knew she was lying about being fine.

"Take a walk with me? I want to show you something you'll like."

She looked back up at his fine strong face and wondered if he'd been planning to show Ann the same thing that morning, or if this was special, for Cindy. And then she realized that was a completely juvenile and pointless thing to wonder, the kind of thing she wondered about boys in grade school, where she spent so much time dreaming of the day Boy X or Boy Y or Boy Z would find her irresistible, which none of them ever had.

"I think I have a class right now." She couldn't remember what. Her brain seemed only to be able to hang on to useless, meandering thoughts at the moment. She was probably acting like someone with Alzheimer's. If she could sleep at night, people might not think she was such a ditz.

"So?" He grinned and bent down to whisper close to her ear. "Play hooky with me."

"Oh." She laughed nervously. Something about the way he said that had sounded sort of naughty. Or would have from the lips of a guy who liked women. "That sounds fun."

"Then let's go." He gestured her out through the comfortable blue-green living room, then out through the door on the opposite side of the cabin so they were walking up the gentle hill away from the sea. They crossed a mown field to another narrow path of matted grass and then, when they entered the woods, of soft leaves and moss.

As Cindy walked, the phone call with her daughter kept looping through her mind. Patrick could show her the pot of gold at the end of a rainbow, complete with sprightly leprechaun, and she'd just nod. Lucy couldn't be harmed in all this, Kevin had to see that. He shouldn't let his trampy girlfriend into their house, shouldn't let her answer the phone and upset everyone. But then that was Kevin—and most men from what she gathered—doing what he wanted and expecting everyone to accommodate him. She'd spent a lot of her life accommodating Kevin, done it mostly happily out of love, but in retrospect that made her part of what was now hurting Lucy.

"Here." They'd left the path, and Patrick held back a spruce branch for her to pass into a small mossy clearing strewn with rocks, ferns, and downed trees so old they squished into moist splinters under her feet. Ahead, dangling from a branch, she saw a strange lantern-looking object with yellow plastic flowers pasted around it, half filled with a bright red liquid, like the lone decoration left on a Christmas tree.

"Hummingbird feeder."

"Hummingbirds?" She turned in astonishment and found him directly behind her, so she stepped back into the prickly embrace of a spruce, and had to rebound with a quick side-step. "I thought hummingbirds were tropical."

"Not all." He gestured to a flat stone roughly chair height, mostly bare of moss, and they sat there, so close together their shoulders touched, and their hips, and all along their thighs, because there wasn't more room than that. She expected to feel awkward, and did a little, but actually it was nice being next to him, since Patrick could hardly take the contact sexually. He smelled good. Not expensive and sophisticated like Kevin, but manly in a different way that seemed to have been absorbed from the woods rather than dabbed on.

"Will the birds come, do you think, while we're here?"

"I'll tell you what." He held his hands up, palms away, fingers spread, sort of like a photographer framing a shot. "If we only allow the possibility that they will show up, then we'll affect the universe in a positive way, and make it easier for them."

Cindy's heart started to beat a little faster. Something in her personal universe that had always felt off seemed about to click into place. She wanted to look at Patrick but was pretty sure the sight of his handsome face this close would unnerve her, and she had to say this before the chance passed without her grabbing onto it: "That's how I think. That's how I feel about the world."

"It took me a long time to learn. With all I went through . . . " He chuckled, though not bitterly, as she might have expected. "No wonder I clung to the negative. It becomes a habit, you know? But in Thailand, with the monks, I learned how I, myself, was playing a part in my own downfall. So I totally let go, all the bad thoughts and expectations and worry. After that, boom, only a matter of time until my life turned around."

"Oh." Cindy's breath caught in a small gasp. "No one else . . . well, other people don't get it. At least not the people I know. They think I'm silly."

"They're jealous."

"Jealous?" Cindy put a hand to her chest, delighted just by the idea. "Of *me*?"

"Not that many people can throw off the negativity surrounding us." He was looking at her intently, she could feel it, but she kept her eyes on a daddy longlegs exploring the world of a lichen-covered stump, drinking in every syllable of every word. "It's safer to be cynical, Cindy. It's easier to hate, to point to misery in the world and then use that hate and misery as a sign that we can only expect more."

"Yes." That was Kevin. In a nutshell. And her brilliant parents. In an even smaller nutshell.

"It takes courage to be vulnerable. To say 'I love. I like. I am happy with who and how I am. Good things will come to me. I deserve them.'"

"Yes." Now her eyes were drawn to his, because there was nowhere else she could look and be satisfied. What he described, she'd tried to do all her adult life, without ever dignifying it with such beautiful, strong words. "Too many people don't want to hear good things."

"Worse, they want to destroy the words and attitudes that can make those good things happen."

"Yes. *Yes*." She knew she was saying *yes* too much, but she wanted to say it a thousand times more besides, yes yes *yes*! Tears rose, along with an absolute tsunami of gratitude for the man beside her. "Thank you, Patrick."

"Hey, you're welcome. For what?"

"Understanding." She smiled, calm and peaceful, sure she could give Centered Betsy a run for her money. "My husband *will* come back to me."

"He will." His earnest and beautiful gaze took on a slight edge. "If that's what you want."

Of course it is was her automatic response, but she only thought it this time, staring into his deep gray eyes.

"He'd be a fool to lose you, Cindy." He was nearly whispering, and was it her imagination or had he leaned closer? She should move back. She should, but she didn't. She simply had the thought that she should and left it at that, as if her brain had lost control of her muscles.

"Most people . . . " She cleared her throat. "Most people think I'd be a fool not to lose *him*."

"You have to follow what's in your heart. Only you know what that is. You have to be at peace with you. No one else."

He could not have spoken any more directly to her inner-most soul. She wanted to seize this moment, bottle it forever so when she felt stupid and young and uncertain, she'd have his deep gray eyes and his validating words to bring back how she felt right now. "You don't know how much it means to hear you say that."

"That's what I'm here for, Cindy. To help."

She was going to say that she was pretty sure he'd helped her more in the past several minutes than anyone could for the next two weeks, but something buzzed by at top speed, like a bee, only too large and too loud, and Patrick's eyes shifted past her. "Look. There, behind you. Turn slowly."

She moved as carefully as she could, then let out an "Oh" no louder than a baby's sigh. A hummingbird, the first one she'd seen except on TV nature programs. Not three yards away, drinking from the feeder as if it was the most natural thing in the world to be doing, while she couldn't get past the idea that something so graceful and exotic should be feasting on brilliant fragrant rain-forest flowers, surrounded by vo-luptuous women in colorful dresses with more of those same flowers tucked behind their ears. Not here, in the browns and greens and grays of the Maine coast, putting on a show for Cindy, who wore Kevin's Princeton sweater and jeans that were too short.

The bird's wings beat into a blur, its green shimmery body hovering, undulating, liquid in the light, darting forward, back, forward, back, inserting its beak into the center of the yellow plastic flower each time, enchanting and endlessly thirsty.

"Ruby-throated hummingbird." His voice barely sounded

in her hair, tickled the strands above her ear. The warmth of his breath made her shiver. "Isn't he amazing?"

"He?" she whispered back.

"Patch of red at its throat. The females are all green. Look. There's another. A female. To the left."

She nodded. She'd seen it. And couldn't stop looking, feeling the warmth of Patrick at her back, the chill of the stone seeping through her pant leg, the cool stillness of the woods and the faint whirring buzz of the birds as they darted back and forth, occasionally resting on a branch gnawed bare by porcupines, then feasting, fast-motion, again.

"They remind me of you, Cindy." He put a hand on her shoulder, heavy and secure. "Full of energy, exploring their surroundings, bright and beautiful."

She bent her head, unsure how to respond, half ready to dissolve into sentimental tears, half ready to get up and dance from the sheer joy of his compliment. His hand left her shoulder, began massaging her neck, working on the tight muscles, which barely got to relax anymore, even at night. Cindy closed her eyes and gave herself over. At home, her massages were administered by a dark, silent woman in an exclusive salon in Fox Point. But this was just as good, if not better, for the deep connection between them.

She'd been after that connection when she brought home a massage video for her and Kevin to practice, but while Kevin had lain blissfully still while she massaged him, when it was his turn, he'd become irritated and uncomfortable, and she'd spent twenty minutes lying rigid with guilt while he grunted in annoyance, until she finally thanked him and said she'd had enough. Which hadn't been a lie.

But Patrick's hands felt sure and strong, melting her muscles, making her realize how much tension she'd been carrying. And the more she relaxed, the more her deprived body craved sleep . . .

"I've met a lot of women in a lot of places all over the world, but I can tell that you're a very special lady, with a lot of power inside you." His other hand joined the ecstasy on her neck, then both moved slowly outward to treat her shoulders—then down, where they remained still, firmly cupping her upper arms, making her stifle a groaning protest. "I'm looking forward to getting to know you a lot better in the next couple of weeks. I know you'll keep going in a positive direction. I'm proud of what you've already done."

"Thank you."

He was proud of her. She wanted the feeling from those words to go on and on and on, so she stayed, head down, not moving, as if his hands clamped on her arms had bound her to the stone beneath her. The hummingbirds had flown away or gone silent, the woods still except for faint noises down from the camp. An occasional voice or screen door slamming, the rhythmic thump of tennis balls against the backboard.

"Turn around, Cindy." His whisper broke the silence.

She obeyed, helped by the pressure of his hands urging her into an embrace against his chest. His lips touched her forehead; she closed her eyes and let herself register as precisely as possible every sensation. The grassy smell of his shirt, the smooth muscle underneath it, the strong encircling protectiveness of his arms. This too her memory would want to call back up in the days ahead.

Because the difference with how it felt when Kevin held her was immediately obvious and immediately shocking. Kevin's touch was dutiful, paternal, part of their familiar and admittedly stale marital ritual. While Patrick, a man she'd known barely a day, held her like he meant it.

Chapter 8

Dear Eldon,

What saves me is that it's so beautiful up here. The colors are so vivid, and the air is so clear and flavorful. It makes my life in Burlington seem even more brown and airless. But there's also beauty about this place that goes beyond visual. A peace, that affects you in deeper ways than ordinary calm. A constant pull to be who you are at your innermost level, as if any sort of artifice would pollute what's around us. I can see why Betsy picked this setting for women needing to reach inside themselves for knowledge and balance. She is a powerful and inspiring presence. You'd like her.

Now that I've been here, I regret more than ever the weekend I suggested we come here that didn't work out. Of course at the time I was less into Maine and more into the idea of being with you outside, in public together, for the first time in over a decade. The chance to have you acknowledge me with more than just your special wave from the speaker's podium. I planned to savor every second of being a "real" couple again. I use the quotes because we were always more of a real couple than most, but in this case appearances mattered, at least to me.

Thank you for arranging for me to be here. Your part in it is the only reason I decided to come, and most of the reason I'm staying. Everything I see, everything I observe about this place and the people, I find myself storing, squirrel-like, to share with you, the way I've always stored up the bits of my life for you. It made for a hyphenated existence, but worth it.

I check the Internet every day for news of you. Betsy understands and allows me to use the computer in her office. It's hard with her hovering over me, wanting to grab at my every emotion, like a frog waiting for flies to buzz by, but it's better than not knowing.

Miracles happen. Come back soon. I'm waiting.

I love you, I miss you,
Martha

Martha opened Internet Explorer on Betsy's computer and typed in the familiar address for Google. She spent a lot of time on her computer at home. Surfing the 'net felt more worthwhile than watching television. Her brain was undoubtedly more active, and she always learned something, even if it was that people would do anything for attention. Particularly, she suspected, those most terrified of finding out they were completely unremarkable.

"How are you today, Martha?" Betsy asked in a voice that meant a response of *Fine, thank you* would not cut it. Being part of this camp meant she was expected to put her feelings and her relationship with Eldon into words, instead of having them reside comfortably in her head where they had for so long. She'd frozen in group therapy, not at all sure how she could bear up under the scrutiny or questions of others. Especially after Ann nearly strangled Cindy with her scorn.

"It's beautiful here. That helps me cope." She took her hands off the keyboard and gave Betsy her full attention. That way she could put off having to type in Eldon's name and read the same news all over again. No change. No change. No change.

Last night she'd dreamed Eldon had been underwater, gasping for air, and that she had dived under too, so her presence could bring him lifesaving oxygen. Sure enough, like the Disney mermaid movie, the touch of Martha's hand had made them both able to breathe, and they'd swum happily around coral reefs together—minus the warbling shellfish.

"I'm glad you're doing well." Betsy smiled, perched on the edge of her desk, but her eyes were cautious and watchful. More even than usual. "Go ahead. I'm here if you need me."

What did she mean? Martha quelled the darting worry by relaxing and loosening her muscles, opening her lungs wide for air.

She typed in his name, wrote *Edlon* by mistake and had to

acknowledge Google's superiority when asked if she meant *Eldon*. Yes. She meant Eldon. She was sorry to have been so imprecise.

The hits came up. Martha scanned the summaries and felt her diaphragm squeeze to a stop. Eldon had pneumonia.

This morning she'd assumed the dream assured her and Eldon of a happy shared future, but the underwater freedom could also have meant a shared future in death.

She opened the first article and read. "Common complication," "antibiotics," "prognosis uncertain." A quote from chilly Bianca, about trusting that the doctors were doing everything they could.

Martha pretended she was still reading, but the words started to blur and jump. Once, she'd made up a story about a man who always ran away. When his life went badly, he'd put on his special shoes, brown and green and blue like planet Earth, and run until he reached a place in which he felt the pull to start over. One day after being fired, he went home and found the shoes in a box under his bed, put them on, and started running, west, as he always did. He left his house, his block, his neighborhood, friends, family, and city behind. Trees thickened into a forest, rose over mountains, thinned to a prairie on whose far edge a strange brown rippling appeared. On he ran, through the whipping grasses, until he realized the rippling was the ground eroding, buckling, collapsing in front of him, falling off the end of the world. He turned back, but the dirt and grass eroded faster than he could run, poured off the edge of shrinking Earth like a brown and green waterfall, until the ground beneath his feet—

"Martha?"

She turned to Betsy. She couldn't speak, but she couldn't

cry either. She was trapped, caught between denial and a harder place. The undersea dream had been about death. Eldon's and hers, if she wanted to stay with him.

"Would you like to talk?"

Martha worked to unlock her throat enough to speak. "I . . ."

She was going to say that she'd like to be alone, but the last time she tried that, on her arrival here, Patrick had burst forth to save the loony from herself.

"I . . . have kayaking now."

Betsy tipped her head gently to one side, watching Martha with gentle patience, wearing a gentle smile, waiting for her to crack and admit that instead of kayaking she was really going to find a stake to drive into her own heart. Which would be redundant because the article had already done that.

Eldon was going to die. Maybe Martha had known it all along, but she hadn't truly felt it until now.

"Okay." Betsy rose and stepped back to let Martha pass. "I'll walk with you. I'm going that way myself."

What a coincidence. Martha stepped out into the humidity of the day, felt sweat gathering between her breasts. She wouldn't be out of anyone's sight for the rest of her stay, she felt it instinctively, a pressure building in her chest. Caged even here, in this beautiful place, caged by grief and fear and people's worry. Then back to her brown apartment, which she'd no longer be able to pretend, even to Ricky, was like living in chocolate, and to her job. Without Eldon for the first time in two decades, since they'd found each other shortly before Eldon graduated from college and were drawn together as if each had a force of gravity meant only for the other. They'd been together four years out in the open. Then

Eldon had settled on a political career and met Bianca, the perfect political wife.

Until this morning, when Martha found herself facing Eldon's death, she'd thought nothing would ever hurt as much as when he told her he was marrying Bianca for his career. Before that day, Martha had been sure love would conquer all. Now she knew that love conquered people, but it couldn't do shit about circumstance. Even the truest of true love hadn't been enough to earn her a right to Eldon's name, and it wouldn't be enough to save his life.

Down by the water, on the coarse pebbly part of the beach exposed by the tide, seven other women had already lined up in shorts and water shoes. Eight kayaks taken from the boathouse, four red, four blue, rested between them and the gently swishing waves.

Six of the women had already paired off. Ann stood to the side, alone, looking at Martha as she crossed the sand. She looked the way boys looked at Martha when she was the only option left during the week P.E. students were taught the basics of ballroom dancing, which none of them would use and all promptly forgot. The scars from the process, however, had miraculous staying power.

Anger surprised her, spearing her chest—lightning in an already tense sky. Anger of an intensity she usually felt only for Bianca and the warden's grip she held on Martha and Eldon's happiness. Martha forced herself to step calmly in place next to Ann instead of hauling off and socking her perfect nose. Years of working at the DOT had taught her to block out negative and frustrated people. They owned their problems, not Martha. Martha owned plenty already. But she still felt the hostility beside her, coming off Ann in waves larger than the ones licking the shore.

She waited, a tiny breeze occasionally cooling her sweat-filmed skin and ruffling the hems of her Indian print pants, while Betsy had a talk with Cheri, the instructor, who flashed concerned glances at Martha, which made all the women turn to see what could possibly be so much more wrong with her than with any of them. Ann's cold hazel eyes stared hardest.

Let her wonder. Let them all wonder. Martha gazed across the bay, at the restless blue-green expanse dotted with jewel-like lobster pots, and felt the urge to swim, swim, swim, even not knowing how, until her head became a dot in the middle of the bay, indiscernible from the lobster pots or clumps of floating seaweed or bumps of driftwood.

Eldon had pneumonia. He was going to die.

The instructor handed Martha water shoes and a bright pink life jacket, then reminded the women of the safety tips they'd learned in the first class on Monday, and had them all practice one more time with paddles until they got the feel and rhythm for the stroke back. Martha had been canoeing a few times before, when her parents and nine siblings swarmed into Gus, the bouncy, squeaky school bus her dad bought to transport their oversized family, and went to visit Aunt Peg in New Hampshire. Canoeing was okay, but Martha had been half as big then, and these kayak looked tiny and unstable in comparison. She stood awkwardly next to the rail-thin women lined up on the beach, who all seemed so comfortable and energized in their bodies.

Maybe men left thin women in greater number than fat. That would be some justice.

"Okay, ladies, let's each get into our kayaks and I'll help you shove off. We'll stay close to shore at first, then we can take a quick paddle out to one of the ledges if you're feeling up to it, since it's so calm today."

Seven women strode toward their boats, pushed them into the water and clambered in, some with grace, some without. Martha put on her water shoes, balancing on one leg, then the other, watching her kayak, blue with a black seat, the front of it already lapped by waves that had been several inches away when she came down to the beach. The boat looked small, graceful and delicate, everything she wasn't. When they practiced getting in and out last time, she'd felt like a buffalo among swans. What if she took a few strokes then sank slowly, inevitably—the *Titanic* going down on its maiden voyage?

The pain of realizing she wouldn't be able to laugh about that image with Eldon propelled her down the beach to push the blue kayak into the sea, just until it floated. This was a mistake. This was not going to work.

Cheri strode up, brunette, size two, with defined muscles and a perky smile. "All set?"

"Sure." Martha hiked up her pant legs, stepped into shallow frigid water, heaving breaths to avoid a rush of tears. Then one leg and her weight into the boat, which wobbled dangerously. In a fit of panic, she yanked her other foot on board and her butt hit the seat with a *whump* that grounded the kayak flat against the sand.

Beached whale.

"Okay, well done. Here's your paddle. We'll wait for a wave and get you going. Ready? Here comes."

The wave slid in; Cheri shoved with her impressive muscles, and the kayak lurched forward, caught the deeper water another wave made possible, then glided smoothly ahead.

Glided. Smoothly. Martha glanced at the sea, paddle clenched in her fists, and noted incredulously, then thankfully, that it wasn't rising rapidly over her boat.

She dipped her paddle in. Took a stroke. Another. The kayak moved straight, slipping effortlessly through the water, more effortlessly than Martha could move herself on land. Exactly as it was supposed to. Another stroke. Another. Practice turning. Practice going backward.

It worked. It all worked. If such a miracle was possible, maybe Eldon would get well.

Cheri called out and they followed her, two by two, past *Stronglady*, the Kinsonu speedboat, then gliding along close to the coast, waves swirling and gurgling around and between the rocky formations. Gulls soared overhead, cormorants skimmed the ocean surface. A light breeze refreshed her face. Martha wasn't sure how, but she felt suddenly light and free. As if leaving the land had made it possible for her to leave her body and her pain behind. She didn't want to stay here near the safe hard coast, she wanted to turn and go straight out into the live, liquid sea.

Fifteen minutes later she got her wish. Apparently satisfied with her fledgling kayakers, Cheri led them a third of the way across the bay toward a ledge, uncovered at low tide, covered at high, now half visible.

Martha stroked and stroked, exhilaration building, working her muscles, enjoying the speed and the space. Eldon would be cured of pneumonia. His renewed health would wake him. His brush with death would make him realize how short life was. He'd leave his wife and come back to her, and they'd live together for the rest of their lives as they were destined to do from the moment they met.

The kayakers gathered around the reef, which had come into view underwater as they approached, like a huge ghostly sea creature. They drifted listlessly, watching the swaying seaweed and grasses, limp and lifeless out of the tide, but here a dancing delicate forest. Mussel shells glinted blue and white, barnacles crusted rocks spotted with pink circular growths, orange and purple starfish clustered among them. A crab slipped sideways through the weeds.

The women had gone silent, paddles moved only occasionally to maneuver. Martha couldn't take her eyes off the view under the surface. This was the world of her dream—set in Maine instead of in coral-filled tropics—but the same type of place where she and Eldon had—

"Hey."

Martha's boat jerked from a minor impact. She'd floated gently into the side of Ann's kayak, and Ann was glaring at her as if she'd committed a crime against humanity.

"Sorry." She didn't bother to add a smile to her apology.

"Watch where you're going."

"Okay." Martha shrugged, again the buffalo among swans, and turned her kayak away from the group, away from Ann, and let it drift to where she could lay a convincing, if false, claim to solitude.

No one called her back, so it was easy to take a stroke, and another, and again, only half listening now for Cheri's signal to rejoin the herd. She stopped paddling and gazed over the side, even though there was nothing to see at this depth, until a slight sound made her look up.

A dark head poking out of the water, large, black, glistening eyes staring at her.

She stared back, and let the kayak drift closer. The seal took in her approach, whiskers visible now on its nose, fur shiny wet. The breeze stopped. The water gently rippled.

Eldon loved animals; the encounter would have delighted him. Why wasn't he here? Why couldn't she show him this? How could he choose to stay shut in a hospital when there was all this world to explore together?

"What's down there, seal?" she asked in a whisper, enchanted, and found herself half expecting an answer.

Once upon a time . . .

Eldon, he replied. *Come down and see. He's calling for you.*

"Eldon?" Her heart was knocking to get out of her chest.

Take off your life jacket and come. He needs you.

If Eldon needed her, she'd go to him. Of course . . .

She took off her life jacket, slowly. The seal tipped up its nose and slid back under. Martha peered again over the edge, hoping for a glimpse of its sleek body—like hers, clumsy and slow on land, graceful and fleet in the sea.

Mesmerized by the sun-illuminated columns plunging until lost from sight, she leaned over farther. Water as freedom, water as pneumonia in Eldon's lungs. She imagined herself slipping under as the seal demanded, welcoming liquid in her own lungs, joining Eldon in the fight for breath.

Then the quick sharp sensation of falling, the shock of the icy, icy wet, and the sudden unexpected terror of the yawning void underneath. She couldn't swim, had never learned.

Her life jacket was back in the boat. Why the hell had she taken it off? She didn't belong in water, God knew what was under her. Whales? Sharks?

The boat. She flailed toward it, imitating swimming motions. Her head went under. She jerked up, coughing, gasping, under again, back up. Ann's kayak, swiftly coming up beside her, Ann's beautiful face set and tense.

"What the fuck are you doing?"

What the fuck does it look like? Martha lunged for Ann's boat. Her head plunged under again. Cold water. Icy water. Frozen water meant for some frozen planet. She emerged, coughing again, moaned without meaning to. Every drop of warmth was being sucked out of her. People died of hypothermia quickly in water like this. Or of cold shock, which was even more dangerous. The boat was safety. Air was safety. She needed out.

Ann spoke, shouted, words Martha couldn't understand. She flailed, tried to kick; her face went under again; more sea in her lungs. She coughed it out, fighting it out. Eldon couldn't. He was going to die.

Another splash and Ann was in next to her, yanking her up so her head stayed above water. "Don't you *dare* drown yourself, you bitch. Get the hell out of this water. *Now.*"

Her furious voice cut through the spinning panic in Martha's head. She stopped moving and allowed herself to be dragged, weeping silently, cold, numb, heavy, through water, then through kayaks piloted by the silent shapes of women, until her feet touched the craggy edges of the reef. She crawled on, shivering violently, aware now of anxious and curious faces, of Cheri and another woman paddling off to save the abandoned kayaks.

"Jesus. *Jesus*. That water is *freezing*." Ann dragged herself up on the ledge next to Martha, crossed her arms and rubbed frantically at her shoulders. "Why couldn't you try to drown yourself in a fucking hot tub?"

Rage rose instantly, buffalo ready to trample the swan, except Martha's teeth had started chattering uncontrollably and she could barely hold still enough to keep Ann in focus. "I f-f-f-fell."

"Then f-f-f-fall in a hot tub. Better yet, do it when I'm not around. I'm not going to rescue you twice."

"I d-didn't ask you to d-do it once."

"Oh, I was supposed to leave you there? Or pile rocks on your back to help you out? Is that it?" Her face screwed up in fury. "You sickos ever stop to think about the people left behind to clean up?"

Martha stared, wanting to pick Ann up and hurl her back into the ice pond.

"Forget it. Forget it." Chest heaving, Ann lifted a Stop hand toward Martha, which pissed Martha off even more because the only person who needed to stop right now was Ann. "But don't *ever* do that to me again, you selfish coward."

"To *you*?" Martha's buffalo trampled the swan. It lay flat on the earth in a broken tangle of red-stained feathers. She shivered and laughed and shivered again. "Funny, I thought the *sun* was the c-center of the universe."

"Shut the hell up, you don't know shit." Ann's furious face crumpled, and Martha wasn't sure she'd ever been with someone about to cry and felt only loathing. Except maybe watching Bianca's cosmetically appropriate grief on TV. "God I need a drink."

"Oh, good idea. Alcohol makes you lose b-body heat."

What was she saying? Who cared? Let Ann drink a case of whatever she wanted and die of hypothermia. With all that hate inside her, what good would she ever do the world?

"I don't give a rat's ass." She raised a shaking hand to cover her forehead and eyes. "I can't face this shit again."

"Again? What the—"

With a sick plunge in her belly, Martha realized. She closed her eyes, wanting to cry again, but this wasn't her moment for tears. Ann's love had taken his own life.

All Martha had been thinking about was her own pain, about Eldon, about that watery connection. She'd gone in wanting that.

The buffalo retreated so the swan could get up, brush herself off and clean her wings.

"I . . . fell." She said it in a gentle voice this time and made it the truth. "I was looking over the s-side and I tipped out."

"After taking off your life jacket."

"I was hot."

Ann looked at her fiercely, her lovely face contorted and blotchy with the effort of keeping back tears and memories. "You bloody well better have been."

A woman arrived silently with Ann's red kayak and delivered it, hand over hand, until it was under Ann's control. Cheri pulled up holding Martha's steady.

"You okay to paddle back?" Cheri tried to smile, but Martha could tell she was frightened.

"Sure." She nodded, feeling foolish and useless. The kayak was pushed in front of her. She stared at it helplessly, blue body, black seat, discarded pink life vest.

"Wait." Ann had stopped, one trembling leg lifted to step into her own boat. "She can't. I'll help."

"I can manage."

"I said I'll *help*."

Martha hauled herself up, feeling twice her usual weight and as if she had access to only half her brain. The blue kayak bobbed in front of her on the tiny waves, sunlight glinting off its smooth sides, dry as a bone inside. Ann held the boat steady and she forced herself to step in. For an awful moment she thought she was going to teeter out and bring herself and Ann back over for another swim, but a surge of determined power kept her momentum directed into the seat with another humiliating *whump* that sent water splashing onto the ledge.

"Thank you." She put on the life jacket and accepted her paddle from Ann, who nodded curtly and climbed effortlessly into her own boat.

Martha hesitated, considering an olive branch, dove to Ann's swan. But then she heard the phrase "stupid cow" muttered from perfect pink lips.

No dove.

She made the trip back one buffalo stroke at a time, occasional teardrops slipping silently from under her lids, trying to reconnect with the positive thoughts the sea had brought on her way out: The seal would bring good luck. She'd fallen in, not tried to go. Her failure to drown meant there was still good reason to be alive. When Eldon faced death, he'd retreat from it as violently and completely as she had.

Her mood didn't respond. Toward the shore, she saw Betsy waiting, and forced new tears to dry, made herself appear calm. Betsy would mean well, but Martha couldn't share Eldon right now. She'd shared Eldon all her life, with his wife and with his children and with the voting public of

Vermont. She wanted him to stay intact inside her, where she could give him undiluted strength to fight through what could otherwise be the last few days of his life.

Betsy was there as her kayak landed, wading in, sympathy in her eyes, a cell phone in one hand. "A boy named Ricky called five minutes ago. I have my cell here, you can talk to him."

Martha stared at the cell, feeling too stupid to understand what it was or what she was supposed to do.

"He says he needs you."

Ricky needed her. She understood that. Betsy dialed. Martha climbed out of the boat and took the phone in her wet hand, pressed it to her ear. "Ricky?"

"Oh, yeah, hi, Martha." He was using his most casual I-don't-care voice, which meant he was upset. "How is camp? I got the number from that paper you left on your television."

"It's fun, Ricky. Maine is beautiful." She had to concentrate to speak without her teeth chattering, her words weighted down by the dull grinding in her chest. A blanket was wrapped around her. She didn't look to see who'd done it or offer thanks. "You would like it here."

"Can I come visit?"

"No, Ricky. It's just for old women."

His giggle softened the tight muscles in her face. "You're not old."

"I'm older than five hundred and forty fruit flies. How is everything there?"

"I'm bringing in your mail every day like you asked." He sniffed, avoiding the reason he'd called, and she imagined him wiping his eyes and smearing dirt on his cheek. "I was wondering . . ."

"Yes?"

"Could you tell me a story?"

Ricky's parents were fighting. He needed a story. She wasn't sure she had any left in her. "A story."

"I want the one about the ugly bug."

The bug story was one of his favorites, a black comedy born on a bad day they'd turned to good with laughter and chocolate. Martha closed her eyes to block out the figures on the beach, still there even after the fat lady suicide show was over. She dug down deep inside her until she connected with the power and clarity she needed to tell her stories, until she could see the bug and his forest home so clearly she might as well have been there herself.

"Once upon a time, there was a really ugly bug who lived in a big beautiful forest. None of the other bugs wanted to play with him, because he was so ugly, which made him very sad. His mother told him that what was inside mattered more than what was outside, but the little ugly bug wasn't satisfied. He knew deep down that somewhere lived an ugly little boy who would understand him, and be his friend."

Ricky made a small soft sound that Martha recognized as the beginning of a giggle, and clung to it hopefully. She shrugged out of the blanket so her arms and body would be free to help her tell the story, even though she knew Ricky wouldn't be able to see. But she felt cramped and stifled not being able to move.

"So one day he left home, and traveled long and far, over bumps, under branches, and through puddles, until he came to the big shining city. He scurried along the edge of the buildings to avoid being stepped on by all the shoes belonging to all the feet belonging to all the people, none of whom was his boy. Nobody took notice of him until he got to a corner. There stood a little ugly boy who was about to cross the street, when suddenly he tugged at his mother's hand, pointed and said, 'Look, look, look!'

"The little ugly bug quivered with excitement. Here at last was his one true friend."

Ricky snorted, trying to hold back laughter.

"'Leave it alone,' said the ugly boy's mother, who was pretty ugly herself, 'it's just an ugly bug.' But the ugly boy wouldn't listen. He came closer and leaned down to look at the little ugly bug more carefully.

"The little ugly bug was beside himself. He smiled his biggest, ugliest smile and waved his littlest ugliest leg. 'Hi,' he squeaked. 'I've traveled a long way to find you. Now we can be—'

"'Wow,' said the little ugly boy. 'That is a really ugly bug.' And he picked up his ugly little foot and stepped on him."

Martha stood, eyes still closed, listening to the beautiful gales of Ricky's laughter, let it wash through her pain and rinse some of it away. Eldon would have loved that story too, a welcome relief from the squeaky clean politically correct world he had to live in without her.

She registered another sound and opened her eyes. Smiles and giggles from the kayakers too. Even Ann seemed mildly amused, wrapped, as Martha had been, in a blanket, standing next to Patrick.

Why were they still here? Weren't they finished gawking?

Except in their faces she saw something new, besides the laughter. Not sympathy, not apprehension, but something pleasant that made her uneasy, but also warmer. In all but Betsy, whose usually kind blue eyes were narrowed thoughtfully.

"Thanks. Thanks for the story. I feel better now."

"You're welcome, Ricky." Martha told him to be good, wishing she could shout the same at his parents, said good-bye and handed the phone back to Betsy, who continued to watch her speculatively.

"Thank you for letting us share your story, Martha. You have a real gift." Something about the way she phrased it made it sound less like a compliment than a condemnation. "You and Ann should go back to your cabin and dry off. I'll have one of the kitchen gals send over hot drinks. And I'll be available in my office if you want to talk."

Martha nodded dutifully and started for the wooden stairs leading off the beach. Just before she reached them, she remembered her other story, and how the man running away from the collapsing prairie had escaped at the last second by leaping into the air and catching hold of a star.

Chapter 9

Dear Paul,

You would hate Camp Kinsonu. You would make fun of every aspect of everything that goes on. I wish I could have seen your face when they said we had to sing "I Am Woman." But you're not here. I hate that I am. I hate that you put me here.

That's all folks,
Ann

Dinnertime at Camp Kinsonu. Ann pushed a piece of yellowish macaroni around her plate. She'd taken maybe five bites of the creamy and faintly curry-flavored casserole, bursting with chicken and vegetables, after a half-sandwich lunch and the microtoast breakfast. Not healthy. At home, or what passed for home these days with her parents, she'd counted on her nightly cocktail to get her appetite going, though her weight continued to drop anyway. Of course, here such shocking indulgence was forbidden. So she starved.

Macaroni made her think of Paul, who detested it, after growing up eating the boxed mix too many evenings while his exhausted mother lay in her room, too depressed to get up and take care of her kids. His father tried hard to be a good dad, but by the time he got home, dinner was over and the sin of mac 'n' cheese again had already been committed.

She knew she should eat; of course she knew. But tonight she couldn't get rid of the queasiness that started out on the bay when she noticed her "buddy" missing and turned to see Martha facedown in the sea. Martha insisted she'd fallen, but Ann was pretty sure that was bullshit. Of course, Kinsonu was buzzing. Bad news was like a bad smell: once released, impossible to contain.

"Ann?"

Ann tried to look as if she were anticipating Cindy's next words with anything but intense annoyance. She wanted quiet. At home after work, she had gotten used to, then enjoyed, the silence in the house with Paul, stupidly not recognizing the red flag. Here there was pressure to be BFF—best friends forever—from the second they got up until they dropped into bed for bad nights of sleep. "What's up?"

"Dinah asked you a question."

"Sorry." She thought about smiling at Dinah, but one look at the empty eyes, bright lipstick, teased hairdo, and turquoise jogging suit over past-its-prime propped-up cleavage turned her smile into a symbolic gag.

"I was telling everyone about my first honeymoon in

Vegas, and my second one in the Florida Keys, and my third one in the Bahamas. Cindy said she'd gone to the Catskills on her honeymoon, and I guess Martha never did get married, so now I'm asking where you went on your honeymoon. If you ever got married." She giggled and her cleavage jostled around, as if it were trying to ingest one of the gold chains. "Though I should probably have asked where you were just now instead, since it was probably more interesting."

Ann blinked at her. "Where I was?"

"Well, obviously you were a million miles away!" More giggles, more jiggles, hahaha.

"Paris." Ann spoke sharply. "We honeymooned in Paris. Stayed on the Left Bank near the Luxembourg Gardens. We walked the city every day and had dinner at a different three-star restaurant every night. We hired a boat and cruised the Seine. We took a two-day trip to the champagne district, and saw the cathedral at Reims. We went to the Loire Valley and tasted Vouvray wine at a farmhouse, served to us by the vintner himself. We went to the church where Joan of Arc worshiped. We saw Napoleon's tomb."

She pushed her plate back, irritation making her stomach even more inhospitable. "How does that compare to Vegas?"

Cindy looked down at her plate. Martha took a sip of water, making her shawl jingle. Dinah stayed frozen for a few seconds, then blinked, showing turquoise eye shadow. "Well lah-dee-dah. I was just asking."

"I was just answering."

But she hadn't been. Not at all. She'd used a trick she recognized suddenly as one of Paul's. Getting Rid of Unwanted Company by Showing Superiority. An ugly trick, one that had embarrassed her every time.

Crap.

"Sorry." She could only manage to direct the apology to her full plate. "I had a shitty day."

"Whose fault was that?"

Ann lifted her head to glare at Dinah, fiercely protective of Martha's weakness. "Excuse me?"

"I think you heard me." She didn't shy away from eye contact, and Ann realized with a fresh wave of anger that Dinah wasn't talking about Martha.

"It's my fault," Martha said flatly. "I upset her when I—"

"It's not your fault." Ann kept her eyes on Dinah. "And it sure as hell isn't mine."

"We've all got troubles. Everyone here. But only you need to *punish* us with yours." Dinah flicked a nervous glance around the group, then waved her hand, shoo, shoo, as if Ann were a fly that had disturbed her dinner. "Now . . . now grow up and take it like a woman. Like the rest of us."

That was it. Forget anger. This called for fury. "What exactly do you mean by that?"

Dinah lifted her chin.

"Um . . . I think what she *means* is that you can control how you react to your day, and you can make that reaction more positive." Cindy snuck a wary peek at Ann, then back to Dinah. "Right?"

"That's the nice way of putting it, yes."

Furious rage. Rage boiling so high and hot that tears snuck into her eyes and she wanted Paul so badly her chest felt as if it were going to implode. He'd know exactly how to take her side. He'd laugh calmly, then come up with the brilliant cutting insult she was too upset to think of. Rat bastard, where was he when she needed him?

"Hey there, ladies." Patrick bent over the table between Dinah and Cindy, glancing first at Martha, then at Ann and her full plate. "How's it going?"

Silence. Ann managed to stay seated, but barely. To hell with fight *or* flight, she wanted both. Take out a few of Dinah's overwhitened teeth, then a few from Cindy's equine overbite, and run.

"Well . . . Ann was just telling us about her honeymoon. In Paris." Cindy beamed up at him. "It sounded really romantic."

"I bet." He turned his gray eyes on Ann again, and even in the blazing midst of her fury she felt the unwelcome shock of attraction. "Paris is one of my very favorite cities."

"Ooh, you've been there too?" Cindy swiveled to gaze up at him like a lovesick puppy. "I've always wanted to go."

Oh *God*. If Ann's own attraction to Patrick was unwelcome, her jealousy over Cindy's was ten times more.

"You'll get to Paris someday, Cindy." He smiled down at her. "If you really want to go."

"You're right. I will." She nodded happily, transported by his apparently all-encompassing wisdom. Ann's stomach heaved.

"How are you doing there, Miss Martha?" Patrick extracted himself from Cindy's gaze and turned to the end of the table.

"I'm fine." Her voice was so weary that some of Ann's rage dissolved into fresh concern. "Thank you."

"Did something happen to you today?" This from Dinah, their china shop's resident bull.

"No," Ann said. "She's *fine*."

Dinah ignored her. "I thought I heard someone talking

about you as if something bad happened, and now Patrick is asking . . . "

Martha heaved one of her endless sighs, looking as if she'd like to tip off the bench and drown herself in the floor-boards.

"She fell out of her kayak." Ann turned away from Martha's grateful look and stared pointedly at Dinah. "Splash. She got wet. She got dry. She's fine."

"Oh good. Because people are talking as if she tried to—"

"For God's *sake*." Ann whammed her palms on either side of her plate. A clump of macaroni separated itself from her serving and toppled over as if she'd shot it.

Silence at their table, silence and stares from the table next to theirs. Ann would be given a shiny new moniker: Camp Troublemaker.

"People think I tried to kill myself."

Dinah gasped and pressed a ringed hand to her mouth, but not before Ann caught her ambulance-chaser smile. Cindy looked stricken. The table behind theirs fell quiet. Martha turned toward the sea, deep blue now that the light was fading, bringing colors vividly to life, before it hid them for the night.

This was sickening. Why wasn't Patrick saying anything? Why wasn't he taking charge, helping Martha out?

"She fell." Ann's nails dug into the tablecloth. "I was there. If people want to turn it into high drama, that's their problem."

"Okay, okay!" Dinah lifted her red-taloned fingers. "I get it. You don't have to bite my head off. I was just asking."

"I was just answering."

"Everyone going to the bonfire tonight?" Patrick's loud

voice cut in—finally—and the tables around them came back to life with comments and chatter. Dinah and Cindy exclaimed their enthusiasm. Martha nodded silently.

Ann laughed without pleasure. Bonfire tonight. Whoopee. She'd forgotten. A perfect shit ending to a perfect shit day. And tomorrow? Even better. Up at dawn for her mandatory lobstering lesson. Of all the useless ways to spend her time. "I'm going to sit this one out."

"But you can't." Cindy stared in alarm. "I mean everyone goes, don't they, Patrick?"

"Usually, yeah." Patrick smiled at Ann, eyes speculative. "I'll talk to Betsy."

She watched him walk across the room in his graceful easy stride, saw women's heads turning to watch his progress. Unless she was completely insane, which at this point was a very strong possibility, he was cooking up something else for her to do, and she wasn't sure if that would be better or worse.

"My first husband, Dan, tried to kill himself, you know, after I left him, did I tell you? Honestly, you have to wonder about people like that, how stupid they have to be not to have the vaguest idea what a ridiculous *waste* it is, to—"

"Dinah. New topic." Martha's low voice carried surprising power and enough threat to stop even Dinah cold. Martha glanced at Ann, impassive as always, but in that second Ann knew she'd figured out how Paul died.

Aw, hell. She sat stunned, previous anger evaporated by the intrusion and shock. After her abominable behavior in the bay, she should have guessed Martha would figure it out.

Ann didn't want her to know. She didn't want anyone up

here to know, except Betsy and Patrick and the other staff, who had to. Paul's death was her business. Her business and her shame. Though if anyone had to know, better Martha than the emotional peeping Toms around here.

"Dessert." Cindy jumped to her feet, holding her empty plate. "I think I saw lemon pound cake out there. I'll bring back plenty for the table."

"I'll help." Dinah climbed over the bench to join Cindy, leaving silence that needed to be broken.

"Thanks." Ann mumbled the word to her hands, twisting on the tablecloth.

Of course, Martha didn't hear.

Ann turned to the spiky back of Martha's head. "I said, thanks."

No reaction.

Ann cleared her throat and reached to touch Martha's large soft shoulder. "Thank you, Martha."

Martha nodded, still facing out to sea, then her body convulsed suddenly as if she had the hiccups.

Shit. She was crying.

Ann wasn't cut out for playing nursemaid. She hadn't been able to deal with Paul's depression, she couldn't deal with emotional collapse from a stranger. Her parents, her brothers, they'd all grown up rough-and-tumble and teasing. "Uh. You . . . okay?"

Stupid stupid question. If Martha was okay, would she be bawling her head off and trying to hide it?

"He's sick." The big low voice was thick and congested. "Pneumonia. He's going to die."

Ann's eyes froze wide. Crap! Who was sick? Martha wasn't

married, so who? Boyfriend? But she had to have lost someone. Ex-boyfriend?

Shit! Ann wasn't equipped for this. Where was Patrick? What was taking him so long? She spotted him, still conferring with Betsy, who glanced over at Ann, who was getting very tired of feeling like a psych ward case.

No help there.

"Oh. Wow. Pneumonia. That . . . sucks."

Christ. She sounded like her neighbor's teenage daughter complaining about too much homework. She had to do better than that. She *would* do better than that.

"Martha . . . I'm really sorry." She made her voice come out gentle and sincere. Her chest responded with warmth, as if the words had triggered truth. "This is all so . . . surreal. For all of us."

A nod. Another hiccupy sob that made her round lumpy body jump. *Damn it.* The others would be back soon. Martha couldn't be caught like this. She'd hate it.

"I don't know if this helps, but, well . . . " She took a loud exaggerated breath so Martha could hear. "If Dinah can get through three deeply felt losses and turn out the way she did . . . then there's hope for all of us. Don't you think?"

Martha's back stiffened. She turned slowly, caught the look on Ann's face and did what Ann had been hoping for. She cracked up. Which made Ann laugh too, and the two of them sat there, snuffling and chortling with intensity usually reserved for grief, until Patrick came back and climbed into Cindy's spot, grinning and wanting in on the joke, which made them both stop laughing.

"So." Ann wiped away a tear, feeling lighter than she had

all day. "Have I been given a reprieve from Bonfire of the Seventies?"

"You've been charged to my care tonight, Annie. I'll come by your cabin at eight to pick you up." He winked, and got up to make room for Cindy and Dinah, coming back with plates heaped with slices of lemon cake.

Ann watched him walk off again, trying to get her brain to process what he'd just said. Charged to his care? Just him and her, alone all evening? *Annie?*

A dark burn of excitement started low in her body, and she had to tell herself she was being ridiculous. Again. Things were not always more than they seemed. Martha had simply fallen. Patrick was gay. She couldn't have saved Paul.

Bullshit. All of it.

The bleakness carried her through the rest of the uneaten meal, back to the cabin where she dodged her cabin-mates and lay in bed, trying to block out the Dinah-drone recounting every microsecond of her coastal Maine flora and fauna class that morning. *And then I inhaled. And then I exhaled. And then I did it again. And then I scratched my elbow.*

Going to the bonfire would have been dreadful, but easy. Spending the evening in Patrick's cabin could be complicated. She wasn't in the mood for complicated. Everything in her life for the past few years had been inevitably and increasingly complicated, though she hadn't tuned in completely until Paul forced total consciousness into her head with the bullet he shot through his.

She got up, accepting the incessant jabbering as part of the cabin's background noise, drifted to the window and looked out at the fading light, darker toward the east, probably a sunset visible from Dinah's and Cindy's rooms. She felt shaky, restless, electrified, possibly manic after a few months of depressive.

An evening with Patrick and no idea what to expect. Anything from twenty games of gin rummy to two hours of intensive new age therapy bullshit. Or worse, some kind of self-improvement exercise where she'd have to crawl around pretending to be a lioness.

Or . . .

No, no, no. He was either gay or pretending to be. He had too much at risk to blow his cover. There was no reason for her to be this nervous. None.

Unfortunately, being this nervous gave her an enormous reason to want a drink. Liquor store, tomorrow. No way could she survive another week and a half of this place without the soothing fortification of something brewed, distilled, or fermented.

Through the thin walls she heard the others getting ready to leave—Cindy, having managed to get a word in edgewise, saying she hoped they'd get to sing again. Oh yes, Dinah agreed, she hoped so too.

Sometimes Ann felt like she'd been sent here in a space pod from some other world. No, galaxy. No, universe.

Heavy steps thudded up to their porch, making Ann's heart echo the beat. Patrick's voice, not as deep as Paul's, but male all the same, and a welcome relief from Camp Kinsonu's twenty-four-hour female channel. Ann had always preferred male friends. Who wanted to talk about feelings or fashion or decorating or endless hygiene and makeup routines? Poopy diapers, potty training, nursery school applications, and at what age to make sure the kids had condoms. Get a life! The world was bigger than wall colors and skin-care products and cloth versus disposable.

"Ann?" Patrick, outside her door.

"Here." She scowled over her fluttering heartbeat, refused to look in a mirror, grabbing the light jacket she'd torn off when she got back from dinner as she went out into the hall. "Ready for my special ed program."

He stood grinning, hands on his hips, looking her over in her jeans and yellow cotton/cashmere sweater until she was squirming with discomfort.

"We staying here?"

"Sure. Standing in the Hall for Fun and Profit."

She rolled her eyes and struggled with her jacket, which had one sleeve inside out.

"Allow me." He took it from her, righted the sleeve and slipped the jacket onto her arms. The kind of gesture Paul would make—or would have made before he descended into permanent gloom. In fact, the Paul she fell for had the same energy and charm as Patrick, though eight or nine times the cynicism.

"Thank you." She zipped up the jacket for something to do with her hands. "What's the plan after this terrific bout of hall-standing?"

"Entertainment at my cabin tonight, Ann."

A nervous chuckle burst out of her; she glanced past him to make sure the others had left. "What does that mean?"

He shrugged, his eyes lit gray, reflecting the beams of sunset coming through Dinah's room. "Means we go to my cabin and hang out so you don't have to sing about being woman and roaring."

Sounded harmless. Didn't it? Harmless was good. Wasn't it?

So nice to be back to her usual decisiveness. "Deal."

"Good deal." He grinned and let her pass him in the narrow hallway. Very close.

Relax, Ann. She stalked through the common area and tromped down the steps into air beginning to cool toward chilly. They'd hang out. Or whatever. Anything was better than facing a beach full of agonized women pretending waving their arms around brought them closer to healing and to each other.

She glanced toward the shore and spotted the familiar trio from Cabin Four nearly at the steps down onto the sand, Dinah and Cindy walking together, Martha plodding behind.

On shore today, after the kayak incident, another of Martha's odd transformations, like when she'd done yoga during group therapy. From bawling mousy suicidal mess into an astonishingly magnetic storyteller, gesturing like a dancer, giving the silly kiddy tale an extraordinary musical delivery that drew listeners in as if she were performing Shakespeare.

"Patrick." Ann stopped, eyes fixed on the large stooped figure. "Maybe Martha should be up here too, with us."

"Betsy's watching out for her." He came back, touched her shoulder. "I'm watching out for you tonight."

She scrunched up her face. "Private tutor or probation officer?"

"A little of both." He smiled his charming lazy smile and led the way, long legs eating up another narrow uneven path, to a small cabin tucked far back into the woods across from the lodge building. Inside, it was comfortable, spare, masculine. A bed with gray wool blankets, made with one long diagonal wrinkle underneath. A desk with computer; bookshelves with a few books, mostly self-help. A file cabinet. No TV. Basic bachelor layout except for the small pine table bearing a silver statue of a laughing Buddha, familiarly seated cross-legged, earlobes stretched long, belly extended, joyous grin on his chubby face. Flanking him, candles in glass holders, a few silk flowers, and a few perfect shells.

"Your altar?"

"Meditating brings me peace."

"Ah." Peace. What a concept. As likely in Ann as it was in the Middle East.

She studied the bald beaming figure, which she dimly associated with China more than Thailand, where Patrick had lived, aware that he'd moved away. She tuned into the sounds across the room behind her—the clank of a bottle on the counter, rattle of ice into glasses, then liquid glug-glugging that sounded so much like it was being poured from a bottle of booze that she actually started salivating. "You think it's possible to be at peace?"

"The monks in Thailand can do it twenty-four/seven. I settle for small chunks. It takes more time and work than most of us can manage and still have what passes for a life in western culture."

Peace as hard work? She'd always thought of peace as something that descended naturally when you got all the ingredients of your life assembled in the right recipe. She couldn't remember feeling much peace in the last few years. Maybe when she and Paul were first married, most often when they lay together after sex—though too often her mind would start a tilt-a-whirl over some job issue. In later years she was always aware of their disconnect, though too firmly in denial to acknowledge it openly. When had that started?

"Here." A glass appeared in front of her, bisecting her view of Buddha so that his head appeared over the rim of what looked—and oh happy day smelled—like scotch.

Ann whirled around, a fiancée-to-be given her first surprise glimpse of the ring. "For me? Really?"

"Single malt. You've earned it."

"Did I die and go to heaven? You can tell me. I can take it."

He laughed and pushed the glass closer. She took it, grinning up at him, gestured to his glass, a fraction as full as hers. "You're having some?"

"A taste. Alcohol and I are careful of each other. After this I'll match your every round with apple juice. So cheers." He clinked with her. "The night is young, and so are we."

"Speak for yourself." She toasted him and drank, closed her eyes and allowed the smooth taste to spread over her tongue. "Oh my God did I need that."

"Yeah?"

"Mmmm." Another sip, to get the mellow soothing started. Then another. Then the glass drained. "Am I allowed seconds?"

"Seconds and thirds and whatever you need tonight, Ann."

"I need a lot." She held out her glass, already feeling the warmth traveling her veins, lifting her mood. "I've got days of horrendous deprivation to make up for."

"I know what that feels like." He took her glass and gestured to the door. "Let me grab your bottle and my juice, and we can sit outside and watch the sunset. How does that sound?"

"Perfect." She stepped out onto the porch, humming a tune she identified as "Tonight, Tonight" from *West Side Story*, which made her stop humming immediately and just stand there, alcohol fueling a buzz of tense excitement and rare pleasure.

In the west, the sun had turned the clouds bright orange and pink. To the east, the sky deepened to navy. Trees had become black silhouettes. A faint glow rose from the beach where the Females thronged around the fire. She could almost imagine finding peace in this part of the country.

"Beautiful, isn't it." His step sounded on the porch boards; she felt him close behind her. "I never get tired of that view. It's hard to be taken over by your troubles when you see a sight like that. It's like the souls of dead artists are up there putting on a show every night. A direct manifestation of a better place for all of us to look forward to."

Uh . . . Ann found herself waiting for the cynical punch line she instinctively expected. Neither Paul nor any of their friends would ever let something so imaginative and naive go by without skewering.

She'd let it pass.

"Have a seat." He dropped onto a simple pine bench softened with cushions, and poured out her second drink, then his apple juice.

She sat, pulling her jacket around her, less for warmth than for comfort. The bench was narrow enough that she could feel the heat of his body next to her. He handed over her glass and she took a big gulp, which joined the other gulps in a race through her empty stomach and into her bloodstream. At the end of this drink she'd be able to relax. Or maybe the next.

"Tell me about today, Ann."

"Uhhh, not one of my best."

"Talk to me." His voice was low in the fading light, his body warm and the drink really good. "Tell me."

"About what?"

"Whatever is in your head."

She snorted. "Trust me, you don't want to hear—"

"Yes. I do." He leaned toward her to give more weight to his words, capture her attention more honestly, but for a silly tingling second she thought he was going to kiss her, and was shocked to realize she would have let him.

"Oh." She felt a little overwhelmed and a little helpless, two feelings she absolutely detested. Worse, his sympathy and strength were bringing on the teary poor-me's, and she hated those too. She drained her drink, damning the scotch for giving her a low when she'd needed a high.

"Talk to me." He was whispering, which made him sound persuasive and sexy, like a boy trying to convince her to go all the way on the couch in his parents' living room. Worse, he reached up and gently stroked back her hair, touching her cheek. "Tell me everything."

"Patrick—" Her voice broke. She was going to tell him to stop. She was going to get up from this bench and walk away while she still had one tiny shred of her pride left, but his hand stroked the back of her neck, began massaging the tight painful muscles, making her want to moan with pleasure. *Yes, yes, right here on your parents' couch.* "I . . . don't want to be here."

Crap.

"With me?"

"At this camp."

"Where do you want to be?"

She bit back a pathetic girly sob and started to loathe herself in earnest. "I want to be returned to my life."

"Before Paul died?"

"Of course. Before."

"You loved him that much."

"Yes. Yes. I did." She answered too quickly and realized too late that her response sounded knee-jerk. Worse, when she looked up guiltily, Patrick was frowning the frown of a skeptic. "He . . . we had a few . . . some problems. Every couple has problems."

"True." He went back to massaging; she went back to loving it. "Tell me something."

"Mmm, what?"

"If Paul hadn't killed himself, what would have happened to the two of you?"

She clutched her drink, felt her muscles tense again. The sun slipped down behind the trees, the light around them deepened and she shivered. For the past six months she'd thought only of Paul's death, tried to come to terms with his loss and her culpability.

What would have happened if he'd stayed around to face their ruin?

"Are you cold?"

"No. No, I'm just—"

"I'll be right back." He got up and went into the cabin.

Ann sat, paralyzed. He'd let a lion out of its cage, and she had to deal with the beast. What would have happened? Ann would still have had to get a job, nothing new there. But Paul would have had to get a job too, and he'd sworn years ago, in a tirade against office politics, butt-kissing, and the dense concentration of idiots in the workplace, that he'd never again work for anyone but himself. Add in his track record of worsening depression, his chances of being hired would be slim to none unless he agreed to seek treatment, which she didn't think likely. He'd bring only scorn and amused superiority into a therapist's office.

Patrick reemerged with a blanket that he draped over both of them, down to their feet, up to their shoulders, creating his and hers against-the-world intimacy.

"Any thoughts?"

"None."

"You thought about it. Tell me."

"It's none of your business."

He put his arm around her under the soft scratchy warmth of the blanket, which smelled of Patrick and wool. "You're a tightly wound spool. I want to find the end of your thread and unravel you."

"Leaving me a hollow wooden core?"

He laughed, easy and free in the darkness. "Good one. How about I just want to be your friend. Help carry your load, be your beast of burden . . . uh, share the yoke . . . what else."

"Lean on you when I'm not strong?"

"Yeah, that." He hugged her to him, kissed the top of her head. Even that brotherly gesture starting a long rusty motor purring. "How about that I think you are one of the most powerful and special ladies I've ever met, and I care about your happiness?"

Again she felt that some acid comment was needed to cut the sugar. "Patrick, I can't just—"

"Okay. Shhh. No worries. Tell me more about Paris. I love Paris."

"Tell me why you love it."

"Well . . . I mean the Seine, the Eiffel Tower, the Arc de Triomphe, the Louvre, the croissants, the baguettes . . . "

She frowned. Not the answer she expected. "That's tourist Paris. You didn't experience Thailand that way, why would you—"

"I was making a joke, Ann."

"Oh." She laughed with silly relief.

"Tell me about your Paris."

"What I love is how everything is so beautiful, and so tasteful, and so safe. Manners are still important, in a way we've completely lost in this country, and it makes the experience so . . . gracious and aesthetically satisfying. Like living in an art house movie. It's why people want to live in gated communities here, only this isn't isolated and fake, it's real, a real city."

"Yes. Exactly. That's exactly why I love it too, Ann. You captured it so perfectly. All the beauty in all aspects. Thailand is like that too. I'd like to show it to you." He was murmuring into her hair, and something warmed and loosened in her heart, making it dangerously gooey.

Who cared? She was drunk and wretched and if Camp Kitchy-Koo turned her brain to treacle, then fine, it would. God knew goo felt ten times better than fury.

"Patrick . . . " She struggled to steady her voice. "I don't know if Paul and I could have . . . we might have had to sell the house. It was really huge. Too huge for the two of us. And the mortgage was shocking."

She moved uncomfortably, feeling like a traitor. Paul had delighted in living on the very edge of their budget, which, granted, was considerable. He'd had complete faith in himself and in his destiny to live and die a wealthy man. She'd shared that faith, simply because his was so absolute.

"You'd have had to embrace a simpler life. That's not a bad thing. On the contrary. I know that so well."

Her stomach turned over; she felt a sudden sense of suffocation, as if truth had taken over her oxygen. It would have been a bad thing. She couldn't picture her and Paul in a simpler life. Not as a couple. Not together. Since they'd started making decent salaries, their life had been defined by money. Where they lived, who they knew, what they did, how they did it.

"Patrick . . . " Her voice shook. She held out her glass and he poured for her, got his own bottle, poured for himself. "I don't know that Paul would have liked a simpler life."

He'd have detested it. He'd have sunk lower into depression, fueled by guilt and shame and resentment, not having the money barrier that made him feel special, that lifted him above the unwashed masses he used to be part of.

Their relationship had been dying for years. Paul had been dying for years.

"Oh God." She gulped her drink, drained it, instantly regretted it. Patrick pulled out the bottle and she shook her head. "No more. It's fucking with my head."

"It's helping you see more clearly."

"No. Not this time. Not this time." She threw off the blanket and stood abruptly, nearly overbalanced. Too much alcohol too quickly, too little in her stomach. She wasn't seventeen, she should have realized. Tomorrow she was going to feel like hell . . . and oh *God*, she had to be up at four-thirty. "I have to get out of here."

"Whoa there." He came up behind her, put his arms around her, firm and steadying. "My bad. I shouldn't have let you have that much. But it also means I can't let you go yet."

She turned in his arms, blinked at him stupidly. "What, I'm a prisoner?"

"No, darlin'." He rocked her gently back and forth, like a tantrum-prone child he had to be careful of. "But I'm not letting you go in this condition. God knows what havoc you'd wreak. And if anyone found you this way, I could lose my job."

"So . . . " She frowned and tried to think. "What am I supposed to do, spend the night with you?"

"Sure." He spoke easily, and a little alarm light went on, too faint for her to care. "Or just hang out until you feel sober enough to go back."

In the face of this momentous decision and the easy rocking against his chest, her brain turned off. It was all too hard. Patrick's arms were strong and capable. She'd deal with reality later.

"You're safe with me, Ann." He spoke earnestly. "You know that."

"I'm not sure."

"No?" He stepped back, took her hands, compelled her to look at him, his handsome face illuminated, the last rays of light from the west catching his gold earring. "I want you to do something for me, or at least think about doing it."

"What?"

"Stop hanging onto Paul and to the past, to the materialistic driven life you led. That died with him. Look ahead. Look around. Open your beautiful soul to other men and other more simple experiences." He dropped her hands, took her shoulders, brought her close again, holding her tightly with his magnetic gray gaze. "The woman you had to be with him is not who you really are, Ann."

She gasped. Then took a long breath, prepared to tell him he didn't know her, that he had no right to say that, no right to tell her anything about Paul or about herself.

Instead, she exhaled a dry sob. *Damn* the damn scotch.

His arms came around her again and she burrowed shamelessly against him, felt his lips on her hair, her forehead. She turned her face up, instinct and need taking over for common sense, and his mouth landed on hers, firm, practiced, and judging by the dark bolt of desire up her middle, exactly what she wanted.

But even while she gave herself over to the kiss that went on and on and on, she distantly noted in his sexy mouth the total absence of the sweet taste of apple juice.

Chapter 10

Death. Imminent. Ann rolled to her side, sending mental instructions to her chirping alarm watch to spontaneously combust. A second later her brain rolled, following her body—only her brain kept rolling, which sounded like a good idea to her stomach so it started rolling too.

Four-thirty A.M. *Oh my God.*

Chirp-chirp-chirp. She groaned, groped, knocked a pen off the bedside table, found the watch, shut the damn alarm off and flung the culprit back onto the table, head pounding, mouth rank. Last night was such a good idea. Seriously. Tossing back three glasses of scotch on no food. Brilliant. A MacArthur genius grant was in her future.

Another good one: letting Patrick kiss her. But wait, there was more! Letting Patrick screw with her head until she decided her marriage had been empty and cold. Nice! This place did wonders for the soul. Next she'd find out she really hated her parents. *And,* she was a lesbian with an insatiable desire for young girls.

At least she'd stopped at letting Patrick screw with her head, and hadn't been stupid enough to let him screw the rest of her. Or wait, maybe he was the one who hadn't been stupid enough. In any case, no screwing had happened. She was too drunk and too freaked out, and he was too employed.

Or no, too *gay*. She forgot.

After that one intense thirty second kiss, her instinct had kicked in with bad-idea messages, and then, thank God, Patrick had drawn back, looking confused, and insisted he hadn't known what came over him, that this wasn't like him at all, that he hadn't been with a woman since high school and that he liked Ann too much to yadda and yadda, plus his job at the so on and so on would be etc., etc., etc.

Right. Even Peter Pan wouldn't believe in that fairy.

She'd come close to asking how stupid he thought she was, but then figured if he wanted to keep pretending he was gay, he could go right ahead. Most likely he worried that if he took advantage of her drunken vulnerability, she'd wake up pissed and get him fired. Instead, she got the fun of waking up fatally hung over on a day she'd have to spend with fish-smelling men in a bob-'n'-weave boat.

Whee.

New experiences, Betsy had said, new experiences to help channel their lives in new and exciting directions. Ann didn't want new experiences. She wanted her old familiar ones back.

She brought herself up to her elbows, squinting and miserable. By five freaking A.M. she had to be dressed and ready to be picked up at the parking lot. Five women, each going out for the day with a different lobster guy.

Her legs made it onto the floor. Her body hoisted itself out of bed, which beckoned, *Come back to me, Ann darling,* the most seductive offer she'd ever had.

Maybe she should call in dead.

But if she didn't show, they'd send someone to see what was wrong, and her simple need for sleep would turn into another excuse for them to reach inside her with pliers and try to yank out her inner feelings. Or, if Patrick was anything to go by, to plant inner feelings they'd like her to have.

Fine. She'd go.

Fifteen minutes later she'd showered away the worst of the self-disgust. Ten minutes after that she'd dressed in jeans, wool socks, and a few layers under her sweater, since it would be cold out on the water at this hour, and didn't that entice her even more.

Forget makeup. Forget hairstyle. Forget breakfast. She was as ready as she'd ever be.

The van ride down Shute's Point on the narrow twisting sand and gravel road was stomach torture, as were the perky driver and chatty passengers. Of course, Ann was the last dropped off, abandoned at the mouth of a side road with cheery waves and enthusiastic "havefuns" that made her want to throw up even more. What was wrong with silence? What was wrong with having a really good bad mood on? Ann had never had the slightest problem with either.

She dragged herself through the woods on the rutted fern- and moss-lined road, which after nearly forever widened into a small clearing, home to a battered white shed surrounded by low blackberry plants and higher raspberry plants. She stopped to pick a few berries, whose sweetness helped battle the sour taste even vigorous toothbrushing hadn't erased.

At the shore, the greenery ended; Ann stepped carefully

down three rock steps set into the eroding earth, onto a wide flat ledge. In front of her a small cove, low tide, of course, so the muddy, clammy smell could be at its ripest. At anchor a dozen or so yards out, her home for the morning, the *Tiger Lily II*, dark green hull separated from white by a neat crimson stripe.

On board, one man, middle-aged in a ball cap, peering at her through the windshield. She gave a halfhearted wave. He returned a quarter-hearted wave and went back to whatever he'd been doing before he spotted her.

Well. How jolly. Did he expect her to swim out?

At home—her home with Paul—she'd still be asleep. At seven, her alarm would go off, she'd plow efficiently through her routines, barrel to the office—in sheer nylons, a wool suit, and expensive-but-tasteful jewelry. All day long she'd network, negotiate, coddle, manipulate, then rush home again to Paul, to neatness, to order, to luxury . . .

She wanted that back so badly, it hurt even more than her pounding head.

The door to the shed opened and another man, about her age, stepped out, dressed in yellow rubber overalls and black boots, carrying another pair of each, which she guessed were her fashion attire for the day. He stopped when he saw her, glanced at the boat, then strode over to greet her. He was medium height, maybe an inch or two under six feet. Dark short hair, dark blue eyes, handsome actually. Tiny bit of a cleft chin. Very serious expression. As if he wasn't exactly looking forward to having her on board.

Which meant they had a lot in common right off the bat.

"Ann."

"That's me."

"I'm Clive." He held out the coveralls and looked her over critically. "At least you're dressed."

She raised an eyebrow. Charmed, she was sure. "You were expecting naked?"

"Some women show up ready for a day at the beach. See if the boots fit."

Yes, sir. She snatched the boots, holding back her thanks. If he wanted lack of manners, he'd found his dream girl.

The boots fit decently, the rubber overalls were beyond special, but they'd cut the wind and protect her from wet, so what the hell. If she was going to play Suzy Fishergirl, she might as well do it up right.

"This way."

She clumped after Clive of the Silver Tongue, over the flat rocks, then gravel, then mud, to a skiff at the water's edge and climbed in, hands on the gunwales, keeping her weight low, thankful for her sailing experience with Paul, so she wasn't a complete dork around boats.

Clive took charge of the oars and pulled the skiff to the *Tiger Lily* with powerful strokes, then skillfully finessed it alongside. "Get in."

Yes sir! She clambered over and was met with a very uninviting whiff of dead fish, which did her stomach no favors whatsoever. Nor was she enchanted by the cloud of mosquitoes, which decided she'd make a perfect breakfast. Did she mention she wished she were home?

"Hi." She managed a smile at the wind-weathered older man—she guessed he was pushing sixty—standing in the open cabin by the controls of the boat. "I'm Ann."

"Arnold. Welcome aboard." He gestured to a chair set near him, and turned back to wait for Clive to tie up the skiff and cast off the mooring.

She sat, bile rising from the fish smell and the gentle rocking of the boat. Arnold fiddled with his shortwave radio, twisted dials on another contraption, consulted a chart on a clipboard, seeming at ease with the silence. Or at least unwilling to break it. Maybe he'd already forgotten she was here.

Perfect. All she'd have to do was sit still, watch, and try not to puke.

A few shallow-breathing bug-slapping minutes later, Clive was on board and Arnold fired up the engines and pulled *Tiger Lily* out of the cove, radio barking static and gibberish at regular startling intervals. Immediately the blessing of losing mosquitoes to momentum was offset by diesel fumes mixing themselves in with the *eau de dead fish*. In the open waters of the bay, the regular climb and plunge only added to the fun.

Ann launched herself out of the chair and moved astern, seeking open air, which blew by in a steady, blessedly fresh stream. She gulped a few breaths, then a few more. Better. Barely. The coastline rapidly miniaturized, while the seascape expanded around them to emphasize shoals, other vessels, and countless buoys. Arnold decreased his speed to pass another lobster boat; the crews exchanged somber raised-hand greetings while the attending gulls outdid them in enthusiasm. *Tiger Lily* caught the wake of its erstwhile neighbor and wallowed.

Urgh. Ann flung herself to the side, hung on grimly, eyes closed, breathing carefully and deeply through her nose.

"Seasick?" Clive's voice, faintly amused.

"Not generally."

"Tied one on last night?"

She didn't move. Screw him. "That's my business."

"Did you eat breakfast?"

"Also my business."

"Not entirely. Did you?"

She began a good glare, then the boat lurched and she hung over the side again, fighting the rebelling noncontents of her stomach. "No, *mein führer*, I didn't."

He muttered something she was glad not to catch and strode to the front of the boat, came back and pushed into her field of vision a large blueberry muffin, carefully wrapped in plastic.

"No." She waved him away when he pressed it on her again. Damn it. She'd left camp to avoid being mothered. "I don't want it."

"Eat. We've got two hundred traps to haul today. I don't need you sick while we're trying to get our jobs done."

This time the boat held steady long enough for her to deliver her best go-to-hell stare. Breeze lifted the dark hair from his forehead; his blues eyes didn't so much as glance away. She wanted to scoop up a bucket of herring bait and dump it over his head.

Except, though it pained her to allow this much maturity into her snit, he had a point. Lobstering was dangerous. Paul had a friend in high school who'd been snagged by a line on its way overboard and dragged to the bottom. Clive and Arnold needed to concentrate on their work, not on a hungover Diva Princess. Ann should have stayed in camp.

"Take the muffin. There's coffee in the big thermos. Don't

drink it until you're finished eating. You don't want that acid on an empty stomach."

She took the muffin from his large sturdy hands, feeling like a five-year-old told which coloring book to use and which crayons. But fine. She'd eat the damn muffin. And when it became fish food, he'd learn to leave her alone to her death wish.

The muffin turned out to be exceptional, tender, buttery, stuffed with intensely flavored Maine wild blueberries, better even than the saucer-sized ones she and Paul got from Pallas Bakery, around the corner from their condo in South Boston. Unsure at first, her stomach rose to the challenge, and after a cup of coffee—damn good coffee—she grudgingly admitted, to herself only, that Commander Clive had been right to insist.

Fine. It didn't mean she had to be nice to him.

Humanity partly restored, she could focus on what was going on around her, which was a lot. Traps hauled in, contents inspected, most creatures discarded back into the waves, sometimes all. Nonlobsters—urchins, crabs, blundering bottom-feeders—got thrown back. Lobsters too small, thrown back. Lobsters too big, thrown back. Most Clive discarded by sight, but those close to legal size he measured with a gauge to make sure the beasts were under the maximum, over the minimum.

She stayed determinedly silent and out of the way, but when Clive cut a notch in the tail of a lobster before he threw it back, curiosity got the better of her sulk.

"Why did you cut that one?"

"Berried female."

"Buried?"

"Eggs on her. Berries."

"So if someone else catches her, she'll be thrown back again?"

"Yup. Larger males and breeding females are safe."

"For lifelong uninterrupted nookie."

He lifted his cap, brushed the wrist of his glove across his forehead, and went back to rebaiting the trap.

Ann rolled her eyes at his back. No sense of humor. Well, okay. Don't mind her, she'd stay here in her leper colony and watch.

The men worked with skilled precision, no movements wasted, minimal communication. Clive threw legal lobsters into a crate, then rebaited the traps with knit bags stuffed with ripe herring bits, and launched them back overboard. Bricks in the bottom carried each trap swiftly down to the place Arnold and his fancy imaging equipment chose.

"How long have you been doing this?"

Clive glance over his shoulder. "Learned from my dad as a kid."

Splash. The trap sank back into the sea; the engine surged as they moved forward, the sea gulls giggled and complained. His answer surprised her. His skin wasn't weathered enough, his hands not rough enough, and something else about him didn't quite fit the lifelong-fisherman mold, though it was entirely possible she was just being snotty. Wouldn't be the first time, wouldn't be the last. She'd had an expert teacher in Paul, for whom the concept of "enjoying the finer things in life" gradually became more important than whether he actually enjoyed any of the things or not.

"You've been doing this all your life?" She tried to keep the incredulity out of her voice, but he sent her a look that told her she hadn't been entirely successful.

"Not all."

"What else did you do?"

"Odds and ends."

"Like . . ."

He set a line around the pulley and started the winch, winding up the next trap from the bottom.

Okay. Private Property. Trespassers will be prosecuted. Which made her even more curious, of course. If Pandora had been Pandoro, the infamous box would have stayed closed. Though mostly because it would soon have been covered by all the other manly junk he piled into his ancient garage.

"How about you, Arnold?"

"Eh?"

"How long have you been lobstering?"

"Learned from Dad."

"Are you married?" She wondered the same about Clive, but the question felt awkward put to a man her age, now that she was single. "Do you have kids?"

"Ayuh. Two sons. Oldest is in the military, youngest has his own boat now. Got his license a year ago. Used to be able to get a license right away. Now it's three to one—three fishermen have to give theirs up before the government will issue a new one." He gestured around him. "Used to be half this many buoys. Now you can walk across the bay on 'em."

After that veritable explosion of dialogue, she settled back and watched some more, sometimes wandering, sometimes sitting, enjoying how the warm sun made the cool breeze comfortable and vice versa. This was good. She was glad to be here. And it hit her that this was probably the first time those phrases applied in a long, long time.

"Feeling better?" Clive stood in the back of the boat, gloved hands on his hips.

"Almost human." Wow. Could he in fact be pleasant? She smiled, just to see what he'd do.

What he did was stride to the front of the boat, grab a pair of gloves and thrust them at her. "You can make yourself useful."

Her smile died. Right. No tolerance of Diva Princesses. Mrs. Clive would be solid, uncomplaining, dinner always ready at five-thirty, fine with her whether Clive wanted sex or to watch wrestling on TV afterward, just let her do the dishes first . . .

"Help stuff the bait bags."

"Love to." She pulled on the gloves and turned to face the drum of stinky herring bits, newly shored-up stomach threatening to rebel again. But Ann Redding never backed down from a challenge. Which attitude earned her a black eye when the challenge was class bully Duffy McPherson, and a scholarship when the challenge was to be the first in her family to get into an Ivy League college. She thrust her gloved hand in among the clouded staring eyes and exposed guts and flesh and bones, and stuffed fistfuls into the bag, vowing that herring would never again grace her table.

"Here." She pulled the string fastener shut and shoved the full bag at him. "Just like Mom used to make."

He nodded his unsmiling approval, then showed her how to hang the bag back between the net funnels the lobsters crawled through to get their sorry asses caught. At the back of the trap was an escape hatch, closed with rings designed to corrode easily in the saltwater. If the trap got lost at the bottom of the sea, animals would eventually have a way out.

She could use one of those. A lot of people could. How about Clive? Arnold? Did they feel trapped in this work, in this life, or set free? She didn't dare ask.

As the morning wore on, Ann found herself caught in the men's rhythm, able to enjoy the air, grin at the noisy persistent sea gulls following the boat with high hopes of herring. Off in the distance, Camp Kinsonu had become a quaint cluster of shingled dollhouses, while around them the sea was live and vast and vivid.

Way earlier than she usually ate lunch, Clive passed around thick ham and Swiss sandwiches. Ann managed half of one, took her cue from Clive and Arnold by eating quickly, drinking more coffee, and going back to work. No extended expense-account lunch break here. Two hundred traps, hauled, emptied, rebaited, reset. The catch of legal-sized lobsters swelled in the crate, claws banded to keep them from nipping fingers or each other.

By the time the last trap splashed back into the sea and they were heading for the pound, Ann was exhausted, elated, face freshened by the wind, hair stiff with salt spray, nose sunburned, stinking of fish and rubber.

She pulled off the guts-splattered gloves and moved her chair out into the open area near the stern, put her feet up on the side and turned her face to the warm sun, closed her eyes, making herself think about where they'd been, not where they were going. At the pound, they delivered their catch, took on more bait, and were on their way, long day over at mid-afternoon.

Too soon the boat slowed, reentered the quiet cove, men

coming home after a hard day's work. Arnold back to his wife, Clive back to . . . who knew?

Her mood downshifted with the motor. Back to the van, back to camp, back to crowded dinners, back to the shared cabin, closed in, watched . . . a zoo animal once more.

And back to whatever had happened—or not—last night with Patrick.

"We tire you out?"

She turned to Clive and found him watching her, hands resting on the mop he'd been using to scrub the deck. Unexpectedly, she didn't have the heart to be snotty to him. Even if he was asking hoping he'd kicked her white-collar princess ass to the moon.

"This was a really great day."

His eyes narrowed, as if he expected the other shoe to fall. Not that she could blame him. Being earnestly grateful wasn't exactly her strong point. But she *was* earnestly grateful. And she wanted him to know it. Even if he was a fascist.

"I haven't had many great days recently, so this was . . . " Her mind spun frantically. *Oh God, she was going to say that word, someone help.* " . . . special."

Ew.

"Seriously, thank you." She glanced back to include Arnold. "Both."

Clive stood watching her until she wanted to jump up and shriek in his face to break the tension. "You hungry?"

She blinked. "Am I *hungry*?"

"I've got food up at the house. Fresh coffee. Save you having to go back to camp yet."

She stood slowly, needing more power. "What makes you think I don't want to go back?"

He shrugged. "Do you?"

She bunched up her mouth, then relented. "No, not really."

"I'll call Betsy and let her know. Drop you back at camp later."

"I haven't said I'd come yet."

"Well?"

She didn't know what bewildered her more, his sudden invitation or her panic over a very simple decision.

Arnold chuckled. "He's harmless. You go on up. Best cook on the point. I've gained five pounds since he's been on board with those muffins of his."

She didn't hide her amazement. "*You* made those muffins?"

"Should I call Betsy or not?"

Ann waited, enjoying his embarrassment. A muffin-baking sailor who'd barely tolerated her all day suddenly wanted her up to his house? Not that she'd been a disciple of Miss Manners either on this trip.

Okay, she'd go. She was too curious not to. A good excuse to put off being another slide under the Camp Kinsonu microscope.

Clive's house was a small neat colonial farther west on Shute's Point, past a stretch of blueberry barrens, off a long narrow road through the woods. The interior confirmed that there was indeed a Mrs. Clive, though no visible signs of little Clives. But this was not a bachelor pad—at least not a straight guy's bachelor pad.

If he turned out to be gay, she was going to introduce him to Patrick and see what happened.

The walls had been painted a warm straw yellow, colorful without being intrusive. Against them, arrangements of dried flowers, curly willow snaking out in all directions; a "Bless this Home" framed circular needlepoint; a hanging figure of Christ on the cross. Elsewhere, coordinated pillows and furniture, and on the fireplace mantel, candles, more dried flowers, and a bunch of those prissy porcelain figurines she detested more than they probably deserved.

The clincher? Wedding pictures, on the end table next to the couch, one of either his parents or hers, and one of the blushing bride herself, a plain stocky woman on whom the delicate veil and poufy Cinderella gown looked utterly wrong.

The overall domestic effect? Cozy Nest, though somehow Cozy Nest self-conscious and untouched. But cozier and nestier than her and Paul's place, which had been decorated Chilly Expensive Chic.

The comparison felt uneasy, but Ann wasn't going to take that feeling out and examine it for all the group therapy in the world.

"Shower?" Clive reemerged from a hallway holding out a towel, which she took gratefully, even as she felt odd planning to get naked in a strange man's house. Which proved her brief run as a wild single woman in her teens and early twenties was way too far behind her.

"I'd love a shower, thanks."

"I'm betting I don't need to offer you a drink."

She winced comically, surprised at his sudden switch into Mr. Hospitality. "No drink for me. I've sworn off. Nothing until . . . oh, let's say . . . tomorrow morning, right after breakfast."

As soon as the joke exited her mouth, she realized he could very well report her back to Queen Bee Betsy for consuming alcohol and planning to do so again. Patrick could get into trouble as her supplier . . .

God, it was all too annoying.

"Clive." She followed him into what was obviously the master bedroom, a king-size-bed-dominated room decorated rather ookily in ruffly peach and beige and light green. "We're not allowed alcohol at Camp Kinsonu."

"I know." He turned at the bathroom door and gestured her in.

"So . . ." She stopped opposite him, clutching her towel, feeling like a complete grade school dork. "I would appreciate it if you didn't—"

"Tattle?" He grinned, and a surprise dimple appeared in his cheek. How did she miss that all day long? Hadn't he smiled? "How you choose to deal with your pain is your business."

"Thank you." She hugged the towel to her chest. "I'm . . . not used to other people's rules."

"Believe it or not, I guessed that."

"Hey, I stuffed your bait bags, what more do you want?"

This time he actually chuckled, which made her feel like she'd won some competition. "Have a good shower. If you need anything, holler."

"Okay." She stepped into the bathroom, but peeked around the door frame so she could watch him stride out. He moved on land the same way he did on the boat, calmly, confidently, but as if everything he did needed to be accomplished in the minimum amount of time. Yet something was different here. He seemed nicer, yes, more relaxed, maybe, but something else. She couldn't place it yet.

The shower was heavenly, though the bathroom was fright-

eningly spotless and as ordered as the living room and bedroom, to the point where her filth seemed an affront and she
peered anxiously in the tub for stray hairs after she stepped
out. What would Mrs. Clive think of her trespassing? Most
likely Clive was calling her right now: *Honey, brought home
another wacko from the camp. Where should we bury this one?*

Refreshed and defished, she dressed again, dropping the
layer closest to her skin so she wouldn't have to put sweaty
clothes on a clean body. Back through the dust-free living
room, she found the kitchen, cheerful in a brighter yellow
with red accents throughout—a bowl of wooden apples; a
red teapot displayed on a shelf; a red, yellow, and white dec-
orative plate perfectly centered on the wall behind the table.
Again, all the right ingredients for "cozy" but . . . not quite.

Clive had showered and changed, jeans and a white long-
sleeve knit shirt that looked thick and soft. Without his
rubber coveralls, she was able to enjoy the view of a very
nice body. Compact, powerful, she could only imagine the
shape his muscles must be in.

As soon as she had the thought, she wished her brain could
spit it out like something rotten. What was wrong with her?
Paul had been dead only six months, and she'd kissed one man
last night and was ogling another today? This was not how a
recently widowed woman should be acting. Hell, this wasn't
how she usually acted. She'd been dazzled by Paul, dazzled
by his talent, his charm, his professional hunger, and most of
all by his interest in her. Once they were a couple, when she
was all of twenty-four years old, she stopped looking, always
felt a little odd when her girlfriends drooled over men not
their husbands, thinking maybe she was undersexed. Paul's
death seemed to change that. Or was it just another part of

the temporary insanity of grief? She needed a guidebook to get through this.

Clive put a big glass of water in front of her and she gulped it gratefully, alcohol, wind, and caffeine having robbed her of liquids.

"When I was young, my favorite meal on a hung over stomach was breakfast."

"You're not young anymore?"

He smirked. "I don't drink anymore."

"At all?" She sounded horrified. *Geez, Ann. Let him not drink if he wants to.*

"Not much." He opened the refrigerator, peered inside and started taking out items: a small plastic container, a carton of eggs, a package of bacon, half an onion. "But I don't drink as an activity, as a way to spend an evening. There lies the path to self-destruction, weight gain, and dead brain cells."

"Gotcha." And bingo, she knew what was different. He was more articulate, more sophisticated. Out on the boat he'd been Mr. Monosyllable. What made the transition happen? Being off the job? Being away from Arnold? Being . . . alone with her?

Stop, stop, stop, and while you're at it, stop.

"Back in my drinking days, my favorite hangover cure was BEPO."

"Beepo? Is it some kind of drug?"

"Bacon, eggs, potatoes, onions. Tastes better made over a campfire, but we'll make do." He put an omelet pan on the stove, added a slab of butter to start melting, sliced leftover quartered potatoes and tossed them in to brown.

Her response was automatic. "I'm not really hungry."

He sliced the onion, stirred the potatoes. "You need to stop starving yourself."

Surprise delayed her reaction, but hello, how are ya, here it came, the all-too-familiar simmer of temper, this time tinged with disappointment. "Gee, I thought I was away from camp. Or are you allowed to boss me around too?"

"I'm making an observation. You're skeletal."

Compared to your bovine wife? "I've been through some rough times."

"No excuse not to take care of yourself."

"For God's sake." She clutched her temples. "Can I not have *one* conversation where someone doesn't point out how I need to change? Anything else you'd like? Boobs too small? Bags under the eyes annoying? Plastic surgery is so good nowadays, I'm sure I can accommodate you."

He stayed calm, chopping bacon. "You done?"

"No, I'm not done. What the hell makes you and everyone else think that losing someone makes me public property?"

"People want to help."

"I'm *so* sorry, of course, you're right. Criticizing me is for my own good. Making me feel I'm even more of a failure at grief than I was as a wife is for my own good. No, even better, 'helping' makes *you* feel good, which is what really matters."

He turned and met her eyes with that hard stare she wanted to scratch off his face. "Done now?"

"Completely."

Apparently there was a clock in the kitchen, because its ticking was suddenly very obvious. No doubt it was red. No doubt he and his anal-compulsive neat-freak wife had picked it out together. Bacon sizzled, the smell making her stomach react as if it had been on a hunger strike only until it got this exact meal.

Her anger started to dissolve into fatigue and hopelessness. And then the unthinkable.

She dropped her eyes.

Ann Redding never backed down. Well, with Paul she never had to; he withdrew rather than fight. But she could stare any coworker under the table, had a reputation as a barracuda. This man's blues had defeated her.

Worse? It meant she knew he was right. She was too thin. She needed to eat more.

Crap.

"Sorry," she mumbled.

"What was that?"

"I'm sorry." Louder than the first time.

"Didn't catch it, what?"

"I *said* I'm *sor*—"

She raised her head and caught him grinning, hand cupped to his ear.

"Okay, okay." She smiled unwillingly. "You won another round."

"You'll have me begging for mercy at some point, I'm sure."

"I'll try."

She watched him break eggs, stir, pour, scramble. *So how long have you been married?* The question wouldn't come out, and she realized with a jolt of horror that right now she didn't want his wife to be real.

"Where did you grow up?"

"Right here."

"You've lived here all your life?"

"Not all. How about you?"

She tightened her lips. Okay, so he wasn't going to talk about himself. Fine. Then she'd tell him about herself. "I grew up in Framingham, Massachusetts, daughter of a junior high science teacher and an insurance salesman. I went to Brown, then to Stanford business school, met my husband Paul when I was twenty-four, got married six months later, started a career in IT sales, got fired, got a call that Paul had ruined us and killed himself, and bingo, just like that, here I am, at your counter, ready to have BEPO."

Her voice had risen steadily so that she was a defiant coloratura by the end. There. He had it all. More than she intended, but Paul's story sprawled out with the rest of it. If he told her she needed to explore her feelings and her rage more deeply, she was going to push his face into the pan.

He moved the eggs around one more time, turned off the flame and added salt and pepper. One glance over at her, then back to his task. "I guess after all that, it better be damn good BEPO."

She gaped for a half second, then burst out laughing. He turned and grinned, and the shared humor made her laugh again, fresh spasms of giggles overtaking her until she got her breathing under control with a slow in-and-out sigh that reminded her of Martha. "I thought I'd heard every possible reaction to my tale of tragic woe. That was the funniest. Thank you."

"You're welcome, Ann."

And there, in his gentle deep voice, was genuine and respectful sympathy and regret, and maybe even admiration for what she'd had to go through.

Her burst of pleasure was nearly sexual. She wanted to waddle over on her knees and embrace his, call his wife and tell her to stay away, so Ann could wallow a little longer in the sensation of not being treated like a patient.

"Here we go." He served up the glistening concoction, put one plate in front of each of them. "Dig in."

She dug. Fifteen minutes later she'd polished off her new true love, BEPO, along with two pieces of wheat toast, liberally buttered, a glass of orange juice, a glass of milk, and a cup of excellent espresso.

"So." Clive's face defined the concept of smug. "She's not hungry."

Ann sent him a look. "Because she's been *starving* herself for so long."

"Is that right?" He shook his head in mock amazement. "You'd never know it to look at her."

She rolled her eyes and got a dimpled smile back. "Can I help with the dishes?"

"Leave them."

"Really?" What, he left messes for his wife to clean up?

"I'll do them later, come on."

She tried to hide her dismay. "We're going back."

"I want to show you something. Outside."

She followed him out his back door, into a neatly mown yard bordered by grasses grown wild, then by more forest, glimpses of the ocean through the trees about a hundred yards off. Down just shy of where the shore dropped in a dozen-foot-high cliff to the rocky water's edge, a small building perched, a lean-to really, walls open on three sides, screened off from bugs.

Inside, room for a chaise and a chair, pulled up to a built-in writing or reading or eating surface with a spectacular view. To the right, the spine of a sandbar curved inward, forming a

shallow clear tidal pool in its arch. To the left, forested mainland ending in dramatic ledges sloping to the sea. Ahead, a
clear expanse of water, and beyond, more green fingers of the
mainland grabbing at the sea.

The sight lifted her mood even higher. Was that what he'd
intended? "It's beautiful."

"If you need somewhere to go, some time to yourself some
afternoon or on a Sunday, just let Betsy know and I'll come
get you." He glanced at her, then back out into the bay.

Wow. She felt shaky and odd and vulnerable again, and
profoundly touched by his offer after she'd been something
of a pig to him, not that he'd been Prince Charming either.

If she didn't watch out, she'd develop a crush on this guy
too. *Widow Becomes Maneating Nymphomaniac.*

"Thank you."

"No problem." Clive glanced at his watch. "I should take
you back."

"Yeah. Okay." To her surprise, the news didn't fill her gut
with as big a ball of lead as before. Not when she had the
promise of escape. Another day out on the *Tiger Lily II* next
week, and the offer of this peaceful glorious place. She might
even survive seeing Patrick again, sorting through her con-
fusing feelings about him and who she was now. She might
even manage not to maim Dinah.

Maybe she'd turned a corner.

"Look." He touched her arm, pointed out over the water.
An enormous bird flapped into sight, glided lower, landed
and stood in the shallows on long spindly legs. "Blue heron."

She stared at the bird, who appeared to be posing for a
Come to Maine postcard, and found herself moved, not only
by the sight, but by the simple fact of standing in silence,

watching the bird with a friend as entranced as she was.

One tear slid silently over her cheek. When did it end, this need to pour out saltwater over something that had happened so many months ago now?

She turned away before he could see, pretending to find something in the woods far more fascinating.

"Grief sucks." His vehemence startled her into unlikely laughter.

"No kidding."

"You'll get through it, Ann. Good things will come out of it. It's just hard to see them at first."

"You've had experience."

"Few people haven't."

"Right." She got the tear under control, wishing he'd tell her his story too. "Right. Thanks."

"And another thing." He took a step away from her, watching the heron intently. "People kill themselves because of who they are, not who they know. His death wasn't your failure."

The tight ball in her throat wasn't a surprise this time. "I'm trying to believe that."

"You can. Once you stop making his death about you."

She bristled. "I don't think—"

"Stop." He turned and looked at her calmly. "Don't take that the wrong way. You proved on the boat that you're not as much of a prima donna as you seem."

She made an open-mouthed sound of indignation. "Oh, *that's* just—"

"Down, girl." He winked and showed his dimple. "I'm teasing you."

"Half teasing."

"Okay, half teasing. I admit, I thought you were going to be a pain in the ass at first. Arnold and I have seen it all."

"Why do you do it?"

"Take women out on the boat? For the cash. Plain and simple."

"Right." Ann forced her tense shoulders to relax, and grudgingly let her anger go. "Well, thanks. I guess."

He nodded. The heron took a few long-legged delicate steps in the background. Some small animal scuttled through the dry underbrush nearby. A mosquito investigated her forehead.

"So . . . " He gestured to the house. "I really do need to take you back."

"Okay." She met his eyes, felt stronger again, and able to cope.

They drove in comfortable silence, his truck bumping and squeaking on the rough entrance road into camp. She was already looking forward to next time, and looking forward to anything was a rare luxury these days.

"Thanks for today, Clive. For the lobstering and . . . everything else."

"You were good company. And a good worker." He slid his truck into a parking place. "It was easy having you around."

"Thanks." He might as well have told her she was Mother Teresa, Marilyn Monroe, and Marie Pasteur all in one. She was definitely going soft in the head. "And thanks for the food."

"No problem. They told me I had to fatten you up."

Oh Christ.

She knew her face fell. Even though she turned away immediately, she knew he saw it fall. Stupid girl, thinking she'd been out of reach of the Grief Brigade.

As if to underline the concept, before she was even out of sight of Caretaker Clive, here came Patrolling Patrick, striding on the path, heading for the truck. *Subject returning. All monitoring systems engaged.*

Clive turned off the motor. She glanced at him questioningly. "Staying?"

"I need to talk to Patrick."

Ann laughed, a bitter unpleasant sound. "Of course. A report on the patient."

She opened the door, slid out of the truck, wanting to put the whole day behind her now.

"I meant what I said about coming by any time."

"Right." Another directive from the Betsy Gestapo. *We believe Ann might do better in a more isolated environment. If you could pad the walls of your lean-to, we think it might be an ideal place to further our experimentation.* "For my own good."

"Ann . . . " He got out of the truck, came around and stopped, eyes focused behind her on what must have been Patrick's approach.

"Hey, there, Lady Ann, good to have you back." Patrick's voice, big and hearty. She turned and saw him, tall, confident, movie-star handsome, eyes glowing with warmth and welcome. "How was your day?"

"You know? I don't think I'm qualified to answer that." She turned and gestured to Judas, standing solidly planted on the gravel lot. "Why don't you save yourself trouble and ask Dr. Clive."

Chapter 11

C indy smiled down at Martha's perfect cookies and tried to suppress the urge to upend the table and send almond crescents hurtling in all directions. Her mandatory baking class, held in a light airy annex to the camp kitchen, was a disaster, as she knew it would be. Why wouldn't they let her try something she could actually be good at? Though she wasn't even sure what that would be. Waiting for her husband to come back from screwing another woman? If they made that an Olympic event, she'd medal.

Martha's almonds ground into perfectly fine and even grains in the food processor. Cindy's clumped into almond butter the first time, and the second, came out half ground, half chunked. Martha's cookies were smooth, symmetrical, evenly dipped in powdered sugar. Cindy's were misshapen, burned, and blotchy.

"You've all done great." Francine, their plump, cheerful instructor walked by and did a double-take at Cindy's disasters, then moved on. "The camp will be lucky to have these for dessert tonight!"

Cindy wanted to crawl under the cookie-laden table. She could see it now, the rush after dinner, the pillaging, the stuffing, and at the end, only her cookies left alone on the table, unwanted and unloved. Maybe she should dump them now, in the trash or into the woods for the birds, to spare them and herself humiliation.

"So ladies, we're ready to move on to the third stage of our bread-making. Your dough should have doubled in size by now. A gentle poke should leave an imprint that does not bounce back. That means it has risen enough and you can punch it down."

The women drifted to their dough balls, each in its own bowl, covered with a blue and white striped towel. Cindy lifted her towel without much hope. Sure enough, the dough looked exactly the same as when she put it in. She glanced at Martha's. Martha's had risen nearly to the rim. Of course.

"Yours looks great." She pointed to Martha's bowl and gestured hopelessly at her own, laughing, so Martha would see how little it bothered her to be such a complete and utter failure at everything she tried. "I guess mine didn't rise."

Martha frowned at Cindy's lifeless lump. "Your water might have been too hot. Or too cold."

"Probably." Cindy gritted her teeth. Those sentences were the most that had come out of Martha's mouth all class, maybe all week. Why had this woman even come to camp if she wasn't going to talk to anyone? Dinah talked a little too much, but at least she had something to say, and tried to get along with people. Ann just sniped. She was a tall skinny sniper rifle. Martha was a big bowl of bread dough. Maybe if you poked her, the poke would stay indented as a sign that she'd risen enough and it was time to punch her down.

Cindy would like to volunteer for that job.

She knew she was being jealous and childish. Martha couldn't help being shy and at ease in the kitchen. Cindy could have paid more attention during those Cook-Easy classes Kevin gave her as a Christmas present years ago. But that had been shortly after his first mistress, and she supposed she'd deliberately not-tried in order to punish him. If someone pushed her to the wall and forced her, she'd admit to sly pleasure serving him bad food and watching his face shut down into stoicism. She knew more about stoicism than he ever would, but she liked giving him a taste anyway.

Maybe Cindy hadn't shown enough interest in Martha, and that's all Martha needed to warm her up.

"So." She punched at her dough, which didn't deflate and sink because it hadn't risen in the first place, but she was going to go through the motions and bake the thing if it killed her. "How are you liking camp?"

For a second she thought Martha was going to ignore her, and that made her feel like turning and screaming the question repeatedly, right into Martha's face. Which was a little worrisome because it usually took something like, oh, say, her husband having an affair, to get her that worked up.

"It's okay."

"How are your other classes?"

"Good." The pudgy heel of Martha's hand pushed the dough; she gathered it expertly, folded, pushed again, earth mother, pioneer woman, salt of the earth. "Are you liking yours?"

"Oh yes. They're all terrific." Cindy laughed and gave her

cold, unresponsive dough a good whack. "Well, baking isn't my thing, I guess you noticed that."

"No one is good at everything."

"Of course not." It's just that most people were good at *something*. "My husband says the same thing all the time."

"Have you heard from him yet?"

Cindy sent her a sharp glance in case Martha was making fun, but she didn't seem to be, just stood there placidly, at one with her perfect bread dough. "Not yet. I guess he'll take a while longer to get this latest one out of his system."

"Right."

Cindy's fingers dug into her failure. "You think I'm crazy, don't you?"

"Not at all." Martha's slightly bulging blue-green eyes actually met Cindy's; she shrugged her large shoulders, for once free of the striped shawl so the movement didn't make her jingle. "You love him."

"Yes." Cindy's response was automatic, while she thought how much wider and prettier Martha's eyes would look if she curled her eyelashes, which grew down quite sharply, like a camel's.

"Then I understand."

"Really?" And a softer hairstyle. That spiky hairdo served only to point out that she was too old to be wearing a spiky hairdo.

"When you've invested your whole life in loving someone who truly completes you, when you've achieved that deep and total intimacy to the point where you can read each other's thoughts and finish each other's sentences . . . who can ever give that up?"

Cindy blinked. Excess acid started trickling into her stomach. "Um. Exactly."

"You hang onto something that rare. Not many couples have it. And if it means you have to share him, then that's your cross to bear, but in the end he's worth it. *Your love* is worth it."

Cindy was feeling more and more bewildered by the second, and getting strangely angry. First of all, after nearly a week of silence, it was disconcerting that this odd woman should spout all this at Cindy, when Cindy had just been trying to be politely friendly. And second of all, what this woman was saying sounded as if it had come straight out of a romance novel. Cindy didn't know any couples like that. After the wedding, most women quickly found out they'd been sold an absolute crock. Their wedding might be the happiest day of their lives, but only because it was all downhill after that.

"Of course. Our love is worth it. That's exactly it." She picked up a knife and hacked her dead dough into pieces, while Martha formed hers into soft factory-perfect rolls. "I can't imagine my life without him."

That much was true, but not the way Martha would take it. It was true because since her teen years, she hadn't *had* a life without him. Kevin or Kevin's money defined her current existence, which meant Cindy minus Kevin equaled pretty close to a big fat nothing.

That depressing thought carried her through dinner, where her cookies were conspicuously absent from the dessert lineup, ditto any sign of the dense masses that were supposed to be her rolls, then through the after-dinner karaoke activity, which she barely paid attention to, though she smiled and laughed and clapped along with everyone else, and then it accompanied her to bed and another night of agonizing wakefulness.

Three A.M. and she'd only managed to doze for an hour before she bolted awake again and started to obsess over what Martha had said about love. What kind of perfect man had Martha met and how did someone get that lucky? Forget Wal-Mart, there should be a store called Wed-Mart, where you could pick out husbands and return or exchange them if they didn't work out, without the pain and shame and stigma of divorce.

Why didn't married couples tell you the truth when you were on your way to the altar? All they said was, "Marriage is a lot of work." The *Titanic* wouldn't even have been scratched by the tiny tip of that iceberg. A couple of times she'd imagined being with other men, but even imagining it made her feel angry and guilty. Patrick was the closest she'd come, the first time another man had touched her that intimately. How did big weird Martha find something that rare and special? Maybe now that Martha had said more than four words, Cindy could ask her. Maybe Cindy would, tomorrow. Make that today, it now being three minutes after three A.M.

She gave in and turned on the lamp next to her bed. If she squinted at one of the assortments of knots on her pine ceiling, the arrangement looked very much like the eyes, ears, and muzzle of Max. She'd taken to talking to this Max at night, which probably meant her sleep deprivation was making her lose it, but in many ways he'd been her best and only friend, so sue her. Right now she and Max were going to discuss whether she should stay in bed, where she was becoming increasingly frustrated and upset, or whether she should get up and take a walk. She loved the woods at night. The stars had been out earlier and the moon should be rising soon, which meant that wonderful sparkling path on the water that looked like an invitation to dance on it.

Max agreed that a little walk would probably do Cindy good, so Cindy got up and slipped into her bathrobe, then into her jacket and her sneakers, which were perfectly named tonight since she needed to sneak.

Outside, the air was chillier than she expected, a crisp nearly fall-like feel. If fall started in August, winter up here would go on forever, probably even longer than it did in Milwaukee, which was even longer than it did in New Jersey, which was plenty long enough for her. She headed away from Cabin Four, her flashlight illuminating a dark dot within a small bright circle, within a larger, dimmer circle, like a woman's breast made of light.

Okay, she was cracking up or something, that had to be the weirdest thought she'd ever had.

She headed toward the shore and the inviting moon path on the sea, intending to sit on the beach, listen to the waves, feel the breeze on her cheeks. Maybe that would put her to sleep. Something had to, didn't it? How long could a person stay caught between two natural states, never tired enough to sleep deeply, never alert enough to be constructively awake? She would probably find out. With luck, before she was institutionalized.

A rustle in a stand of immature evergreens made her jump and, she was embarrassed to say, give a little shriek. Probably a mole or something. *Honestly, Cindy.* She shone the flash-light toward the noise at the same time she took a few hurried steps away, which turned out to be a mistake because she tripped over a root and couldn't help another little yell of surprise on her way down. Ouch. She hadn't really hurt herself, but it felt like it from the blow to her pride, if not her tailbone.

Guess what? She couldn't even take a stroll in the moonlight without screwing up.

Clumsily back on her feet, she brushed herself off, even though she couldn't see anything to brush with her flashlight dropped and gone out. Tomorrow her bathrobe would probably be full of pine needles and twigs and people would think she'd been rolling in the woods.

More sounds in the brush to her left, this time made by something much larger than a mole. She groped for her flashlight, really hoping it was a person. She wasn't in the mood to tackle a moose.

"Who's there?" Patrick's voice.

"Oh." She breathed in a gasp and breathed out a nervous giggle, found the flashlight but didn't turn it on. "It's Cindy. Matterson."

"Cindy." She saw him in the faint glow from the half-moon, walking comfortably through the dark woods without any other light to guide him, which struck her as mysterious and alluring. "What are you doing out here?"

"I'm . . . I'm . . . walking."

"Yeah?"

"I was heading for the shore."

"Sounds chilly."

"Oh." She frowned at the bay, black but for the moon's dance floor. "I thought it sounded lovely."

"Lonely." He laid his hand on her shoulder. She could feel

its warmth through her jacket, bathrobe, and nightgown, all the way down to her bare skin.

Patrick and Cindy, alone on a moonlit night when she was having dim thoughts of marriage and tortured dreams of ideal love.

Damn the whole gay thing.

"Come on over to my cabin, Cindy. We'll see if we can get you sleepy."

She twisted again toward the beach, spread silent and empty, and now that she thought about it, it did look chilly and lonely. "That sounds even nicer."

"Come on, then." His hand traveled down her arm; he interlocked his fingers with hers and led her back the way he'd come, supporting her effortlessly with his considerable strength when she stumbled, which made her ridiculously weak in the knees, which made her stumble more.

She wasn't quite sure that being with Patrick was going to make her sleepy, even if he curled up on her tummy like Max. Her heart seemed to be beating pretty fast right now. Gay thing aside, going to a man's cabin in the middle of the night would be about the most adventurous thing she'd ever done. Wouldn't Kevin be surprised? He, who was always trying to get her to be more sexually adventurous, wanting to do it where they could be discovered, which instead of exciting her, only made her obsess about being put in jail. Naturally, Kevin had stopped asking—at least he stopped asking her. She supposed his other women had no problem getting it on in public bathrooms and parked cars and empty classrooms and quiet graveyards.

Did Martha's soulmate ask her to do things she didn't want to?

A few more stumbles through the trees, into a tiny clear-ing, up wooden steps and into Patrick's cabin, which fit him just right, like Goldilocks's bed. Plain and comfortable, his mystical side on display with the pretty little altar on the east wall. Cindy loved Buddha looking so happy. Who wouldn't want to pray to someone who seemed to be having so much fun all the time? That was a concept of God she could really get behind. Too much of western religion depended on the negative.

Behind her she heard the *thunk* of a bottle on a counter and the rattle of ice into glasses. She turned and found Pat-rick pouring out scotch.

"Are we allowed to? I mean . . . " She laughed awkwardly, cursing herself for sounding like Ms. Goody Two-Shoes. They were both old enough to drink, for heaven's sake. Though she thought she remembered Patrick talking about an alcohol problem that night of the first bonfire, or some addiction, hadn't he?

"Medicinal purposes." He crossed the room and handed her the glass. "It will help you sleep."

"Oh. Right." Medicinal only. That explained it. The first sip of scotch startled her with its strength. The second went down a little easier. She took a third to be polite and a fourth because he was examining her with his beautiful gray eyes and making her antsy when she desperately wanted to be calm.

"What do you think, should we stay in here or sit together on the porch? I have a blanket we can throw over us."

Cindy tried to picture both. Outside would be intimate, the two of them snuggled up under a blanket. Maybe a little too intimate. He might be gay, but she wasn't, and with her fifth and sixth nervous sips of scotch already ancient history, she was terribly afraid she'd get sloppy and do something embarrassing. "I think I'd rather stay in here. It's so nice and warm."

"As you wish, milady. Maybe some music?"

"Yes, please!"

"What are you in the mood for?" His voice was low and sexy, his shoulders high and broad, his earring pirateworthy.

What if she said, *You?* Not that she ever would. "Something soft, easy."

"Yeah, I don't think head-banging rock would do much to help you sleep." He rummaged through CDs on a shelf at the back of the room and selected one. "Mellow jazz?"

"Perfect." She smiled, feeling like a girl on her first date, even knowing that Patrick was— She stopped herself. Gay. Right. Gay. She wasn't going to think about that anymore. She was just going to enjoy herself, and if that meant pretending in her foolish romantic head that he was straight and that relationships like Martha's really were possible, then fine. She would. No one could stop her anyway.

The music swelled, replacing her nervousness with a slow, steady beat. Patrick smiled, moved across the room with a graceful two-step and turned out the lights. The slight glow of moonlight entered through the three sea-facing windows. Green lights glowed on the CD player; red ones streamed and receded with changes in volume. Otherwise darkness. A woman began to sing, deep and sultry, crooning about love as if she'd done it all and planned to do it all again.

"Dance with me." Patrick approached, one arm up, one reaching for her waist.

"No, no." Cindy shook her head, feeling instantly sick. "I'm a terrible dancer."

"No, you're not." He took away her scotch, put the glass on the altar to Buddha, and took her into his arms.

"I *am*. The worst." Oh gosh. The last thing she wanted was to ruin this beautiful night by bumping into him and trampling all over his toes. "Forget two left feet. I have at least four."

"Shh. Give yourself over to me, Cindy."

And didn't that sentence, whispered into her hair, send thrills all the way down to where it shouldn't. He was moving already, urging her into his rhythm, swaying with her, letting her know what he wanted with subtle touches and gentle pushes. Stiff at first, she found herself responding, slowly understanding where she was to go and when. *Give yourself over to me, Cindy.* Oh, she was, she would, she had. She relaxed further, let her body go, let herself fall into the music and into him.

"Who told you you couldn't dance?"

Kevin's name came to her lips, but she couldn't betray him that way, couldn't admit to the memory of dancing with him, feeling his rigid disapproval as she stumbled through the steps. Or maybe she just didn't want to say his name during this magical moment with Patrick, and make him real again. "Well, actually—"

"That's who I thought." He pulled her closer, their bodies touched, hers thrilled again. "Put your head on my shoulder, Cindy. Close your eyes. Try to empty your mind."

Oh, yes. Cindy put her head on his shoulder and closed her eyes. She could not empty her mind, though. Not with so much Patrick to think about, how tall and solid he felt, leading her gently around the room until she imagined herself Ginger to his Fred.

"Tell me . . . "

"Mmm?" She found a more comfortable spot for her head, pillowing her cheek on firm, smooth muscle.

"Does he make you feel good at anything?"

His question stole back at least half of the delicious relaxation he'd given her.

"Patrick . . . " She turned her forehead to his chest. "I don't want to talk about him. It doesn't feel . . . right."

"I see." His hand moved from her waist around to the center of her back. "Why do you think that is?"

She couldn't tell him that. "I don't . . . I mean—"

"Shh. You don't have to answer. Just think about it. Okay?"

"I'll try." She wouldn't. The music floated on, the woman's voice bringing hot, easy Bourbon Street to chilly New England. All she could think about was dancing and Patrick and how she already knew she'd miss him and this night when she was back home with her discontented board of a husband.

"What song is this?"

"'My Foolish Heart,' by Carmen McRae. Do you like it?"

"Oh, yes." Her voice came out small and breathless, probably girlish and foolish too. She didn't care. Being held in Patrick's strong embrace, smelling his wonderful smell, she felt protected and cared for in a way she hadn't in way too long.

"Patrick?"

"Mmm?" His low dreamy voice actually made her shiver.

"What do you think about love?"

His hand slid up her back, his fingers into her hair. "It's a many splendored thing."

She laughed softly, moved where he guided her, infatuated with her own grace. "Do you think it's real?"

"Ah, Cindy. The world would be a sad place without love."

He hadn't understood. Or maybe the question was too big, too complicated, too scary to be tackled while dancing to jazz on a moonlit night.

"I mean romantic love, do you think it can last?"

"As long as the two people are meant to be together, yes."

She laughed bitterly. "All brides and grooms think they're meant to be together."

He lifted his arm, turned Cindy under it and brought her back against him; all his toes remain unharmed. "Why do you want him back?"

"He's my husband."

"And if he doesn't come back?"

She sighed. "He will."

"If he *doesn't*?"

"Patrick . . . " She tried to move away but he gripped her shoulders and wouldn't let her. She tried harder and his grasp became hard enough to hurt.

"If he doesn't come back, Cindy?"

She stared up at him, breath coming high and uneven. Her giddy mood dissolved. Her head dropped. She stared now at their feet, recently dancing, still pointed toward each other. "I don't know any other way to be but married to him."

"That's what you need to learn, Cindy." He spoke urgently, with a faint note of triumph. "How to be you."

She leaned against him, this time in exhaustion. She was already her. How could she be anyone else?

"If Kevin loved you, he couldn't cheat."

"No." She shook her head wearily. "It's not that simple."

"It is, Cindy." His arms came around her again, she tried to relax back into the music, and into him. Patrick believed in love the way Martha did. The way Cindy once had, so long ago she could barely remember. What had she missed out on?

"That . . . man that you—" She tried to get herself to say the word "loved," but couldn't bring herself to think about Patrick with a man. Not when he was once again making her feel like the girl during the high school slow dance everyone assumed would go all the way later in his car. "The one you were . . . with. You loved him?"

"Yes."

"How did you know?"

"I just did." The abrupt words were not what she'd expected.

She wrinkled her brow against his chest. Maybe this was a bad subject to bring up. Maybe the pain of losing this man had been so great, he still couldn't talk about it.

"Was he—"

"Cindy." His voice was slightly hoarse.

"I'm sorry. I know how painful it must be to—"

"No. It's not that. It's just that with you here, he seems so . . . "

The song drifted gently to a close. Cindy stopped dancing, heart pounding; she lifted her head, gazed at the dim outline of his face. Maybe Patrick didn't want to bring up a loved one's name just now either, for reasons that still scared her enough not to want to name them. "He's so what?"

"Far away," he whispered. His face drew closer, and for a breathless second she thought he was going to kiss her.

Of course he wasn't going to kiss her. Gay men didn't— He kissed her.

His mouth was warm, soft and achingly tender, and even

as she knew she wasn't supposed to respond, that he didn't mean it, that she *couldn't* mean it, she surrendered to the sheer physical pleasure of kissing someone who wanted to kiss her, who wasn't doing it out of habit or guilt or love so complicated and worn that it barely resembled the bright shiny passion they'd started with.

He drew away, then came at her again, more passionately this time, as if the first delicious exploration had only unleashed a stronger hunger. She responded, feeling female parts that had been wounded and betrayed and dormant for too long stirring to life. His leg moved between hers and she welcomed the intrusion, found herself wanting, yearning, lusting for intrusion to a far greater and more satisfying degree.

How could she?

Why shouldn't she? Kevin had never hesitated, she was sure of it. The first woman to give him a come-hither stare had him naked, coming in her hither, before five seconds had passed.

"Patrick." She buried her mouth in the smooth firm skin of his throat, moaned and pushed against his leg like a lovelorn poodle. This was insanity. This was ecstasy. This was also a little . . . strange. Him being *that way* and all.

He bent and lifted her; she wrapped her legs around his waist, her arms around his shoulders. He walked them over to his bed, sat, then lay back so she sprawled on top of him. Now she was able to make her mind go blank. It was the only way. His hands were inside her jeans as fast as hers were inside his. Pants and underpants discarded, condom on, they were joined so quickly that even if she'd been capable of thought she wouldn't have had time.

She rode him insistently, flushed and panting and triumphant. *Take that Kevin. Take that.* She imagined her husband naked and erect, lying on his back, Patty, who she imagined looked like Ann, straddling him. Cindy and Patrick, Kevin and Patty, all making love together—no, screwing. They were screwing together. What's more, Cindy was going to come. Easily. And Patty was going to have trouble.

As soon as she had the thought, Patrick found her special place with his thumb and she came so quickly thinking of her husband and another woman, with Patrick inside her, that she barely had time to realize what was happening. Patrick followed soon after, with a low groaning noise that unfortunately sounded exactly like Kevin after Mexican food.

There. *There.*

She'd done it.

She slumped onto Patrick's broad chest, wrapped her arms around his shoulders and felt the most deep wracking need to cry she'd ever felt in her life.

"Cindy." He took her shoulders, lifted her away so he could see her face. His had gathered into anxiety. "I am so sorry."

She could only stare dully, fighting the pain in her throat. What could *he* possibly have to be sorry about? He hadn't cheated. Except on his sexual orientation.

"I don't know what happened. I don't know what came over me. I . . . haven't been with a woman since high school, and that was a disaster that never got off the ground. But you . . . " He caressed her cheek reverently, brought her close for another kiss and cradled her tenderly against his chest. "You woke something in me I didn't even know was there, Cindy."

She reached up and touched his shoulder, stroked it. The

urge to cry receded and a deep and growing warmth took its place.

"Oh. Wow." All thoughts of Kevin vanished. She couldn't see herself but she was sure that if she had access to a mirror, she'd discover her eyes were shining.

Patrick was her first, in a way, and she was his first in another way. Maybe there was something really special between them, something powerful enough to supersede the fact that Patrick only liked men, and that she had vowed only to be with Kevin. Maybe there was such a thing as never-ending love after all. Maybe she'd simply missed it the first time.

Maybe she had a chance to find it now.

Chapter 12

Martha sat out on her favorite ledge in her favorite meditation pose, but she wasn't meditating. She simply sat, watching the beautiful view as if it was her favorite TV show. The islands turned bright to dark in moving patches as clouds drifted through their morning sunlight. A steady breeze kept away mosquitoes and created carnival rides for birds up so high they looked like a child's double-arched representation in black crayon. One pair gracefully circling and twining the drafts she suspected were hawks—maybe osprey, maybe eagles. Dinah had spotted an eagle visiting its nest on one of the islands and had bludgeoned them with facts, including that eagles mated for life.

Obviously, Dinah wasn't an eagle.

A quick scent of pine entered the breeze, and Martha arched up to meet it, eyes closed, head back, smelling and feeling and being. She knew someone on the camp staff was close by keeping tabs on her. She knew if she picked up a big rock and heaved it in the water, the splash would bring attentive feet running. But in this beautiful spot she could at least pretend to be alone.

This morning she'd woken up strangely peaceful. Maybe she'd taken a few more steps toward accepting Eldon's illness. Maybe denial was just giving her a break from the painful and frightening emotions. Maybe her revolt against death had shocked her gratefully back among the living.

Wednesday at dinner after her kayaking accident, she'd told Ann that Eldon was sick, acknowledging him out loud for the first time in well over a decade. She'd felt she owed Ann after having figured out Ann's husband killed himself. Finally making her relationship with Eldon exist outside of her own secrets had not felt like a violation, but a glorious validation. Ann accepted what she'd said and offered her own clumsy brand of sympathy and caring without question.

That night, Martha had gone to bed repeating the conversation over and over in her mind. Four simple words, *my boyfriend is sick,* and Martha's relationship with Eldon was instantly as real as anyone else's, and she had the right to grieve deeply and openly for his impending loss. Yesterday she'd been bold enough to talk to Cindy about their love, and the envy in Cindy's eyes had fed her starving soul.

Maybe that breakthrough was responsible for her mood today. All she knew was that colors were brighter, smells more vivid, and sensations sharper.

"Martha?"

Martha started. Her stomach sank. She hadn't heard Cindy pushing through the alders to reach her rock of solitude. "Hi."

"Wow. This is beautiful." Cindy put her hand like a visor

over her eyes and scanned the view. "Not that it's so different from over on the beach, but the perspective is shifted or
higher or something."

"Yes." Martha could not have been less in the mood for
Cindy's nervous edges and anxious chatter.

"So, well, anyway." Cindy turned and examined Martha
instead of the horizon. "Betsy wants to talk to you in her
office."

What had happened? In went Martha's breath for nine,
held for three, out for fifteen. She wished now that she had
been meditating, so she could face whatever this was about
evenly. Eldon was still alive; she would have felt if he'd
passed. But she caught Betsy staring at her a couple of times
at the bonfire two nights earlier, and this morning at breakfast she'd stopped by their table, started to speak to Martha,
then changed her mind.

Martha stood, reluctantly leaving contact with the warm
steady rock, and followed Cindy to the path, wishing she had
her shawl on for comfort.

"I keep meaning to ask how you are doing after your kayaking spill, and I keep forgetting."

"Fine." She glanced at Cindy striding gawkily along, returned her eyes to their destination, then glanced over
again, suddenly wanting another fix of her new drug. "I was
distracted when I fell in. I found out my boyfriend in the
hospital contracted pneumonia."

"Oh. That's terrible!" Cindy was so distressed she stopped
walking. Martha's pleasure rush of adrenaline was immediate
and energizing. Now Martha and Eldon existed concretely
for Cindy too. "Do you think . . . I mean is Betsy going to . . .
Do you think he's okay?"

"If he died, I would have felt it."

"Oh. Right." Cindy's eyebrows drew down. She seemed annoyed. Martha should have let it rest. "I'm going back to the cabin to read for a while, so if you need someone to talk to after you see Betsy, that's where I'll be."

Martha nodded, and answered Cindy's wave when she turned off the path. If Martha needed someone to talk to. About Eldon. She could hardly dare to imagine it. Two women chatting openly about the men they missed. Just the thought would sustain her through whatever Betsy had to say. *Once upon a time a woman spoke to the world of her great and beautiful love, and the world became a better place . . .*

Betsy sat at her desk, peering at her computer screen over black half-glasses, but looked up with a big smile when Martha walked in.

"Hi, Martha. Come on in, have a seat." She gestured to a cozy-looking window nook in her living room, whose windows faced the sea.

Martha dutifully parked herself on the cushion, hoping Betsy didn't choose to sit next to her. She liked Betsy, but instinctively felt the need for space during this discussion. She now suspected that since she hadn't sought Betsy out for counseling after her tumble into the bay, Betsy had decided the talk would need to happen on her invitation.

Martha didn't want to hear about how suicide was not the answer, and how her life meant too much to waste because of Eldon's tragedy. Doubtless Betsy would consider all the hours and weeks and years spent waiting for Eldon wasted too.

Unfortunately, Betsy must have felt that this was a girl-friendy occasion, because she did sit next to Martha, then turned sideways toward her, drawing her knee up onto the seat and clasping it. "How was your morning?"

"Fine." Martha shifted on the cushion, arranged a throw pillow more comfortably behind her.

"I sense that you are settling into camp a little better."

"Yes."

"I've noticed you seeming more animated, and talking more with the other women."

"Yes." Martha looked out the window, envying the outside its freedom. The sun sparkled on the sea, giving it a warm radiant look that made it hard to remember how cold and inhospitable it had felt surrounding her body.

"Do you remember, when I wrote to you earlier in the summer, I mentioned that an anonymous donor had secured a place for you in this session?"

This unexpected comment made Martha stare until she realized of course Betsy would know that Eldon had paid for her to come. "Yes."

Betsy's smile became forced, and Martha sensed that more of a response was expected of her. She didn't mean to sound recalcitrant, but didn't know what else to say.

"You and I have never talked about it, have we?"

Martha started to feel uneasy. Were they supposed to? What was the point? "I know who it is."

"I see." Betsy sounded surprised. "She is quite a generous woman, isn't she?"

Martha's body turned still. "She?"

"Bianca Cresswell."

Bianca. The ice woman. Martha stared until comprehension dawned. "She might have signed the check, but the instruction would have come from Eldon. He'd have wanted plans in place to have me taken care of in case anything ever happened to him."

Betsy's eyes narrowed, as if this troubled her. "You think he would have discussed his wishes regarding his mistress's care with his wife?"

Martha didn't know what to say to that. Bianca turned a blind eye to Eldon's personal life. Eldon had arranged for Martha to be here. Why else would she be? Certainly Bianca wouldn't have offered this succor out of the frozen waste-land of her heart. "I guess he must have."

"And you think she would carry them out?"

Martha's breath began behaving strangely, and she tried to force it back into its proper rhythm. Betsy was right. This didn't make sense. Why would Eldon ask Bianca to arrange this? Why would it be her signature on the check? Why not one of his aides, or a banker he trusted?

"Martha . . ." Betsy laid a soothing hand on Martha's knee, which, instead of being comforting, made her want to push it away. "Bianca wanted you here for observation. She and Eldon believe that you are suffering from erotomania. Do you know what that is?"

Martha shook her head. She was trying to get her breathing to cooperate, and it wasn't. Hearing any sentence containing Bianca and Eldon in proximity, especially balancing the two of them against her, was nearly more than she could stand.

"Erotomania is a delusional disorder. A typical sufferer is female, a loner, who believes that a celebrity or other public personality is in love with her. A famous male example is John Hinckley, who shot President Reagan for the actress Jodie Foster. Do you understand?"

Martha stared blankly, and then suddenly, oh yes, she understood. Bianca was behind this. Of course she was. She wanted Martha out of the way, in case she tried to get close to Eldon, in case she made a scene, in case the truth of Eldon's love came out and the media got hold of it and ruined Bianca's photogenic near-widow experience. "Eldon loved me. We were meant to be together. Always, we were meant to be together."

"The love is usually idealized and intense and imagined to be returned just as intensely by the object."

Eldon was not an object to Martha. *Once upon a time there was an evil witch who tried to—* "I'm not imagining what I feel or what he feels for me."

"Sometimes the condition manifests itself after an actual love affair ends." Betsy pressed her lips together as if she didn't want to say what she felt she must. "Eldon did leave you to marry Bianca."

Martha knew exactly how the man in her story had felt, the one under whose feet the earth crumbled away faster than he could run. "He had to. He needed a political wife. The marriage was for convenience only. He loved me. Even when he was on TV, he was thinking of me."

"Yes. I read about the 'special waves' in your letter." Betsy's tight mouth turned down. Her eyes grew sad. She was distraught. She felt sorry for poor insane Martha, who couldn't tell love from old-maid fantasy. "Sufferers from erotomania often believe the object's communication with the general public contains special signs or messages meant only for them."

Martha stood. *Once upon a time . . .*

Nothing came to her. She had to get away from Betsy.

Something horrible was going to happen, she'd stop breathing, or have a heart attack, or die of shock. This couldn't be happening. Eldon's special signals *were* meant for her.

"Please sit down. I want to help you. Bianca wants to help you."

"Bianca does not want to help me." Martha's voice came out low and shaky and strange. "She wants me out of the way, so I can't go to Eldon, so I can't help him. She probably knows that my voice would wake him up."

"Martha . . . " Betsy's voice was so serenely and perfectly gentle that its sound waves probably didn't even disturb the air molecules they traveled through. "I have to tell you that people with the condition often vilify the person they see as an impediment to their love. Bianca would be that person to you."

A sob broke from Martha's throat. Bianca had planned this so perfectly. Who would believe Martha? What proof did she have? None here. None even at home. She'd always destroyed everything—e-mails, cards, phone bills. If anything happened to her, she didn't want anything that could shame Eldon or hurt his career. All the years waiting for him to be free—what were they for now if Bianca took them away?

"The good news is that often the disorder is part of a larger treatable condition, like bipolar disorder or schizophrenia. I'm not qualified to make that assessment, but I'm going to recommend that you be evaluated by a psychiatrist so you can get the help you need. In many cases medication can completely correct the problem."

Problem? Medication? Martha looked down, frightened by her own sudden rage. For all her wise and spiritual ways, Betsy was a fool, taken in by Bianca like the rest of them.

"Medication cannot erase what I feel for Eldon, and not even his death can erase what he felt for me."

Betsy let the silence go for a while, watching Martha, while Martha watched a small beetle negotiating the landscape of Betsy's rug. Whatever sounds the beetle was making, no one could hear them over the raspy shallow heaves of Martha's lungs.

"Will you sit down, Martha?"

She opened her mouth to refuse, but right now her only weapon was to act as sane as she knew how. "Yes. Okay."

She sat, feeling as if she were perched on a bomb set to go off any second.

"Thank you." Betsy smiled warmly, oh-so-pleased by nutty Martha's compliance. "I'd like to share a story with you."

Martha nodded, because if she opened her mouth, she was going to say, *Well, I don't want to hear it.*

"When I found out my son was gay, it took me a while to adjust and to accept it. During that time, and even later, sometimes I would still fantasize about weddings and grand-children, the same way I had before I knew. I wanted those things to be real so much that I couldn't let go of the thoughts or my plans." She leaned forward with a sympathetic smile, while Martha calculated how long she could sit there until she actually did go crazy. "I can understand how the shock of Eldon breaking up with you all those years ago and marry-ing Bianca might have led you to pretend that you were still together. I truly can understand that. I know what a good imagination you have, how you love to tell stories . . . "

Of course. The stories. Martha had played into Bianca's hands perfectly. She might as well admit to having the disorder.

"It's not like that. I don't know how else to tell you." She spoke dully, but managed to look Betsy in the eye, and in return she saw a flicker of doubt. "Bianca is afraid I will go to him. She sent me here to make sure I was out of the way."

"Really, Martha . . . " Betsey gestured helplessly. "I don't think she sees you as that much of a threat."

"Of course she wouldn't let you know how much of a threat I am. Why would she tell you that?" Her voice rose in spite of herself. The earth had already finished collapsing underneath her. She was floating in a meaningless void. First Eldon had been taken away by Bianca and his career. Taken away a second time by his stroke, which also threatened her hopes for their future. Now even her memories, alive only in her brain and his, were endangered. "What happens now?"

"Because I've seen such progress here already, I'd like you to be able to finish out the session of camp. Then, I'll recommend someone you can see in Burlington."

"And if I refuse to see anyone?"

Betsy's sad eyes grew sadder. "I can see why you might not want to accept help from Bianca. But I would hope that you would accept it from me."

"I would accept help from you." Martha stood up. She couldn't bear another second. "If I needed it."

She flung herself out of the cabin, ignoring Betsy's calls, hurried away—not toward the sea this time, because they'd look for her there first, though all she wanted was to take a kayak and go and go and go until no one, not even Bianca, could reach her.

Toward the woods this time, finding a path, following it blindly through the trees, until she heard a voice, then an-

other, and turned back, too late. No trees large enough here
to hide behind.

"Martha?"

She turned around again, facing quite possibly the last
person she wanted to see besides Bianca. Patrick, returning
from the woods with a flushed camper in tow, the shapely
one in preppy clothes Martha had avoided on her very first
day. Martha didn't like Patrick. She didn't like the way he
popped up suddenly, like some devil spirit appearing out of
nowhere. She didn't like the way he hovered over Ann, or
the way Cindy hovered over him.

She started backing down the path away from them.

"Were you just talking to Betsy?"

"Yes."

Patrick glanced down at his belt area, and pulled up a
beeper. "Hey, look. Betsy wants me to find you, and I already did!"

She didn't return his grin. She didn't care when he spoke
to the camper in a low voice and sent her away with a friendly
wink. She didn't want to speak to him or to anyone. She
didn't want to stay here knowing now why the letter about
camp had come to her brown apartment. She wanted to be
home, waiting again for Eldon, waiting for him to wake up
and come back to her.

"So, Martha, what's going on? How are you feeling?"

She held up her hand. "Stop that."

"Whoa." He chuckled, but his eyes held an edge. "What's
this about?"

"I don't want to talk to you."

"Oh?" He cocked his head, puzzled puppy. "I thought we

had friendship and trust going here, but okay. You want to take a walk instead? I've got something to show you I think you'll like."

"The way that other girl liked it?"

His smile faltered, then hardened. "What's that supposed to mean?"

"Nothing." She was suddenly exhausted, not up to sparring. She wanted alone time to figure out what to do. Stay here? Get in her car and go? "I'm going back to my cabin."

"Okay." He indicated the path behind her. "I'll walk you."

Right. No problem. Escort the crazy lady. Bianca had made sure that Martha's time here would be hell, that moving back to Burlington would be hell. If Martha dove again into the sea right now, would she still want to cling to life so stubbornly? She didn't think so.

"Do you think your life would have been better if you'd never loved him at all?"

Martha stopped walking, whirled around and faced Patrick. She'd never been so furious in her life. Not even when Eldon told her he was going to leave her for his career. "How dare you even suggest that."

His smile was not only a surprise, it was charming and genuine. "Then you have nothing to regret, Martha."

Schloop. The wind fell out of her sails. "No. I don't."

"Loving someone is never a mistake."

Her body felt turned to diamond. Rock simply wasn't hard enough. Who was this man, who undoubtedly had never loved anyone but himself? How was he able all at once to seem so completely full of crap and eerily perceptive at the same time?

"I guess Betsy hit you with the erotomania thing, huh?"

Her diamond/stone lips barely moved. "Yes."

"So? *Did* you make it all up?" Under his nonchalance she sensed his eagerness, hound nose snuffling, picking up a promising scent.

"What does it matter what I tell you? The main symptom of my 'illness' is that I believe it's all true."

"I want to hear you say it."

"Why?" Her throat closed. Her rock body shook in a silent earthquake. What did this jerk want from her? "Because one good liar can always spot another?"

"You—" He took a furious step toward her. "What the hell was that for? Haven't I always been a good friend to you? Is that how you repay me? By not trusting me? Calling me a liar? What grounds have I given you for that kind of accusation?"

His eyes blazed, his face contorted. A fleck of spit flew out and hit her forehead, but she didn't dare brush it off. She'd never seen anyone change personalities so suddenly and completely. Bianca could probably do it, leave off the Jackie O routine and ice over into the woman who made Eldon so unhappy, but right now it could not have been much more shocking if Patrick had turned into a werewolf.

"Okay." She stepped back. "I apologize. You've been a good friend."

He put his hand to his chest, took a couple of quick deep breaths that made her doubt further that he'd ever been a serious disciple of Buddhism. Martha had met people who'd been to Thailand or India to study, and all of them gave off an unmistakable aura of centeredness that Patrick, surfer-dude of spirituality, lacked.

"I'm sorry, Martha. It's a crazy, crazy hot button. I . . . I had this friend once, um, who—"

"It's forgotten." She wasn't interested in sticking around for any more of The Patrick Show.

"Thank you, Martha." He made his eyes go gooey-warm, which brought on that intense male magnetism that fascinated and repelled her. "You are a very generous and remarkable person. I told you the first day that you have a special power, and I meant it."

It was all she could do not to tell him straight out to cut the shit. "Thank you, Patrick. You are quite a remarkable person yourself."

"Friends again?" He held out his hand, missing her sarcasm, which had been worthy of Ann.

"Yeah." She shook his hand reluctantly, half expecting to encounter a tranquilizer dart in his palm, managed a smile, then could not begin to describe her relief when he turned, walked a few steps, turned back to wave and wink, and walked back toward camp.

Alone. Thank God. She blundered up the path several more yards, then pushed into a small mossy clearing and collapsed on a rock. Patrick was right. Loving Eldon was no mistake, no insanity. She'd cling to that.

She closed her eyes and cleared her mind, relaxed her body absolutely, ignoring the sting of a mosquito on her calf. When she entered the special place, felt that rush of warmth down her limbs, that perfect clear stillness, she sent her love out to Eldon, felt a rush of joy she recognized as the moment their minds connected. Of course he was thinking of her.

Send me a sign. Send me a sign to know what to do.

Time lost its meaning; she no longer felt its passage.

Send me a sign.

A buzzing sound flashed past. She opened her eyes and

saw a hummingbird at the feeder, its slender body quick and alert, movements sure and impossibly fast. Martha sat, enchanted by its glimmering grace.

Eldon had sent her this bird. Eldon or whatever power in the universe brought them together. God, or Love, or Fate, or the collective wisdom of man.

A sign. And in that next instant she knew what to do. She'd battle Bianca in her own quiet way. Continue what she'd already started, and make sure as many people as possible understood about the rare and special nature of her and Eldon's love.

Chapter 13

Ann looked critically at the painting she'd just completed of one of the islands out in the bay. Getting the rocks at the shoreline right was a killer; their shades were so subtle and their shapes so complicated, but over all she'd take it. Painting gave her the closest thing to serenity she'd felt in a long time, second to sitting on a lobster boat stuffing stinky herring into bags. Even when her thoughts wandered, at least part of her stayed calmly centered on what she was doing. Back home when her body had been calm, her mind always raced ahead to the next thing. After Paul died, it still raced, but always to the past.

The watercoloring women of camp Kinsonu, seven in this class, had brought their paper and paints down to the shore, seated themselves in a row facing the bay, and started trying to capture the sparkling sun, the blues and greens of water and trees, and the brown-grays of the rocky island shorelines.

Too bad they couldn't capture the fresh scented breeze or the swish of waves, or the whiny complaints of gulls.

Beside her she heard the latest groan of exasperation, followed by a high-pitched giggle. Apparently Cindy wasn't pleased with her painting. She'd been making grunts and miserable sounds during the entire class, which was getting incredibly tedious.

"Not happy?"

Cindy gave another of her weird giggles, eyes unnaturally wide and deeply shadowed, skin a sickly color reflecting her bright yellow top. Ann was starting to think she was nearing the edge. Maybe she thought her husband should be begging her to come back by now. Like *that* was going to happen.

"I see it with my eyes, but I can't get down on the paper what I see. I thought I could learn here. I thought I could." Cindy's voice bordered on hysteria, and Ann wanted to shout, *Who cares, it's just a painting!* but was afraid she'd push Cindy over.

"Maybe you're trying to draw too exactly. Maybe you should try to capture the essence of what you see, or the mood of what you see. Or forget what your painting looks like and enjoy the process."

"Oh. Yeah. Maybe I should." Again the giggle.

Ann wasn't sure Valium was fashionable anymore, but it seemed to her Cindy could use a case of it.

"Okay, ladies." Jenny, the art teacher, who reminded Ann of Betty Friedan, clapped her hands. "Please bring your supplies back up and put them away. It's nearly time for your next class."

Ann gathered her things and started toward the art building, annoyed when Cindy fell into step beside her. The last thing she needed was to get stuck playing Nurse Ratched.

A lobster boat revved its motor out on the bay, and Ann wondered for only the fortieth or fiftieth time whether the sound belonged to Clive and Arnold's boat, working its route. Ann would be back out with them next week; she looked forward to more time on the open water, away from the walking wounded. She looked forward to seeing Clive again and apologizing for her outburst. Of course, everyone who worked with the campers would need to be up to speed on what was happening with each of them and would report back. She didn't have to like it, but she got it and had gotten over it. Not Clive's fault, not a personal betrayal, for God's sake. They barely knew each other. She'd overreacted.

Ann had also been thinking about capturing the view from that little lean-to in back of his house. Maybe she'd take him up on his offer of spending time there some afternoon.

"What do you have now?" Cindy stumbled over a root on the path and barely caught herself before she fell.

"Archery." If Cindy said *Oh, me too*, Ann would—

"Oh, me too!" She turned to gaze at Ann as if they were suddenly best friends, and with her eyes off the path, she stumbled again. "Gosh, look at me. You'd think I'd been hitting the rum."

"You are a little unsteady."

"I can't sleep." Her voice sounded a little more desperate and nearer to tears than usual.

Ann hoped they'd get around other people before she let any flow, since Ann wasn't the huggy-huggy I'm-so-sorry type. Which had never seemed a liability until she was around so many women who were.

"I haven't slept since Kevin left me. I think I'm cracking up."

"I'm sure you're not." Ann used what she hoped was a soothing tone, while starting to walk faster. "Have you tried warm baths? Hot milk? Incessant masturbation?"

"*What?*"

Ann sighed. "I'm sure they can give you a pill or something."

"I don't need a pill. I need a husband."

"A new one?"

"No, not a new one. Kevin. The old one. The only one."

"Right." Ann was not going to get into this discussion. If Cindy wanted to whip herself with the shards of her broken marriage, that was her own masochistic fun.

"Were *you* married before . . . this?"

"Yes."

"Divorced?"

Shade cooled their entry into the woods. Ann wearily shifted her painting from her right hip to her left. "Widowed."

Cindy's gasp made Ann roll her eyes. "I'm so sorry!"

"Thanks."

"Was he . . . your true love?"

Ann stopped walking. What the hell kind of question was that? "My who?"

"The love of your life, The One, who completes your sentences and shares everything with you."

"God, where did you come up with such bullshit?"

"Martha found it. She told me."

"Martha has been smoking bad weed. Either that or she lives in a happy place the rest of us can't get to."

‎

"I think she found it. I don't have it with Kevin, I know that." Her glance at Ann contained the obvious question.

"Paul was . . . we were good together." Ann entered the art building and hung her painting carefully where it would dry among the others. They hadn't been good together at the end. Paul hadn't been good to anyone. Least of all to himself.

"I bet he would have been really proud of your painting." Cindy looked at her own ruefully before she hung it away. "Kevin would be disgusted by mine."

Ann rolled her eyes, wondering who'd beaten Cindy down to where she thought this Kevin was worth staying with, then realized she wasn't sure what Paul would have thought of her painting. Because her favorite pizza, in New Haven, Connecticut, wasn't anywhere *near* as good as the pizza he'd had at that tiny hole-in-the-wall restaurant in Rome. And the wine at one of Boston's finest restaurants might send her into ecstasy, but he'd had *much* better in this or that château in France or Italy. She was proud of her painting. Doubtless it would not measure up to Renoir.

Were they good together?

She and Cindy stepped out of the shady building and headed toward the sunny archery field, a few dozen yards up the hill and west of Betsy's cabin, Cindy constantly glancing at Ann. Her yearning for communication was starting to feel like wet clothes on a swimmer, a constant drag. Something about needy people made Ann want to put them out of their misery rather than help. Another attitude she shared with Paul—or learned from him? Another one that wouldn't exactly put her in line for sainthood.

"Where did you grow up, Ann?"

"Framingham. Massachusetts." They walked on, and the more steps they took, the more Ann's reply sounded brusque and rude, and the more obvious it became that the silence needed to be filled. By her. "How about you?"

"Princeton, New Jersey." Cindy sighed. "Daughter of two brilliant professors who had and still have no idea how I came out of their gene pool."

Ann nodded, feeling an actual pang of empathy. Ann's low-strung, placid parents and brothers thought she was an alien for her intelligence and ambition and drive. "I know what that's like."

"*You?*"

Ann sent her a look. "Why not me?"

This question appeared to flummox Cindy entirely. "Well, I mean, I thought, I assumed . . . women like you have it all together."

Ann snorted. "Which is why I'm here."

A few more steps in silence, while Ann hoped the subject was closed. "It's funny, you know not to judge a book by its cover, but we all do all the time. I never expected Martha would have been in such a perfect relationship. I figured you'd had it easy every day your whole life. I thought Dinah had no depth."

"Wait, she does?"

Cindy giggled and slapped Ann's arm playfully, which had to be one of the most annoying things anyone could do. "Tell me more about your family. Tell me how you were different. Tell me—"

"Whoa, one at a time."

"Sorry." She laughed that brittle alarming laugh. "Kevin says I talk too much and say too little."

By some miracle Ann managed not to say, *Kevin is an asshole*. She could tell plenty of Paul stories that wouldn't endear him to anyone either. "Let's say I was determined not to be satisfied with a high school education, a small brick house in a crowded neighborhood, and a job that never offered new challenges."

"And I bet you weren't. Did success make you happy?"

Ann stared longingly at the approaching archery field and its cluster of women who were not Cindy. What kind of naive question was that? "Sure, I was blissfully happy every single waking hour of my life."

Cindy stopped walking and stood there in her denim wrap skirt and denim tennis shoes with bright yellow ankle socks that matched her top, giving Ann a look that made her feel like a puppy killer. "I just wanted to know."

"Who the hell is happy? What kind of question is that?"

"I was happy. In my life. I was happy."

"Happy being betrayed and devalued? Sounds like a regular twenty-four/seven orgasm."

"Most of the time it was fine. Most of the time it was—"

"Why did you put up with it? For the sake of women everywhere, count yourself lucky he's gone and start over now that he's given you the chance."

"I don't know how. I'm not strong like you." Cindy's dark deer eyes filled up with tears, and she turned and walked off toward the targets set up on the field.

Ann threw up her arms to the sky. Great. Terrific. Fantabulous. She should start a new career as an advice columnist. No, a therapist. No, an international diplomat.

Cheri, the kayak-turned-archery instructor, called the

class to order; the eight women lined up two deep in front of four padded targets, white with colorful circles, mounted on wooden frames. Bows and feather-tipped arrows were handed to the first in line, while Ann indulged a few sick thoughts about the wisdom of arming desperate women. Good thing she was two lines away from Cindy.

After several minutes of instruction and practice with the bows, the women first in line were told to ready their arrows, aim, and fire at will. Ann's arrow hit the target with a satisfying *thunk* in the white outer ring. Not exactly a bull's-eye, but she did hit it. In the line to her left, Martha's arrow had nearly made the center circle. Cindy's missed the target altogether, and she stood staring in heartbreaking disbelief. Ann felt her second pang. Cindy couldn't seem to catch a break. No matter what she did. No matter how hard she tried.

Was that how Paul had felt? That the forces of the universe were lined up against him? If he'd only told her . . . If he'd only asked for help.

But he hadn't. Cindy had tried, and Ann had squashed her. Nice.

She fitted another arrow to her bow, readied, aimed, fired at will. *Thunk.* Another one out by the rim. Martha's second shot extended firmly from the bull's-eye. Cindy's stuck straight out of the ground like a croquet stake, six yards past the target.

"Change up." At Instructor Cheri's command, the women in front moved to the end of the line to give the next group a turn. Ann sneaked over and poked Martha's squishy upper arm. "Let me guess. You were an Olympic archery champion several years in a row."

Martha turned her unnaturally peaceful eyes on Ann. "I relax and center my body, then I imagine that I am the arrow."

The next line of archers shot. A sudden breeze lifted Ann's bangs. Martha didn't blink.

Uh . . . was she kidding? She looked completely serious.

"Really. Thanks." Ann walked back to her line and waited again. When her next turn came, she only shot marginally better. Martha again sank the bull's-eye, nearly dead center this time. Cindy missed.

Ann fitted her next arrow to the string, adrenaline rising. She'd gotten where she was in life—sorry, make that where she *used* to be in life—by being a competitive bitch. Two weeks ago, she never would even think of this, but if becoming the arrow would get her ahead, then damn it, she'd become the arrow. She pulled the string back by her right ear, made sure she centered her body, relaxed all but the muscles she needed, aimed, and imagined herself as the arrow, straight and strong, heading for the dead center of the bull's-eye. *She was the arrow. She would hit the target.* An extraordinary sense of calm enveloped her, the raucous cries of sea gulls faded. *She was the arrow.* Ann let herself fly.

Thunk. Not a bull's-eye, but nearly. She gaped at Martha, who grinned and gave her a thumbs-up. Paul would have made terrible fun of her. So much fun that she never would have been able to become the arrow. She never even would have tried. She might never have hit the bull's-eye and been able to indulge this rush of triumph.

Paul would have kept her from hitting the target.

A chill passed over her. She was only barely aware that she still stood there clutching the bow, and it was no longer her turn. Paul's sarcasm made him so admirable and proud and smart and omniscient, or so she used to think. Now he just seemed sad and bitter and isolated and afraid.

Change had happened up here in the clean Maine air, a rebirth, a gradual process that began with the horror that was "I Am Woman," proceeded through an afternoon with a compelling lobsterman's assistant, and then on to her very first time becoming an arrow.

Gentle throat clearing reminded her to hand the bow to the brunette behind her. In the middle of the exchange, a commotion broke out two lines over. Someone shrieking. Ann joined the gawking crowd and saw Cindy, refusing to give up her place in line, clutching the bow and arrow, shouting.

"I want to hit the target. *I want to hit the damn target!*" Tears ran down her face and she sobbed in that grimacing horrible way that every woman on the field understood all too well. Cheri approached her, took her arm, but Cindy shook her off, yanked the bow to her shoulder and let off an arrow that went wild to the right. "I can't do it! I can't do *anything.*"

She yanked up another arrow from the quiver beside her, made a wrenching guttural sound, pointed the bow up to the sky and shot off another one.

Five seconds later, five yards away, a gull fell to the ground like a meteor, with Cindy's arrow sticking out of its belly.

Thud. The bird struggled briefly then lay still, a growing spot of blood staining its white feathers.

Cindy lowered her bow, put a hand to her mouth. "Oh no. Oh no. I can't believe it. Look what I did. Oh no. Look what I did."

Oh God. A few women in the crowd began to sniffle.

Ann felt her own panic growing. That would do it. That was enough to do it. "Cindy—"

Cindy burst into more of those horrible raw tears and bolted, dodging the scattered women like a professional running back. Instinct drove Ann to lunge for the tackle. When Cindy collided with her, she wrapped her arms around the shaking body and hung grimly on, rocking her, trying to stem the rising pressure inside herself.

"Don't do this, Cindy. Don't give up. You're never out of hope. You're never out of people who love you. You're never . . . fully dressed without a smile, I don't know, just don't do this." She went on talking, soothing, encouraging, until she realized she was holding Cindy but talking to Paul.

Paul was gone. He couldn't hear her. But at least she'd tried.

A giggle mixed in with Cindy's sobs. "I'm not . . . myself."

"None of us is the same. And we may never be again. But it doesn't mean we're nothing. It doesn't mean we're not worth it. We're never going to be that. I promise. You get through the pain and go on. You don't give up."

"No." Cindy raised her teary blotchy puffy face up to Ann as if she were witnessing a miracle appearance of the Virgin. "You don't. Thank you. Thank you, Ann."

"You're welcome."

She smiled, and Cindy smiled back, and despite Ann's utmost sincerity in everything she said and felt, she'd reached the absolute limit of sentimentality and psychobabble that she could stand. Happily, New Age Betsy, expert in all things gooey, arrived and she and Cheri led Cindy away, each holding an unresisting arm.

On the archery field, the bird lay still. Women wept. In spite of the scene being perfect material for a surreal Monty Python sketch, a ball of tears rise in Ann's throat too. Camp Kinsonu did not feel like a joke anymore.

"Hi, ladies." Patrick strode into the clearing, the backup cavalry. Ann's heart swelled at the sight of him, strong, in charge, steady. "Change of plans. Meet in front of the lodge, Cheri will take you on a hike to get everybody calmed down, then we'll convene back in the lodge for tea and conversation about what happened, or anything else you need to talk about."

Ann had started to move with the rest of the still-sniffling crowd when Patrick pulled her apart and examined her face with concern.

"Hey there, Annie." He spoke gently. "Are you okay?"

Despite strict instructions to the contrary, a dry sob wracked her. She cleared her throat angrily. "God, look at me. Miserable over a bird I never met and a woman I don't even know."

"You're grieving for Paul. It's supposed to happen." He stroked his thumb down her cheek, leaving her skin faintly tingling. "I'll get a shovel, then you come with me. We'll take the gull into the woods for a decent burial. Okay?"

After her nod, he strode off among the women heading for the lodge, tall and purposeful and reassuring.

Grieving for Paul. He knew. Probably they all knew, from her first day of bad attitude. Grieving his loss, yes, but also grieving how she'd wanted him and their marriage to be different. Did anything in life turn out as expected? Was there ever a time in a woman's life when she could feel truly and justifiably fulfilled, apart from others' expectations of her?

Patrick came back into view holding a shovel and a cloth bag.

"Come on." He took her hand and they trudged over the mown grass to where the poor gull lay. Ann had to look away while Patrick took out the arrow, making herself concentrate on the edges of the clearing, identifying goldenrod, purple asters, and white Queen Anne's lace. Grisly job done, the bird in the sack, Patrick led and she followed into the woods, passing bright mushrooms, Indian pipes, and mossy logs instead of gravestones—a funeral procession like something out of an art film. He strode confidently, cradling the dead bird, stepping over logs, ducking under branches, finally stopping in a beautiful clearing, ringed with spruce and birch, carpeted with varying shades and shapes of moss, some like sponge, some like tiny pale Christmas trees. A red plastic hummingbird feeder hung off the branch of one tree, otherwise the place felt untouched by humans.

"It's like a chapel." This kind of church she could believe in. Natural and silent, uncompromised by mortal man's needs and egos.

Patrick laid the bagged bird on the moss and turned to her, his strong lean body close enough that she could smell his woodsy scent. The clearing lost its holiness and found a clandestine intimacy. "Yes. Yes, exactly. I found this nearly a week ago when I was taking a walk. I thought of you immediately."

"Why me?"

"I'm not sure." He touched a finger to her chin. "I just sensed that you would love it."

She stared at him, wondering why the hell that touched

her so deeply. And why she wanted to kiss him again so incredibly badly. "You hung the feeder?"

"Yes. I love hummingbirds. Sleek, colorful, agile. They remind me of you." His gaze dropped to her lips, then just when she was starting to buzz with adrenaline, he turned and picked up the shovel. "Better get the job done."

He started digging, leaving Ann feeling jilted. She watched the hole grow, glad they could save the bird from being devoured by whatever devoured dead birds around here. Foxes maybe, or—

"What are you going to do when you go back home?"

The question startled her unpleasantly. She didn't want reality. Not here in these peaceful pine-smelling woods. The last week or so, she'd stopped worrying about the future, not because it was resolved, but because she'd been focused on camp life. "I'll go home to my parents' house, get a job, and try to get myself back on my feet, to the point where I can buy a house—"

Her words choked off. Her stomach dropped along with her mood. How long would it take her to save enough to buy a house? What the hell kind of house would she be able to afford around Boston?

Paul had taken a lot more than his own life. He'd taken most of hers, her independence, her retirement, her safe future . . .

"There." Patrick picked up the bird in his large hands and laid it carefully in the grave. "Rest well, bird. Be at peace. Come back strong and whole in your next life."

Ann tossed in a small handful of dirt, and Patrick picked up the shovel again and went to work. Clumps of earth fell around the sack, peppering the burlap with tiny grains.

Shovel after shovel until the bird was covered, the dirt level with the forest floor, and Patrick had carefully replaced clumps of moss he'd kept intact.

Unless you were looking, and even if you were, it was nearly impossible to tell that anything had just been buried there. The moss would keep growing, as if nothing had happened. The woods would remain silent. She and Patrick would walk back to camp, people would forget, the gull would crumble into the earth, and that would be that. His worries were over. Paul's worries were over. Hers had quadrupled. She was alone, penniless, forty years old and everything she'd worked so hard to accomplish was gone. The moss had been put back over her old life and no trace of it remained.

An upwelling of black rage shocked her. Furious thoughts crowded into her brain, double-shocking her. *How could the selfish asshole do this to her? After a decade and a half of marriage. After they'd shared so much, built so much together?*

He should have stayed around . . . so *she* could kill him.

"Ann." Gray eyes searched her face. "What is it? Tell me."

She shook her head, breath coming too hard, feeling like a cartoon character who'd eaten hot sauce, building up a head of steam before she blew flame out her ears.

"It's Paul, isn't it? You are finally letting it out." Patrick was whispering, bent so close she could see the pinpricks of stubble on his jaw. "It's okay, Ann. All of it. Hate, love, anger . . . and desire."

She cupped his head with her hands and brought his mouth to hers almost violently. His response was immediate, and their chemistry, building since that first night when she saw him through the flames, exploded. He backed her up against a tree, and she lifted her leg, to give his thrusting pelvis better access to where she wanted him. She had never been this intensely and painfully and furiously aroused. She wanted to shout at him to fuck her, hard. Now. Only the pristine silence of the woods stopped her.

His hands fumbled with his pants. Hers did the same with hers. *Hurry, hurry, hurry.* Before she stopped to think. Before her rational brain could chime in with what a bad idea this could turn out to be.

"Condom?"

He grunted confirmation and produced one from a back pocket. Later she was going to wonder what he was doing inviting her into the woods with a condom in his pocket, but right now she just wanted him inside her as fast and hard as possible. She wanted to be punished for hating Paul and she wanted to punish Paul for what he'd done to her.

With their pants down and her leg back up, Patrick wasted no more time than she wanted him to. She cried out at the feel of him filling her. God, she'd missed this. He swept his arm under her knee so she'd no longer have to hold her leg up herself. His thrusts were coarse and savage, exactly what she wanted. A bare minute later her orgasm hit so quickly, she yelled in surprise, letting the overwhelming pleasure sweep through her with vicious satisfaction.

Oh. Yes.

Absurdly, she remembered a commercial from her childhood, where a man, slapped in the face, responded, *Thanks, I needed that.*

Did she ever.

Patrick continued to grunt and strain and push, and she was ashamed of herself wishing he'd hurry up. Her leg was cramping, the bark of the tree rubbed her back raw, even through her top. She lifted her eyes to the patch of sky visible over the clearing, watched the clouds push by, the dark green of firs framed against its brilliance. *Thank you for Maine and for erect penises.*

Patrick's breathing changed, his body tensed in climax, and he let out a noise that should have been erotic and exciting, but which was frankly a little comical.

Over. Done. Back to their regularly scheduled programming. Thank you and good night.

"Ann." He was breathless, disentangling his arm from her leg. He cupped her face in his hands; his penis slipped forlornly out of her. "I'm sorry."

"Sorry?" After that? "For what?"

"I don't know what happened, I never meant to . . . it just . . . I don't know what happened here, but it was totally unexpected."

"Which was why you had a condom in your pocket."

He looked startled, then his eyes narrowed and chilled for only a second before he shook his head and smiled sheepishly. "I had planned to go cruising in town tonight."

"For men."

Again that flash of cold suspicion. "Yes."

"Ah, okay." If he wanted to be keep pretending he hadn't been planning this all along, she'd allow him, though she wished he'd stop insulting her intelligence and lose the act, at least around her. He could keep it up for Betsy if he needed to. "And now?"

He shook his head, dropped his hands from her face, peeled off the condom and yanked his pants back up over his beautiful long thighs. "Now I don't know. I don't know about anything anymore. Except that was amazing."

She laughed, flushed and giddy. "It was, thanks."

"Ann . . ." He looked genuinely tortured. "What I mean is, this was so good, and you are so incredible, and—"

"Patrick. We're grown-ups. We both needed this, it was great, and we're friends."

"Yes. Okay." His relief was obvious. He squatted, poked the condom under a patch of moss, then made a show of gallantly checking her back for scrapes, brushed stray bits of bark off her shirt while she did up her pants. "Ready to go back?"

"Ready." She took his offered hand and followed him, glancing back at the beautiful spot to fix it in her mind. This had been good for her. She'd been with someone else, someone who wasn't Paul, and enjoyed herself. There were still pleasures to be had, after all. Maybe she and Patrick would get to visit here again before she left. Maybe not. But she'd always love thinking about the serene peaceful gull, carefully buried in a makeshift chapel, a mere foot away from one of Patrick's used condoms.

They walked back through the woods in silence. Everything seemed lighter, more lovely, beckoning with possibilities. The archery field came into sight, and it seemed days since they'd stood there trying to hit their targets.

"What's next for you during free time, Ann?"

"I'm going to work on a painting. I want to start a new one soon." At Clive's house, the view from his woods. She felt a rush of excitement at the thought, and she wasn't entirely sure it was only the paint she was pumped about.

"Painting was part of my physical therapy. I totally got into the peace it brought me."

"Yes." She laughed for no reason except that she felt like it. They dropped hands crossing the archery field, passed

Betsy's cabin, and as they came to the path from the parking lot, there he was, conjured by her thoughts. Clive, holding a paper bag, stopped in his tracks, watching them approach.

"Hi." She smiled too brightly, surprised to find herself feeling awkward and guilty over what had happened between her and Patrick. "What are you doing here?"

He was looking between her and Patrick in a way that suggested he knew exactly what they'd been up to in the woods, which made her even more uneasy. How could he know? He couldn't. But still she fidgeted. Her body became unable to assume a natural position. What the hell? She was free to do whatever she wanted. Or more to the point, whomever she wanted.

Clive gestured with the bag. "I brought you muffins. In case you still weren't eating."

Heat rose in her face. He'd been worried about her? She was touched. More than she should be. And she suddenly and inexplicably wished for a chance to take back what had happened in the woods.

"Wow. Thank you."

"You're welcome." He glanced again at Patrick, and passed her the bag with the barest touch of chagrin, like a man offering a daisy to a woman who'd just received a huge bouquet of roses.

"Thanks, Clive." Patrick's voice held a dismissive edge. His hand touched the small of Ann's back. "I'll make sure she eats just fine."

Ann felt a flash of annoyance. What was this, High Noon in the Wild, Wild East? Were they going to start dueling?

Except Ann belonged to neither. Patrick was a lying

player, and Clive was married, which made the dynamic even crazier.

She thanked Clive again, told him she'd be by one day soon to paint, letting him know with her eyes how sincerely she appreciated his gesture, then smiled briefly at Patrick and excused herself, not only to escape the weirdness, but also because the scent of muffins had just wafted out of the bag like a wizard's enchanting potion and made her instantly ravenous. Something about Clive made her want to eat.

She jogged back to Cabin Four, leaving the men to snarl manfully at each other or whatever they planned to do— and Patrick better not discuss her recent "progress" in the woods—hoping no one she passed on the path would ask what she was carrying, so the gift could stay private. Back in her room, she'd eat one muffin—or maybe two—and hide the others before she checked in at the lodge and resumed painting.

Then at some point soon she'd make sure she found a nice and safely platonic way to let married Clive know that lying player Patrick had brought her the daisy, and the huge bouquet of roses had come from him.

Chapter 14

Cindy walked along the path toward the building where they had group therapy. It was foggy today, dense and close, drops gathering on spiderwebs strung between birches and pattering dismally off leaves and ferns. All noises were amplified, as if the world had shrunk down to a movie sound-stage. Seals barking out in the middle of the bay might as well have been on shore. The few lobstermen who ventured out shouted conversations to each other that weren't as private as they thought. The edge of the shore faded into gray, the tree trunks were gray, the rocks were gray, the sky was gray, the air was gray. Even their oatmeal breakfast: gray.

Approaching group therapy felt completely different today. A week ago, last Monday, Cindy had been so excited, so full of optimism. Everything in this camp would be great! She'd have a wonderful time! Make lots of friends! Spend a fabulous couple of weeks until it was time to go home to Kevin.

Now she didn't feel like herself at all. Since she'd been with Patrick, she couldn't shake off what she'd done. How could she have enjoyed being with another man so much? She hated the revived memory of how exciting and compelling someone new could be. Was this what Kevin felt with other women? Was her marriage really as sad and lifeless as the night with Patrick had been joyous and vibrantly alive? She hated Kevin's other women twice as much for bringing him what she couldn't.

Except after five whole minutes lying in Patrick's arms, full of afterglow bliss and conflict, he'd gotten weird. Nervous. He'd wanted her out of there, though too sweet to say so with words. She understood, of course she understood. He couldn't be seen hosting campers in his cabin at night. If word got out about them, he'd lose his job. Maybe even his Ph.D. program in Minnesota would rethink its offer of candidacy. She understood that, she understood all that.

But she'd barely slept the rest of the night in her own bed, and she woke up the next morning and every morning in between—double yesterday and this morning after she'd become a gull murderer—raging with guilt and adrenaline, feeling as if nothing was ever going to go right again. Cindy was pretty sure she could spend the rest of her life on that field aiming into the sky and not come close to another bird. The death of the gull had to be a sign. She just didn't know what kind of sign, except maybe one to show that she destroyed everything she tried to make beautiful and good.

Or maybe that she shouldn't plan on a career in archery.

Now, as she strode along the path, her stomach and chest and brain burned and she didn't know how to make them stop.

How did Kevin put up with the guilt? Maybe he never felt any. Cindy hated this crazy mania. She wanted to go back to where everything was predictable, certain, and easy. She wanted to go back to her big overdecorated house and her quiet life and Kevin, and she wanted to find some way to bring Max back, too, because he adored every failing inept inch of her.

A root tripped her, and she stumbled off the path into an empty spiderweb whose sticky threads caught her face and showered drops on her pink sweater. Ironically, she did not want to go to group therapy, the place that could most help her, except she couldn't tell anyone about Patrick or talk out any of her confusion. Maybe he did have feelings for her, though he'd been very careful in their encounters after that night together not to show any glimmer of what lay between them. Maybe he was discovering he wasn't so gay after all. Maybe whatever they had between them was so special that it transcended his gayness.

Or maybe that was all crap. She wished she knew. She didn't feel like she knew anything anymore, not about herself, not about her life. And this place was supposed to help her!

She stomped up the steps to the therapy cabin and flung open the door to the cozy room, warmed by a fire dancing in the corner wood stove. The door swung too quickly and crashed into the wall. Not surprisingly, happy Betsy, chatty Dinah, snotty Ann, and weird Martha all snapped their heads around to look.

"Hi." She gave a high, squeaky laugh that she hated herself for. "Sorry I'm late. Sorry I slammed the door."

Sorry I exist.

"It's fine, Cindy." Betsy smiled, eyes watchful.

The rest of the women kept staring. Cindy imagined herself giving off weird vibes or aura or whatever it was people like Betsy saw. She probably looked like she had a flock of killer bees swarming all around her, her personal attack force. Like she was some superhero or supervillain able to summon the powers of nature to do her bidding. She wished.

"Have a seat, Cindy. We're just starting."

"Did I miss yoga?" She'd dallied in the bathroom, flossing, fussing with her hair, fussing with her clothes, anything to avoid facing her day. She was so, so tired.

"Yes. We've done yoga." Betsy spoke somberly, as if she were telling a desperate mother that the last loaf of bread had already been handed out.

"Okay." Cindy bent her head so her expression of relief would go unnoticed. Even she could tell this was not a good time to be faced with something else she couldn't do well. For all she knew, she'd been terrible in bed too, or broken some cardinal rule of sneaking and illicit sex that everyone else took for granted, and that's why Patrick hadn't tried to be with her again. She crossed to the empty chair, admonishing her bees to keep quiet and behave themselves.

"We were just about to write our second letter to the men we are here to heal from." Betsy passed Cindy a clipboard gripping a white sheet of paper and a black pen. "Okay, ladies. Write to those men and tell them what's in your hearts."

Sure. No problem. Except the only thing she had to say was, what the hell was taking him so long to come back to her? She did not like the person she was becoming. She did not like her life here. She needed him to protect her, to prevent her from losing it, and he was letting her down. Again.

Pens were scratching all over the room, even Martha's,

even Ann's. Apparently a week in this place had given them all a lot to say. Cindy had no desire to share with Kevin happy stories of her camp life. Partly because there weren't any.

A few sentences later she laid down her pen and sat watching the others. Dinah looked the way Dinah always looked. Cindy wasn't sure Dinah had ever actually *had* an emotion. Ann's eyebrows were up and met in the middle, like she was sad and earnest, which Cindy thought didn't fit her personality at all, except for that amazing hug Ann gave her when she needed one so badly. Martha was frowning as if she were concentrating heavily to get exactly the right words out. For a second Cindy forgot her anger, and her own heartache, thinking of Martha writing to her dying boyfriend and maybe having to say good-bye.

Or maybe she was just telling him how great her rolls had turned out.

"Everybody finished?" Betsy came around and collected the papers, glancing at Cindy's few scrawled sentences, then at Cindy, then back down at the paper. Cindy felt herself wanting to fidget like a schoolgirl caught failing an exam. Yes, her letter was different from the last one. *Read it and weep, Betsy.*

"So. Let's start sharing some of our thoughts and feelings this week. Who wants to go first?"

Cindy threaded her fingers together and looked down at her clasped hands. She wanted to push out her lower lip, hunch her shoulders, and play the sullen, scowling child. Last session she'd been happy to talk. This week she didn't want to say anything. The angry bees were buzzing too loudly, and no one would able to understand what she was saying.

"I'll go first."

Cindy stared at Martha, along with everyone else staring at Martha. Even the birds outside had probably stopped singing and were staring at Martha. One of them should fly down and let Satan know hell had just frozen over.

"I want to talk this week." Martha looked around as if she were asking if anyone wanted to listen. She looked oddly animated today, as if she'd finally had that cup of coffee her body needed.

"Of course, Martha." Instead of the look of triumph Cindy would have expected on Betsy's face, with this newest offer of a soul for her collection, Betsy's expression had turned apprehensive. "We're all listening and happy to hear."

Cindy took in a deep breath she thought worthy of Martha herself. She wasn't sure she could stand this. She wasn't sure she could stand hearing about Martha's perfect love, and how her man had completed her so completely, and how his loss had left her only half a person, and how her heart would never heal, blah blah blah. While Cindy only had that from a dog.

She blew out the breath. What was she thinking? How could she be this negative? Martha had been lucky enough to find love. Real love. True love. Cindy should be happy for her and leave herself out of it.

"Some of you know that my . . . that the man I love is very sick." Her face crumpled; she inhaled and exhaled in such a way that clearly showed that Cindy was an absolute amateur and had no business comparing herself at all. "What you don't know is that he was married. For over twenty years, I was his mistress."

Cindy decided it was a shame they hadn't done yoga after all, because she was pretty sure she could not become any stiller than she was at that moment. She'd get the prize for pose-holding for sure. Her sit-in-the-chair-and-gape pose could go on for weeks. Martha's words had not penetrated yet, they'd simply frozen her to her seat. *For over twenty years, I was his mistress.*

"I knew him since we were in college together. We were best friends, then lovers. He was my soulmate. No two people could be closer than we were."

A murmur swept the room. The jury was out on whether people were touched or censorious, or holding back gags.

"So . . . then why didn't he marry *you?*" Cindy barely recognized her voice. It sounded as if someone had taken a cheese grater to her vocal cords.

Martha turned her bulgy lash-covered eyes toward Cindy, nearly quivering with excitement over the prospect of sharing her superiority in finding love. "Because he wanted a very public career, and he needed a beautiful outgoing and gracious wife. More than anything, I wanted him to be happy, so . . . I let him go."

"Not for long, obviously," Cindy mumbled, then put on a fake smile when she caught Betsy staring.

"How did you two get back together?" Dinah was all agog, and Cindy was betting the rest of the camp would know the entire story by lunch.

"He couldn't stand being away from me, and couldn't stand being in a relationship that didn't give him what he truly needed." Martha bent her head meekly, as if she wasn't worthy of such an honor as Mr. Cheaterpants picking up an extra slut so he got everything he wanted and his wife got crap.

"Oh, that's so romantic!"

Cindy shifted her eyes to Dinah, and understood for the first time what it felt like to want to kill somebody.

Ann snorted. "I doubt his wife would agree with you."

Cindy was grateful. At least somebody was making sense. Cindy had a lot to say on the topic of affairs, but she was afraid. The bees were buzzing in their hive—if she let them out, they'd sting up a storm.

"You don't understand. He and I were meant to be. We always were, and we always will be. His wife was a necessity, a decoration. I understood that. But he only loved me."

The hive busted as if someone had swung a shovel at it. Cindy turned on Martha. "Bullshit. He just said that so he could get into your pants. He loved his wife. I can't believe you fell for that."

Martha stared back at Cindy, and her eyelids twitched. What the hell was the matter with her? *Had* she smoked some bad weed?

"What he and I had was—"

"What you had was a totally immoral cheating affair. *You* allowed him to abuse his wife. *You* helped him do that. *You* encouraged him." She found herself standing, fists clenched, without remembering how she got there. "You never gave him the chance to love his wife. How could he, when he had you to compare her to? He never saw you angry or over-whelmed or lonely from how much time he spent away. He never saw you sick and hideous. He never had the chance to get bored of your day-to-day reality."

"We knew each other too well to—"

"And you had the luxury of always thinking he was per-fect. That's what he wanted from you. You never had to pick up after him, clean up after him, cook for him, do his er-rands, try to please him day after day, year after year, while you got your emotional needs met by the family pet. You never had to listen to him snoring and farting, never had to pretend to have a life while he was out at all hours doing God knew what, never had to lie there without knowing if he was out banging someone else. You never had to—"

"*Cindy.*" Betsy's voice penetrated, and with it came the impression that she'd been calling Cindy's name several times.

Cindy blinked, found herself breathing much too hard, bees buzzing so loudly in her brain that her face had gotten hot with the energy they created. "I'm sorry. I just don't know how you could do that to someone. I don't know how you could call that real love, when it was nothing like real love. It wasn't even close to what real love is about. What's more, you were *hurting somebody.*"

More murmurs. Cindy didn't know who was being condemned and who pardoned.

"His wife got what she needed from him." Martha said "wife" as if she meant *bitch*, and "needed" as if she meant *deserved*. "A chance to be in the public eye, children, plenty of money."

"No, *you* got what you needed from him. She got nothing. She deserved more."

"You know, she should have left him, that's what she should have done." Dinah looped a finger in her gold necklace and worked it back and forth. "I never would've stood for that kind of behavior from any of my husbands. In fact I didn't. I always told them, I said—"

"Cindy, do you think maybe you're projecting your situation onto Martha?" By now that gentle "therapist voice" of Betsy's was enough to make Cindy shriek like a banshee.

"I'm doing much more than projecting." Cindy made claws out of her hands and clutched her temples. "I'm holding her responsible for what my husband did. Her and women like her. How can you talk about love when you split him in half with someone else? Love is between two whole people. You split him in half, and ruined any chance he had of loving his wife completely."

"There was no way he could love his wife."

"How do you know that?" She was shouting, louder than she ever shouted at anyone, and she couldn't make herself stop. *"How can you say that?"*

Martha gazed at Cindy with narrowed eyes, which would have made her feel a little scared, except that she was already feeling too much crazy hysteria to fit in fear. "Because he loved me so much there was no room for her."

Cindy backed away. She could swear that the floor was tipping her away, as if a giant hand had reached down and picked up the cabin from its foundations, as if they were all about to be tossed down the gullet of a giant foraging for food. Or maybe hurled by a tornado into the land of the Wizard of Oz. Anything would be an improvement over Camp Kinsonu and the twisted women who came here.

She turned and hurled herself out of the cabin, into the foggy woods. She raced down the path toward the shore then cut off sharply to the left, to Patrick's cabin, wet ferns soaking her ruffled ankle socks and the too-short hems of her jeans. *Please, God, let him be there.* She took the three steps in one leap, skidded on the wooden porch turned slippery from the wet.

"Patrick." She pounded on his door. "Patrick."

She waited, heard him swear briefly, and her body relaxed a little into relief. He was here. He would fix everything.

The door opened. "Cindy. What is it? What's wrong?"

The concern on his face was enough to make her start crying. She tried to explain what had upset her, amidst sobs and hiccups and more buzzing.

"Wait." He glanced behind him, as if something in his cabin was going to come out and attack him. "Let me get my jacket, tell Betsy you're with me, then we'll go for a walk and get you calmed down."

"Oh, thank you. Thank you, Patrick."

She waited, shivering, from the damp and her still raging bees. Every part of her wanted to be wrapped in Kevin's arms again, to make everything else go away. But he wasn't there, for God's sake, again he wasn't there. Patrick was all she had.

She slumped onto the bench on Patrick's porch, gazing out at the claustrophobic gray that obscured the view. The minute she relaxed even that much, the thought she'd been holding off with her panic burst through.

What if Martha's man did love Martha? What if he really didn't love his wife? What if Kevin—

"Here I am." Patrick emerged in a black nylon jacket and grinned at her. "Let's walk."

She got up and followed him, feeling as if her body weighed about twenty pounds more than it had half an hour earlier, feeling as if there was too much humidity in the air for her lungs to process it properly.

When they reached the shore path, Patrick turned left instead of right toward the beach, where most of the camp activities took place. Ten yards into the woods, he stepped off the path and pushed through a stand of dripping alders, gestured her onto a foggy sloping ledge. A gull took off at their approach, disappearing rapidly into the thick static mist. Patrick lowered himself to sitting on the damp rock. She plunked down next to him, their hips and thighs touching, absorbing his warmth.

"Talk to me, Cindy. Tell me what's going on."

She told him as best she could, aware as she spoke that she was not coming off as the rational or well-behaved half of the conflict. Which only made her hate Martha more.

"So that's what happened." She looked hopefully to Patrick, his handsome face sharp against the fuzzy backdrop of woods. Could he tell that she really needed him to take her into his arms, tell her she was right in all that she was feeling, that he was there for her until the end of time? Then she could nobly tell him she was sorry, but Kevin came first, and would always come first . . .

He didn't take her in his arms. Nor did he tell her she was right or that he was there until the end of time or anything he was supposed to tell her. Instead he wrapped his arms loosely around his bent knees, staring out into the fog as if he could see through it. "Your husband is an asshole, Cindy."

Cindy gasped, put a hand to her chest, preparing a defense for Kevin, until it occurred to her that maybe the insult was a prelude to Patrick revealing his jealousy and declaring his strong feelings for her. Probably a stupid fantasy, but at this point stupid fantasies beat out her reality by a long shot.

"Kevin is . . . " She couldn't think what to say since the words that came to mind to describe him were arrogant, shallow, manipulative, deceitful . . . asshole.

She didn't like thinking that way. What happened to looking for the positive, only seeing the good things and thereby helping the universe provide them?

"You deserve so much more than what he gives you, Cindy." Patrick whispered these words out to the invisible sea, then turned his glorious eyes, gray as the fog, back onto her. "You deserve so much better."

Cindy's stomach hovered between a rise into hope and a plummet into despair. "Where would I find anything better?"

"I know out there somewhere is a guy who can give you everything you need, everything you deserve, and more." His voice was low, rumbling comfort, except that the implied ending to his speech was, *but that guy isn't me.*

"First you have to believe that you deserve better." His eyes were kind, but not loving, not tender.

Cindy put her hands to her head. She was on the edge of a giant abyss. Behind her Kevin and safety. Any step away from them would plunge her into terrifying nothingness. Patrick and what he'd made her feel that night stood across the chasm, unattainable, unavailable. Gay. Or . . . whatever.

"I went through a totally hard journey, Cindy, like the one you're facing. Years of self-scrutiny, observing and recording my patterns and destructive behaviors, to get to the core of who I really am, you know? To capture my own essence. Meditation was the key to setting myself free of my own demons."

Meditation. Oh good. Another thing she could be bad at.

"I don't want to go on a hard journey. I'm not that deep of a person. I like to be happy and I like to be comfortable." So why was she sitting here, wet seeping through her jeans, talking to a man who couldn't love her?

Where else would she go?

"Oh, but you are, Cindy. You have tremendous depth." He reached across the abyss to lay a comforting hand on her cheek. "I see in you a light and a spirit and a strength beyond anything you know that you have."

"Really?" She was tired, terribly tired, and becoming quite damp, and now that she thought about it, his eyes were also the color of the oatmeal they had that morning.

"Oh yes, Cindy. Oh yes."

She stood, suddenly irritated. Forgive her for unkind thoughts yet again on this soggy gray day, but she thought he sounded like he'd watched too much Dr. Phil, or like those monks in Thailand had scrambled his brain. She knew who she was. A nice person, not very strong, not at all remarkable. She'd love to believe what he said, but he was wrong about her. Entirely. And if he was wrong about her, what was to stop him from being wrong about Kevin also? Maybe she was too trusting. Maybe she needed to stop trusting anybody but herself.

She lifted her arms and opened her mouth, full of the need to speak, but the futility of not knowing what to say overcame her, so she let her arms drop and started back toward the trees.

"Where are you going?"

"Away. Just away."

He must have bolted after her, because then he was there, catching her hand, turning her to face him, staring at her with his cooked oatmeal eyes. "You shouldn't be alone, Cindy. I can help. Let me—"

"I want to be alone. I need to be alone. I don't want to be with you right now."

His gaze changed from oatmeal to concrete. His grip tightened. "You need what I have to give you, Cindy. Don't turn away from me."

Cindy stared at his changed eyes, his hardened face. She felt like she was in a scene from some late night horror movie and he was the evil villain just now showing his true self right before he bared fangs and drank her blood. "What, Patrick? What do you have to give me?"

"The strength to be yourself. The strength to leave your husband." He leaned closer, and he looked sort of odd and manic, like a religious maniac. She didn't think monks in Thailand behaved like that. Not that she would know.

"I don't want to leave my husband." She tried to pull her hand away, and he tightened his grip harder.

"Not even for me?"

Cindy stopped trying to pull away, and her stupidly optimistic heart gave a little flip of excitement and hope. "What are you saying?"

"Didn't you feel what was between us the other night?"

She nodded slowly, not sure why, when he was finally saying what she wanted him to say, the words and the man saying them didn't make her feel at all what she'd assumed they would.

"Let me be your strength, Cindy."

She took a step back so their arms stretched out. He sounded like a stranger offering a child candy. She didn't want any strength from him. She didn't want anything from him.

However, an entirely new and startling thought did pop into her head.

She might not want Patrick's strength. But she suddenly did want her own.

Chapter 15

Dear Paul,

I'm getting used to it here. Sort of. I still hate feeling like a lab rat, but I have to say it feels better than being home with Mom and Dad freaking out. I guess I've either adjusted or the mind control drugs they slip into the food have had their effect. It's beautiful, for one. The place seems to cradle you—and I can see you smirking at my choice of words all the way from the afterlife, so stop it.

I've rediscovered watercolor painting, which I hadn't done since college, and now I'm not sure why. I guess you get into ruts in adulthood, or maybe I was living too much your life and giving up too much of my own. Looking back, I think I bought into your ideas of how people with our wealth and stature must behave. Somehow I lost how I behave.

I met someone wise who said good things can come out of pain, and I've been looking for them ever since. I wish you'd looked for more good things in your life—in our life. Cynicism can become a kind of straitjacket.

I'm sounding very philosophical right now. How unlike me. But I've been thinking a lot. Which is different than brooding, which you did all the time, turning over and over the same angry thoughts. As you've all too clearly shown, people self-destruct from that kind of thinking. It's easy to hate, and easy to feel superior if you tell yourself you are. It's harder to slog it out in the trenches and be vulnerable and open to new experiences and ideas and people, but I'm trying. Not always successfully, because sometimes you meet people who simply need a kick in the butt and always will.

I wish I had discovered—or rediscovered—this while you were still alive, and I wish I could have taught it to you. Though I'm not sure you would ever have listened or heard me.

I miss you. No, I miss who you used to be. No, who we were when we met, full of hope and possibilities. Somewhere along the way you felt you'd run out of both. I'm starting to realize that's never really true.

Love,
Ann

"Thank you." Ann smiled warmly at Arnold, who was standing at the helm of the *Tiger Lily* as she'd always picture him. "I had another wonderful day."

Arnold touched the brim of his cap. "Pleasure having you. Come 'round anytime."

"I'd like that." She didn't bother saying it was impossible. Camp ended in three days, and who knew when or if she'd ever be back here. The thought left her more empty and depressed than it should.

She shook Arnold's hand and climbed over the gunwale of the *Tiger Lily* into the skiff, where Clive waited until she was settled, then pushed off and started for shore. The day had been much like the last one, plus warmer temperatures, minus the crippling hangover and hostility between her and Clive. There still hadn't been much chatter, but she felt the acceptance of the men—even managed to haul and rebait a few traps mostly by herself—and experienced the same satisfying immersion into routine, the suspension of time and worry in the small fishing boat out on the big salt pond, similar to how she felt on the days when she'd painted at Clive's place.

Coming back, watching the shore grow from a postcard fantasy to an actual destination with responsibilities and the burdens of reality, her mood had lowered. No, sunk. No, crashed. Camp would be over and calm moments of forgetting like this would end. Her life would again be on track someday, but this little taste of surface calm would make descending back into the grief mines that much harder.

Last night she'd dreamed again of Paul, the first after several relatively peaceful sleeps. He'd been alive, but the farther and faster she ran toward him, the more he shrank, until he was a tiny stick person someone picked up and struck against the rough strip of a matchbox. Just before his head disappeared into a ball of flame, he'd burst into taunting laughter.

"You coming to the house this afternoon?"

Ann jerked back to Clive's broad shoulders working, and the gurgling of oar-made whirlpools in the sea.

"Yes. If it's convenient. I'd like to paint again, the view from your . . . backyard." The word seemed ridiculously inadequate, conjuring a manicured fenced-in lawn with a swing set and patio, not forest, sandbar, islands and ocean.

Clive simply nodded, but she had the feeling he was pleased she wanted to stay, and that pleased her; and there they were on a bay in Maine on a sparkling clear day, in a compounded pleasure situation.

On shore, they washed their fashion forward coveralls and boots and put them away in the shed, then climbed into Clive's truck and started off.

"You hungry?"

Ann raised an eyebrow. "What is it that makes you want to shove food at me?"

"Gee, I don't know." He tapped his finger against his chin in deeply exaggerated contemplation. "Maybe the fact that you weigh about three-quarters what you should, and—"

"Aw come on."

"—I get hungry just looking at you."

Boom. My my. "Oh *real*-ly."

He chuckled when she waggled her eyebrows, which made her smile. She liked a guy who could take a joke. She also liked the way Clive came to life when he was off the boat. Maybe this afternoon she'd feel comfortable enough to ask why. The last couple of times she'd been over, he'd had to work, and they didn't get much time to talk.

Her stomach got another sour dose of that desperate feeling she loathed: time running out and too much left to do.

The truck jostled and bumped down his long rutted driveway, stopped in front of the silent white house with black shutters. Inside it remained frozen, as tidy and untouched as if he and his wife lived in a tent in the woods and only came home to host visitors. Clive heated some excellent sausage lentil and spinach soup, and rolls too fresh to be from a supermarket. Ann ate ravenously, enjoying the silence between them, which didn't feel either awkward or hostile, sensing him glancing his approval as her first bowl emptied, then her second.

"I guess the sea air gives me an appetite."

"Your body gives you the appetite. You just haven't been listening to it."

"I've had a few other things on my mind." She tried to keep the poor-me annoyance out of her voice and failed.

"Forget yourself. Just eat."

"I *try*. But since Paul died, if it hasn't been my parents hovering, it's been Betsy or Patrick or my roommates." She cleared her thickening throat and attempted a smile. *Lighten up, Ann.* "I can eat around you, though. Which must mean you make me hungry too."

The intended joke came out like a wobbly schoolgirl crush confession and abruptly complicated their easy silence.

Crap.

"I mean those muffins you brought Saturday were the best things I ever ate. Those tiny cranberries? They were incredible. Are they local? I've never seen them that small in Massachusetts." She yanked up her conversational emergency brake. She'd already thanked him for the muffins when she came by to paint. The babble was only making it worse.

"They grow wild here. You should try them in pancakes

sometime." He got up and cleared their dishes, which cleared the awkwardness too. "You do have a point, though. For all the good camp does, it's not the place to forget your troubles. Better for wrestling them to the ground so you can move on faster."

"I didn't think I could survive two weeks there." Ann drew her finger along the edge of his counter. "I had a pretty crappy attitude."

"You were angry and protecting yourself."

She looked up to find him busy at the sink, apparently not interested in watching his dropped bomb hit the target. Protecting herself, yeah. The same way Paul had tried to protect himself. And guess how successful that turned out to be. "How do you know all this? Please tell me it's not in my camp file."

"I've done it too." He crossed to the refrigerator and searched inside. "Want some raspberries? Cream and sugar? I picked them yesterday, they won't last forever."

Done it too, how? She wished she'd be here long enough to find out. "How can I say no to raspberries and cream?"

"You can't." He set a delicate white bowl in front of her, and she dug her spoon into one of her favorite combinations. Fruity, flavorful berries, sweetened cream . . . Chocolate would make it the holy trinity of desserts, but she wasn't complaining. Back home she'd have to rethink her Lean Cuisine lifestyle and see if she could—

"Ann."

She looked up with a spoon still in her mouth, startled by his serious tone. "Mmm?"

"What's going on between you and Patrick?"

She put the spoon back in the bowl, staring at the cream

turning pink from an overripe berry, sure her cheeks had turned the same color. "I don't think that's any of your business."

"I'd like to make it my business."

She lifted her head. "Why?"

"Good reasons."

"Your reasons? Or Betsy's?"

"Mine." He watched her calmly, but his body had gone rock still. "Are you involved with him?"

"I . . . I'm . . . " Something was riding on her answer, she felt that instinctively, but she didn't want to say anything until she figured out what. "Why do you want to know?"

He smiled dryly. "Okay. Since I brought it up, I guess it's up to me to speak plainly."

"Shoot." She picked up her spoon, to have something to do.

"It is my considered opinion that Patrick is massively full of shit."

Ann burst out laughing, feeling manic and off-balance and now a little sick. "Please. Don't hold back. Say what you think."

"I don't want you to get hurt."

Her laughter died. For a moment the careful blankness of his eyes was replaced with concern that ran through her body like a thrill. Right then she decided Clive's wife was a lucky bitch and that she hated her.

"Patrick is . . . he's helped me in some ways."

"Right." His jaw set.

What was this about? He couldn't be jealous. The odd interest he'd taken in her had felt one hundred percent brotherly.

So what about Patrick? Was she involved with him or not?

She wasn't. She couldn't be. Next to Clive, he was about as substantive as space gas. "He can't hurt me."

"Okay." Clive didn't sound convinced. "Ready to paint?"

She nodded unhappily. More needed to be said, but the topic was enough of a mine field already that she didn't have the courage to trudge on, in case she detonated some, or worse, planted more.

She finished her last bite and spooned up the remaining drops of cream, wasted since her taste buds had become as disoriented as the rest of her. "I'll help you with the dishes."

"The dishes will keep longer than your afternoon light. You can help me do them later if you really, really want to."

"Oh, I really, really do." She slanted him a mischievous look, trying to recapture normalcy between them, and put her bowl and spoon in the sink. She did want to help him. Outside, painting, she'd be on her own, and then she'd have to say good-bye and go back to stinking reality. For whatever reason, Clive felt like a loose end, and she hated having so little chance to tie him off.

Except today after she'd retrieved her bag from his truck and he led her to the lean-to, instead of running off to do his lobster guy duties, he settled on a chair in the far corner while she set up her paints and watercolor pad. Normally she despised being watched, but now she was glad of his company, to keep her thoughts from directions she didn't want them going in. Being around Clive made her feel peaceful and centered, like when she'd tried to be the arrow. No wonder she craved him like a drug—her personal antidepressant.

She pulled the camera from her bag, which she'd finally

remembered to bring, and took a picture of the scene so she'd be able to finish the painting back home. The light was perfect for what she wanted to capture, not the hard-edged light of noon, but the softer, more golden tones of late afternoon, which brought colors to their richest and most vivid hues.

"Nice if you could paint from the real thing every day."

"It would be. But tomorrow is packed, Friday is our cabin's day trip, and I leave Saturday. I doubt the view will fit in my suitcase." In spite of her efforts, misery showed in the words. She took out a pencil and started a new sketch of the island to her left.

"Do you have to leave?"

A jolt of emotion, too complicated to understand. She turned to stare at him blankly. "Camp is over. Betsy gave me a free ride this session, I can't ask her to do it again, and I can't afford to—"

"I'm not talking about camp. I just asked if you have to go back." He spoke calmly, as usual. And as usual, his expression gave nothing away. But she sensed the same tension in him as before . . . or was it coming from her?

"I have to go back and get a job." Her voice wavered. She resumed her sketching, bumbling a line, clutching the pencil too hard. "I have to restart my life."

"And there's only one way to do that, and one schedule of how fast it has to happen?"

Ann dropped her hand to her lap. "Why don't you tell me what you're getting at."

He got up and stood next to her, staring out into the bay with eyes that didn't appear to register its beauty. "I was wondering if you wanted to stay for a while."

"Stay." Another jolt. What was he talking about? "Where?"

"Here."

"Here?" She gestured around her, indicating his property. "As in right here? Or here as in Maine?"

"Right here. There's plenty of room in the house. I'd like the company, and you can paint this view as many times as you want and give yourself more time to relax."

Ann put her pencil down. Her heart was beating very fast. "You're not married?"

His dark brows lifted. "Not as far as I know. You thought I was?"

"I . . . the bride picture in your living room. And the . . . " She groped for the right words. " . . . female look of the place."

"That's Angie. My sister. She lives in Rockport with her family. The house belongs to my parents. I grew up there." A wry smile curved his mouth. "The taste isn't mine, but I haven't bothered redecorating."

Ann nodded, her body buzzing with peculiar excitement. "Where are your parents?"

She needed to ask questions until her brain could catch up to the concept, and then she'd need even more time to figure out how she felt.

"My father died a year ago. Four months ago Mom had a stroke. I couldn't care for her and I had to find a place that could." He was choosing his words carefully, struggling with emotion, but she also sensed a bigger story lurking around his edges.

If she stayed, would he tell her? Would they be platonic roommates or did he have more in mind? Why would he ask her to stay with him after he'd known her such a short time? Unless . . .

"Was this Betsy's idea?"

"It was mine." He pulled the chair closer, sat with his hands loosely clasped between his spread knees, crowding her, and also . . . not.

"Why on earth would you want to invite in a woman you barely know?"

"Seemed like a good solution. You're lost and I'm lonely."

The bristles went up instantly. "I'm not lost."

Clive sighed loudly, exasperated and amused, which made her want to giggle and laid her bristles flat again.

"Okay, maybe slightly lost."

He shrugged, looking past her into the woods. "People who are never lost are just traveling paths that are too easy and too obvious."

Ann's heart gave a small jab of pleasure. There was a lot more to this man than good food and bait bags full of herring. "What would I do all day?

He chuckled. "You can take the rat out of the race but you can't take the race out of the rat?"

"Hmph. Let's just say I wouldn't be happy keeping house for you."

"I'm not asking you to do that. Betsy said she could use your help next session."

A tug of disappointment. "I thought you said this was your idea."

"I talked it over with her. And before you do your insta-huffy thing, if our positions were reversed, you'd check me out too. Betsy and her staff have seen more of you than I have."

Okay. Cancel insta-huffy thing, she'd give him that. But *her*, a staffer at camp? "What part of you thinks I'd be any good cheerleading for basket-case women?"

"When you back off the attitude, you're a good person. And a natural leader."

Ann frowned. "That *has* to be from Betsy's files."

"She confirmed it."

Another jab, pleasure mixed with annoyance. "I can't give you an answer now."

"I didn't expect you to. I've had time to think it over, I knew you'd need time too."

"Right." She fidgeted. "Have you done this before? To help other 'lost' women?"

"No."

"Why me?"

He shrugged again. "Just a feeling it would work out. For both of us."

"I'd get a reprieve from my 'lost' life. What would you get?"

He shifted position uneasily. "Company."

His discomfort put Ann's insta-huffy thing on orange alert. "Uh, how many bedrooms are we talking here?"

"Two." He held up two fingers. "Scout's honor from a genuine if lapsed scout. That's not what I had in mind."

Ann nodded, head throbbing, so irritated and confused by not understanding what she was feeling and what she wanted that she registered neither relief nor disappointment. The idea of staying here was crazy. But it was mostly crazy to the old Ann, a woman who counted every second not sprinting forward as time spent slipping behind.

Part of her wanted to hang on to the New Ann, who'd

been here for the last week or so, gradually slowing down, starting to realize that part of her had remained undeveloped and unattended in her marriage; to grab that woman by the tail and see where she could fly. Back home next week, she'd spend all her time and energy trying to re-create her old life from ashes, because she didn't know how to create anything else.

And yet, she didn't want to be one of those New Yorkers who traded in the big city for a farm in Vermont and in the simple beauty of their new lives slowly lost their minds. Being here awhile longer with Clive could represent a middle ground. A taste of that different, simpler life without having to make a full investment.

Then there was the man himself. "You have Betsy for research on me. What do I know about you?"

"What would you like to?"

She picked up her pencil again and started roughing in the gentle familiar curve of the sandbar, her movements stiff and clumsy. "You grew up here, but you haven't always lived here."

"I left after high school."

Ann sent him a withering look. "Am I going to have to ask a separate question for every piece of information?"

He grinned. "What's the matter, you don't like talking to me?"

"O-*kay*." She rolled her eyes. "Tell me where you went after high school."

"Away."

She growled her frustration and he chuckled.

"I was Kid Fuck-up. I stayed out of jail but I deserved to go. My father came down hard on me and I pushed back even harder. I left swearing I'd never come back. I bummed around long enough to know I needed college, put myself through and worked my ass off. Blah blah blah, ended up on Wall Street and discovered I could handle it like the big boys. After a few years I was on top of the world, making ridiculous amounts of money, planning to marry a beautiful woman. I was going to ask my dad to the wedding."

Ann stopped drawing, kept her eyes on the water, knowing what was coming and hating it. "Before you could talk to him again he died."

"Heart attack hauling a trap. My last words to him at age eighteen were about making sure he knew how pathetic his life was and how I hoped I'd never turn out anything like him."

Ann squeezed her eyes shut against the empathy pain. "My last words to Paul were, 'Could you please get something accomplished today for a change?'"

He whistled. "And he did."

"Oh yeah. He did." She shook her head, throat tight, wanting to fling off the memory and the guilt. "You never get those words back."

"Nope." He sighed and rubbed his forehead. "After he died, everything I was doing in New York seemed pointless. My relationship tanked, I quit my job, sold my condo, and came back here to help Mom and to honor Dad's memory by doing what he loved."

Tears slipped effortlessly from Ann's eyes. She tried to speak but her throat wouldn't work.

"Arnold was one of my father's best friends. He'd lost his stern man and was having trouble finding another one he could work with. He took me on. "

Ann stared helplessly, tears making her cheeks a water

slide. He told the story with such simplicity and humility, the emotional punch hurt ten times worse. She couldn't help thinking of Patrick's self-conscious bravado that night of the first bonfire, bragging about his struggles. She'd listened, heard the words, but they hadn't touched her, not like this.

"So that's my sad tale."

She wiped her eyes. "Obviously I don't think it's sad, or I'd be crying."

"Obviously." He grinned at her with warmth in his eyes she hadn't seen there before, and she felt their connection pop, like the moment of contact flipping on a light switch. It startled her to realize she hadn't felt that with someone in a long, long time. She and her family had little in common. She and Paul had grown so separate. "You don't need to be sad, Ann. I wish things had gone differently, but I've made peace with it. I hope you can do that too, with your sad tale. This part of the world is great for soul-searching. In the city you can hide who you are behind all there is to do. But it's pretty hard to bullshit yourself in these woods, and on this water."

"I'm sorry about your dad."

"Thank you." He stood and stretched, flexing his shoulders, then caught hold of a rafter and hung on so she had to tip her head back to see his face.

"Will you go back to New York someday?"

"Will you go back to Boston?"

Ann opened her mouth to say *Of course*, when her subconscious rose like a mighty mob and shouted, *Hell no, we won't go*. Damn it. Since when did she hear inner voices? Where else was there *to* go? "I don't know."

"Then we're in the same boat, figuratively this time. I don't know either." He grinned, hands braced against the rafters as if he were holding up the roof. "I miss many things about my old life. A few I miss a lot."

"Your fiancée?" What the *hell* prompted her to ask that?

"Ex-fiancée. And no." His voice went flat. "When I lost interest in making money, she lost interest in me."

"I'm sorry." She wasn't at all.

"Better to find out before the wedding than after." He brought his hands down, put them on his hips, gazed out through the trees. "I miss the culture, the opportunities, the energy. I don't miss the rest of it, the crowds, the stress of daily life. Too much happened. Too much of me changed."

"I know what you mean." Exactly. She knew exactly.

"I had an idea we might find some answers to our separate questions together." He was looking full at her now, measuring, asking, and she stared back, her mind too jumbled to come up with a coherent way to respond, feeling his pull much the same way she'd started to feel the pull of this beautiful place. The current between them was overwhelming, enticing and terrifying, made her want to run away and dive in all at once.

She heard her voice answer before she'd consciously ordered it to.

"I don't know. Maybe we could."

Chapter 16

Dear Eldon,

*There are things going on I don't understand. People
trying to tear us apart and deny what we have. You
must come back and claim me. You must see that this
is no longer a time to hide and be careful, but to burst
free and shout out what's rightfully ours. You must
see that. Wake up.*

Martha

Martha stood on the scattered rocks at the edge of the sea.
She'd given up trying to meditate, even trying to sit still. It
was all she could do to stand here and not fling herself into
the drink. She hadn't slept since the middle of the night. The
camp's wake-up bell would ring any minute.

For the moment, no boats disturbed the stillness. Fog still clung to the flat glassy water turned orange by the rising sun, making the islands appear ghostly and insubstantial. A gull flew overhead, wind whirring under its wings. The air smelled of sea and the freshness of sunrise.

Last night she'd dreamed again of Eldon swimming, beckoning her to join him under the water. This time she'd been afraid to go. This time she shook her head and urged him out onto dry land instead. But once again he hadn't chosen to be with her. He'd given her a look of longing and disappointment, then dived deeper until the green sea swallowed him up.

She'd woken up and known he was gone.

Later she'd ask to use Betsy's computer and read the details of his death. Later. Right now she could only handle being in the tranquility of this beautiful morning, suspended between knowing what had happened and having it confirmed. Until she read the news in black and white, her dream would stay a dream. The pain would stay bearable, the fear manageable. Barely.

She'd tried to make him real, to make them real as a couple, but saying words out loud to show the world how strong and good they were together had convinced Betsy that she had a mental illness, which had been unsettling, to say the least, and made Cindy hurl those words back into Martha's face. Even as she understood that Cindy's anger stemmed from her situation with Kevin, Martha still got the same sick feeling she did when she read letters from fellow Other Women to Dear Abby. "He says he loves me, he says he'll leave his wife, but he never does." Then Abby's answer, always the same, "Wake up, honey."

Saying the words out loud couldn't make them a real

couple again. And now that he was dead, even time wouldn't make them a real couple again. Bianca had won when she married Eldon, and now she'd won again, having lost him while they were still together.

If Bianca were like Cindy, if she and Eldon had married for love, real true love, Martha couldn't have come between them. But then if Bianca were imperfect like Cindy, Eldon wouldn't have chosen her. Martha had always considered Eldon's marriage the betrayal, not their affair. Love gave her and Eldon the right to be together. Love was much more binding and went much deeper than a ceremony and a certificate. Society could think what it wanted. Society needed rules to feel comfortable. Rules could never be justified in every situation under their control.

Until death do us part.

Martha had to believe strongly in love to wait and wait and wait all those hours and days and weeks and years alone in her brown apartment. Precious chances to be together got canceled, e-mails were scarce, phone calls scarcer. Sometimes it seemed to her that weeks went by between the times she heard from Eldon. Then always with his greeting, "How's my girl?"

She waited gladly because of the way they felt about each other, but today with Eldon gone, and with her beautiful forever-after future with him gone, it seemed their love for the past twenty years had been more about frustration and sacrifice than joy and sharing.

The morning bell summoned campers from sleep, the clanging sound rolling down to the sea and out over the water. Women would be getting up, dressing, going to breakfast. When Martha was missed, someone would be sent to find her. She needed to go to breakfast. She needed to go to classes. She needed to find some way to cope with the rest of her life, year after unending year without Eldon to wait for. Without Eldon to hope for. What else was there?

Once upon a time there was a good and remarkable man who loved and was loved by an unremarkable woman. Their bond began before they met, and strengthened each year, each season, each day, until dark death took the man away from this earth. When doctors performed an autopsy, they found in his chest two hearts, one his, one hers.

On television Bianca would beautifully grieve, their children would beautifully grieve. The state would grieve its lost senator, also beautifully, and move on. What would Martha do? She had nowhere to move on to.

A seal—she was sure it was the same one she'd seen from her kayak—poked his head above the silent still water and looked at her with soulful black eyes. She stared back through tears. The seal wavered, then became a small boy like Ricky, with a dirty face and black hair, floating, smiling, eyes enormous and still beckoning.

Come with me, he said. *Come swim with me.*

Martha couldn't swim. She stood and watched the seal boy.

Come with me!

She took a step, walked toward the water, stood at its very edge. The tide was coming in. If she stayed here, in a few hours she'd drown.

Come with me! We'll swim to him.

If she swam with the seal boy, she'd see Eldon again. She'd get her heart back. Or get half of his and leave half of hers so they'd be linked together forever. She took another step; the icy ocean licked and swallowed her toes.

Come with me!

Another step, then another, up to her knees. The seal boy raised his head higher; his eyes glistening liquid glass.

That's it, that's it. Now you're doing it. Good girl.

The water reached the tops of her thighs; already she'd started to shiver. Another step then another. "Eldon."

Come with me . . .

Her chest hurt from the pressure of the cold. The boy became a seal again, tipped his nose up and disappeared.

"No." She searched the water, shivering, panic rising, and anger. "Don't leave. *Don't. Where will I go?*"

Eldon had already left her once. Now again. She'd waited so long for him to come back. She'd waited so long for their time together. So many dozens of nights she'd sat home, hoping he'd call. So many dozens of days she'd barely left her computer, hoping he'd e-mail.

Martha turned and waded out of the water.

The seal resurfaced several yards away. *Tell me a story.*

Martha frowned at it. Boy or seal, she wished it would make up its mind. "No. Go away."

Please, Martha. I need a story.

The large black eyes undid her. "I only have one story right now."

Tell me.

She closed her eyes, reaching for the peace inside her, reaching for the beauty of what she and Eldon felt. "Once upon a time there was a man and woman who were best friends and lovers. The woman knew no one had ever loved her as much as he did, and the man knew the same about her."

Aw, you're not going to make this a kissy story, are you? Ricky Seal was disgusted.

She opened her eyes and scowled at him. "Okay, no kissing. One day the man was enchanted by a wicked witch who—"

What was his name? What was the girl's name? Ricky Seal rose slightly out of the water and back down. *What was the witch's name?*

"The boy's name was . . . Elton. The girl's name was . . . Marta. The witch's name was . . . Politica. Politica enchanted Elton, then forced him to marry a horrible woman named . . . Binaca, who was always cold. Even in bed at night under fourteen comforters and fourteen blankets, she never warmed up, and she made Eldon cold as well. Marta was very sad, but she knew love would never die, and that underneath his enchantment, Elton still belonged to her."

A suspicious look from Ricky Seal. *Are you* sure *this isn't going to be a kissy story?*

"Yes." Martha drew in breath, made herself calm down. "Marta hoped for a long time that Elton would find some way to break the enchantment. He visited her when he could, but he could never get free entirely. Eventually she stopped hoping and trusted instead. Twenty years went by."

Twenty years? Ricky seal's scorn made the water turn hot around him. *He couldn't get free in that long? He must not have tried.*

Martha flinched. "He—"

Either that or he was a wimp.

"He was *not* a wimp, he was noble and strong."

Then why couldn't he get free? A hero would have been able to.

She took a step back and nearly unbalanced when a rock under her foot proved unsteady. "It . . . was a very strong spell."

Oh come on. Why didn't Marta do something to help him get free if she loved him?

The dull pain in Martha's chest grew sharp. "She couldn't fight the spell either."

Why not? Ricky Seal made a wet sound of derision. *Twenty years? She's a wimp too. I like stories with heroes.*

Martha stopped telling the story. She unwrapped her arms from around herself and took in a long breath.

"Boo!" she shouted as loudly as she dared.

A splash, then nothing but smooth water.

The seal was just a seal. She was wet and cold. And tired of everyone making it sound as if she'd wasted most of her life and happiness waiting for Eldon.

Dear Kevin,

I'm still at this camp that you and Patty picked out for me. It feels crappy, really, like you've shoved me into rehab when all I'm addicted to is trying to be happy. I don't think you need to be institutionalized for that. Maybe I'm wrong. You seem to think I am.

Cindy

Baking class. Cindy walked into the camp kitchen feeling as if she were approaching a gallows. Or maybe an audition for *American Idol*, where humiliation would inevitably result. Except instead of Simon Cowell, she'd get Mistress Martha.

But . . . Hadn't she resolved to dig out whatever fragments of internal strength she might manage to find? Yes, she had, and she would. That included trying to recapture her trust and faith in the positive, which would include trying to think better of Martha. Things would work out. She needed to stop measuring herself by other people's standards. She needed to follow where her heart led her, as Patrick had told her that time they sat together and waited for hummingbirds.

She couldn't help feeling wistful about Patrick, the way you felt when you had a really good exchange one day with the most popular boy in class and came away glowing, even knowing more than that was never meant to be.

Really, she was glad she'd spent those naughty hours with him. Kevin wasn't the only one with secrets now. Maybe at some point when she and Kevin were at dinner, she could casually mention the hot night she'd spent with the sexy camp instructor. It would teach him to take her for granted.

Martha was already standing at the counter, waiting for class to begin, looking sadder than even her usual. She quickly looked away when she met Cindy's eyes, which Cindy expected. Cindy would have to take the lead. She doubted Martha had ever taken the lead in anything. Even in ruining someone else's marriage—her boyfriend had doubtless gotten her into it.

"Good morning." She took her place next to Martha, determined not to be kept away by the conflict. "What are we baking today?"

She braced herself for Martha's monosyllable reply. The class could, after all, in spite of her recommitment to thinking positively, turn out to be completely unbearable.

"I'm not sure." Her voice was leaden but firm. "I did see boxes of baking cups, so I guess either muffins . . . or cupcakes."

"Oh." Cindy had not expected Martha to be so friendly. But now that she had been, Cindy needed to be that way too. "Well. I didn't do very well last time, but this week I am going to kick some cupcake butt."

Martha actually smiled, even though it was a sad smile, and Cindy felt even better. See what happened when you spread good and positive feelings around? People responded. She'd gotten trapped in negativity for far too long. This was her power, and it was back. Everything she needed to know she'd learned from her dog.

The instructor arrived, and yes, they were going to bake cupcakes, but first—*oh no*—more bread. Cindy started getting a headache, and it wasn't until she realized that she was clenching her jaw as hard as she could that she was able to get it to ease at all. Flour, oats, a touch of whole wheat, sesame seeds, wheat germ, that much she could do. That far into the class she managed to keep her cheer and confidence going. It wasn't until the dreaded moment when the yeast was to be proofed in sugar water that had to be exactly the right temperature that the veneer of her new attitude cracked. She immediately felt like crying. Just telling herself she was confident was not going to make it happen. Who was she kidding? Measuring water was enough to make her break down.

"I can't do this."

"Yes you can." Martha's gentle, steady voice made Cindy turn her head.

"I've never been able to do it, what makes you think this time could be any different?"

"You're fighting yourself. You're panicking. You must concentrate and become the yeast."

Cindy's sighed. For a moment she had actually dared to hope that Martha could help her. Unfortunately, when it wasn't even in her power to mix ingredients the right way, transforming herself into a hungry, gassy little organism was even less probable. Maybe Martha was way off the deep end. Maybe her life and her true love cheater were figments of a schizophrenic mind. "I'm sorry?"

"Try becoming the yeast. Imagine yourself about to be mixed into water." She got that weird dreamy look in her eyes and gestured as if she were tracing the horizon. "What is the best temperature for you to thrive in?"

"Uh . . . "

"I know it sounds crazy, but give it a try." Martha seemed to come out of her trance. She blinked her permanently lowered lashes solemnly. "I think you'll be surprised."

Cindy narrowed her eyes. "Something is different about you. You're talking more. You're helping me, and you should be furious for the way I screamed at you."

"Cindy." Martha took one of her funny endless breaths. "We've all been tested here. We've all had to look our tragedies straight on, and we've all discovered things we didn't expect to see. In short—all of us are ready to crack up."

"You're always so calm."

"Calm is a state of mind you can choose, the same way hysteria is."

"Not me." Cindy laughed. "Calm and I are strangers."

"If you are at peace inside yourself, then you can be calm."

"Oh." Cindy half expected her to say *grasshopper* at the end of every sentence. "Do you know if your friend is feeling better?"

"He died. Last night."

Cindy felt a jolt of adrenaline and dismay. She stared at Martha, waiting for the tears, the regrets, the outpourings of devotion. But no. Only sad resignation, which tore at Cindy's insides more than if Martha had been hysterical. "I'm so sorry. How did you hear?"

"I haven't heard yet."

Okay, now Cindy was getting really freaked out. Was this odd woman all there? Was she about to go nuts and shoot up the room and/or herself? "Then how do you know?"

"I felt it." She tested her water with her little finger, stirred in her sugar and yeast.

Cindy was pretty much convinced now that Martha was a lunatic. Cindy had been with Kevin for twenty years, but was pretty sure he could drop dead and she wouldn't have the slightest clue until she heard from the police. Or Patty. "Well, wow, you seem pretty . . . "

She was not enamored with the word *calm* anymore.

"Chances were pretty good he had brain damage from a stroke. Even if he had woken up, he might not have been the man I knew." She frowned at her measuring cup, yeast already frothing and bubbling happily on top.

"I'm sorry." She was surprised to find that she *was* sorry, and wondered whether the man's wife couldn't help a small feeling of relief mixed into her grief, that she'd finally gotten rid of a snake like that.

Martha turned her sad bulgy eyes on Cindy. "You don't think I deserve to lose him?"

"I'm not sure I believe that's the way the world works. I didn't deserve what Kevin did to me." The words rolled bitterly out of her mouth, and she stopped in absolute astonishment, having no idea she'd been about to say them.

"Has everyone's yeast proofed yet?" Francine, the baking instructor, held up her hand and swept the room with her eyes. Everybody nodded except Cindy. She picked up her measuring cup and went over to the faucet, ran the water with her finger underneath it. How the hell was she supposed to know how this worked?

She thought about what Martha had said. What temperature would feel good to her if she were a piece of yeast, ready to dive in? What temperature did she like when she was tired and cold and needed a hot bath to bring her back to life?

The water turned slightly hotter, warm on her finger with only the tiniest bite. Exactly how Cindy liked her bathwater. She filled her measuring cup to the proper line and brought it back to the table, added sugar, cut open her yeast packet and dumped it in, waited a few minutes, couldn't stand it when nothing happened, and turned away to think about Martha.

What would a woman like Martha do after losing her unhealthy fraction of a relationship that she called true love? "Where do you go from here?"

"I don't know."

"Maybe you should get a job telling stories. To children, or old people at libraries, or hospitals."

Martha gave her a look as if she thought Cindy was crazy, which Cindy couldn't help feeling was the reverse of how it should be. Though she couldn't really blame Martha. The idea was pretty stupid.

Except then Martha's eyes turned thoughtful. "I'll think about it. Thank you."

Cindy blinked. Had she just given someone good advice?

"Look." Martha nudged her and pointed to Cindy's measuring cup. On top of the warm water, the yeast was bubbling, frothing, fornicating furiously. "That will make a wonderful batch of rolls."

Cindy put her hand to her cheeks, which had flushed hot. "Oh my gosh. Oh my gosh. Look at that!"

Martha helped her stir the precious fluid into the flour mixture, and though Cindy's kneading stroke was still clumsy, the dough felt warm and alive under her fingers this time. While it rose, she attacked cupcakes, letting Martha guide her, urging her to cream the butter and sugar together more thoroughly, keeping her from beating too long after the dry ingredients were added to the wet. And while the results wouldn't win any prizes, she was pretty sure they would be among the cakes served to the campers for dessert at night. She might not even be able to tell which were hers.

Everything got better. Her dough had risen as high as anyone else's. She had trouble getting all her rolls the same size, but they even rose a second time, and baked to a brown crusty finish.

Cindy was quite sure the world had never looked, smelled, or been such a wonderful place. Even Martha, who could just as easily have hated her, seemed proud, and only betrayed a slight horror when Cindy gave her a hug of gratitude and sympathy.

She even asked the instructor if she could take one of the rolls back to her cabin to show Dinah and Ann, and was given permission. Cindy practically danced down the path from the kitchen to their cabin, and only stumbled once. She flew up the steps, yanked open the screen door and held a piece of bread up triumphantly. "Look! Look what I did!"

She laughed, knowing that she was being completely ridiculous getting this excited over something so simple. Something most women probably learned to do when they were ten.

Dinah had been sitting in the common room reading *People* magazine, but she got up and gamely celebrated. Even Ann emerged from her bedroom and grinned at Cindy's achievement as if she'd just announced a major publishing contract or a lottery win. Ann didn't even pull away all that much either when Cindy hugged her.

Martha joined them, back from baking class a little more slowly than Cindy's jubilant pace, and they split the roll in the common room of their cabin, exclaiming as if they were dining in a restaurant in Paris.

Tears filled Cindy's eyes. She could not be more grateful for these women and their nutty excitement over her bread.

A knock at the door. Four shouted "Come ins," then odd and immediate silence when Patrick walked into their sanctum. His eyes picked Cindy's out immediately, and for the first time since they'd been together, she saw the warmth in them, and felt herself flushing and feeling even giddier.

"Cindy." He glanced around the room, and brought those beautiful gray eyes back to hers. "You have a visitor."

Cindy had so much adrenaline going that she would not have thought any more was possible, but it was. At the same time, paradoxically, a huge stillness settled over her and apparently the rest of the room.

"Who . . . is it?"

Patrick's smile held a hint of sadness. "It's Kevin. He wants to see you."

Chapter 17

If Cindy thought there was true silence in the room before, when Patrick walked in, she was mistaken. Because when he said Kevin was here, that Kevin had come to get her back, exactly as she predicted, exactly as she told everybody in this camp from the first day she got here, it was as if everyone had stopped moving and breathing and digesting.

If Cindy thought that baking a decent roll had made her feel triumphant, she was wrong. She'd only experienced the tiniest fraction of triumph compared to this. She'd told them all, and Kevin had come back.

"Well." Her voice sounded too high and too breathy. "How about that?"

She turned then, with an uncharacteristic toss of her head, unable to wait a second longer to see her roommates' shocked and abashed faces, to enjoy the moment, to look each of them in the eye and telepathically send them the biggest, smuggest told-you-so that she could manage.

Except while Martha, Ann, and Dinah might have looked shocked, they didn't look abashed so much as horrified.

Cindy sighed. She didn't expect them to understand, but she thought they might find it in their hearts to be happy for her in this as well as her baking.

"He's waiting for you in Betsy's cabin." Patrick sent her a puppy dog look—or was it hangdog? Some kind of dog. Not Max.

"I'll go right away." She was glad to discover she still held a piece of roll in her hand. She could show it to Kevin, let him taste it. He'd be pleased, she was sure. He of all people would understand what an achievement this was for her, after suffering through her cooking for so many years.

She followed Patrick out of the cabin, without looking back at the girls again. Their reaction had made her kind of queasy, and jittery, and she didn't like to think about what they'd be saying once she left. That she was weak, that she was foolish. Though it occurred to her that maybe of all of them, Martha would come closest to understanding.

Irony at its finest.

"Will you go back to him?"

She was about to say *Of course* when she realized that were their positions reversed, she'd be devastated if Patrick brushed her off so lightly. "I'll see what he has to say."

She kept her voice cold, but couldn't help a smile. Didn't she sound strong and reborn!

"Just because you planned all along to go back to him doesn't mean you still have to, Cindy. Your will is your own, and your life is your own, and your pride and self-respect are your own. None of them belongs to him."

Patrick's brave voice made her breath go all stuttering and unpleasant, and she wanted to reach for a tree to steady herself, but they were approaching Betsy's cabin and there were no trees nearby, just the sad roses and scruffy lilacs, and neither of them would offer her support.

She stopped at the doorway and turned to face Patrick. "Thank you."

He looked around furtively, then grabbed her shoulders and hugged her tightly. "Be strong. Be confident. Be who you are."

Strong? Confident? She'd tried that briefly and it hadn't worked out. She smiled into his beautiful gray eyes and loved him desperately for saying such nice things. His belief in her even made it seem possible again that he was right. Then she opened the door and walked into Betsy's cabin.

Kevin had been sitting in a chair near Betsy's desk, and he rose to his feet when she came in. He looked tired. Older. Anxious, and contrite. Her heart swelled and softened at the sight. He was suffering.

"Cindy." He seemed surprised, as if he'd expected someone else. "You look . . . beautiful."

He might as well have told her she was the Queen of England, for how it made her feel. She bet if she extended her hand, he'd drop to his knees and kiss it.

She was going to enjoy this.

"Kevin would like to talk to you, Cindy." Betsy sat at her desk in her black half-glasses, arms folded across her chest. Cindy imagined that Kevin had not been having a lovely time with her. "How do you feel about that?"

"Fine. I feel fine." She beamed at Kevin, even while she

had a funny buzzy feeling, like she'd had many too many cups of coffee. He was back. He was here. He'd left Patty and wanted her back.

"If you're sure, Cindy, you can take Kevin into the room where you spoke to your daughter."

"Sure. This way." She walked through the beautiful living room, past the window nook, into the room where she'd taken the phone call what seemed like years ago.

See? She'd been right. Patty had not moved into her house, just as she'd told Lucy.

She closed the door, sat on the bed, and patted the mattress next to her. Kevin sat in the chair by the phone, where she'd sat talking to their daughter. Cindy rolled her eyes. He never did want to do anything she suggested.

"Well this is a surprise." She smiled at him, pretty sure that if she told him she knew all along he'd show up, he'd get annoyed. This would be hard enough on him.

Kevin fidgeted in the chair. He hated sitting still. Any second he would stand up and start pacing.

He stood up. He paced to the end of the room, looked out the window for a few seconds into the woods, and paced back.

"I suppose you are wondering why I'm here."

"Yes, of course." Not.

"Cindy, I've . . . " He thrust his hand through his hair, turned away again, paced to the window, paced back. "I've been a fool."

"Oh?" She blinked innocently at him, surprised to find herself wanting to sock him in the gut. Why was he the last person to figure that out? Even people here at camp who didn't know him knew he was a fool. Or worse. He'd been called a bastard and a jerk and, she believed, an asshole.

After his next round of pacing he stopped in front of the bed, looking down at her with a perplexed expression. "There is something different about you."

"Camp has been good for me. You and Patty were right."

He winced at Patty's name, as she knew he would.

Cindy felt suddenly serene and powerful, like she'd turned into Martha. "I've learned a lot here. About myself."

Now he was looking worried. She wasn't sure she'd ever enjoyed herself this much with him. Not since the beginning when everything was so innocent and new and passionate between them.

"I did quite a few things for the first time." She thought of Patrick underneath her, and felt her smile grow wicked. "Today I made a decent loaf of bread. I even brought you some to try."

Kevin stared blankly at a piece of bread she held out to him. "Bread? Cindy, I'm trying to say something here, and you want to talk about baking?"

She felt her spine stretch up until she was sitting as straight and tall as a woman in a yoga mountain pose. "Yes, I do. I made bread today and cupcakes. I've never been able to do either of those things before."

She extended the piece of roll farther toward him.

"Patty was a mistake. She . . . wasn't who I thought." His voice cracked and he abruptly pressed his lips together.

"She left you." The bread in her hand started to tremble. She didn't want him coming back because he was cast off.

"No. I left her. She wasn't . . . she wasn't you, Cinds."

"Oh." The bread decided trembling wasn't nearly enough and started shaking in earnest. Yes. Yes. This was how it should go.

Kevin took the bread from her hand. He tossed it onto the bed beside her, reached for her waist and lifted her up and against him. "Please come back."

His voice was rough and low, and she knew how much it cost him to beg.

But she found herself turning to look at the discarded crust of bread, which had deposited a few crisp brown crumbs on the blue and green floral quilt.

"Kevin . . . "

He gathered her hands, clasped them together in his. "I know that I have not been a good husband to you. But I swear this time I've learned my lesson, I have come to understand how valuable you are to me, to my life, to our life together."

Cindy found herself wondering if maybe Patty didn't like to do dishes, or have meals ready for him when he got home, or let him retreat into his study in the evenings when he was too tired to interact with anyone. Maybe Patty didn't like the way Kevin put work first, put himself first, put everything ahead of his partner.

"Why didn't you try the bread I made?"

Kevin's eyes narrowed. How often had she seen that displeasure? "What is this fixation on bread? I'm asking you to come back. I'm telling you it's over with Patty."

"I'm telling you I made that bread and I want you to try it."

He stared, incredulously. "You want me to try bread."

"Yes. I do. I'm very proud of it."

"Okay. I get it. This is you telling me that it's going to be more about you from now on, is that it?"

"No, this is about me telling you I want you to try the roll I made."

"Jesus, Cindy, what is it with you? Haven't you heard anything I've said?"

"Yes. I have. I've heard everything you've said. For twenty years I've heard everything you've said. And for twenty years I don't think you've heard a single thing that I have." She was terrified. She could not believe these words were coming out of her mouth. It was as if someone else had taken possession of her body, someone much stronger and angrier than she was.

"I'm going to try harder from now on. I promise you that."

He still made no move toward the piece of bread that he'd thrown onto the bed behind her. Cindy felt that it was utterly ludicrous that the fate of her marriage should depend on flour, wheat germ, oats, sesame seed, honey, and yeast. Risen twice. Baked at 350 degrees for twenty-five minutes. But it did.

She wasn't going to ask again. But she sat down on the bed, folded her hands in her lap, and turned to look at the crust, then back up at Kevin. "No more women? No sex with anyone else but me for the rest of your life?"

"No one else."

He answered calmly but couldn't hold her gaze. And it hit her out of nowhere with quiet certitude that he would do it again and that nothing she could do or be would stop him.

She picked up the bread and took a bite, chewed happily, savoring the fresh natural flavor. She'd made this. She had.

"Thank you for coming here, Kevin. Thank you for admitting that you made a mistake."

"You're welcome. Darling. Cynthia." He held out his arms, eyes warm, smile meant only for her.

She took another bite of bread. "This is really delicious. You totally missed out."

His smile faltered. His arms floated down. "You're still angry. I don't blame you. I'm staying at a hotel nearby. I'll come back tomorrow after you've had time to cool off."

"Tomorrow I'm on a trip with my friends." She smiled and popped the last of the bread into her mouth. "I'll be busy all day."

"Okay." He put his hands on his hips. "I deserve this, I know. I'll wait, though. And when camp is over, I'll bring you home with me."

Home. The bread lost its taste, and she swallowed before she'd chewed long enough and nearly gagged. Home with Kevin. Lucy's home, the one she still needed even though she was nearly grown up. Nowhere else in the world was home to Cindy except camp, and her parents' house. She couldn't stay here and she'd rather eat live snails than crawl back to her mother and father now. Their daughter, the consummate failure.

What had she been thinking? That a new life would fall into her lap just from needing one? Hadn't she just learned during baking class that wanting to be different, or deciding to be strong, wasn't enough to make her that way? Where else would she go but home with Kevin?

He had come back. But now instead of welcoming the long-awaited chance to return to her life, she felt trapped, suffocated, claustrophobic. Probably how he felt all those years with her. Why were they together? She'd forgotten.

"Okay, Cindy?" His voice was tender, warm, the voice he used to get her to do what he wanted. His gentle touch on her cheek, his hands raising her to standing again; neither his tenderness nor his strength impressed her. His lips met hers; she responded by habit. "I'll be back to take you home on Saturday."

She thought of Patrick's kisses, thought of Ann's embrace on the archery field, thought of Martha's forgiveness and her calm guidance. Thought of how it felt around the bonfire with dozens of her fellow campers, singing with all their hearts "I Am Woman."

She'd never be the same. Camp Kinsonu had changed her. But enough to turn her back on the entire lifetime that had come before?

"I'll think it over."

"That's my girl." He held her chin, tipped her face up and kissed her mouth, the way she always thought was so sweet and sexy. Then he drew back and smiled, and she knew that he knew it was only a matter of time until she got over her cute little pretend show of strength and came back where she belonged. "I'm at the Harrington Inn if you change your mind sooner and want to come home."

He went to the door, turned and winked before he left the room. She heard him speak, and Betsy respond. The front door to Betsy's cabin opened, closed. She heard his voice again, slowly fading as he walked away, talking on his cell.

Cindy sank back down on the bed. She couldn't go back. But neither could she go anywhere else.

The phone in the room rang and made her jump. She heard Betsy answering it, then her steps coming closer to the bedroom. A gentle knock. "Cindy? It's your daughter. Would you like to speak to her?"

Lucy. What timing. Unless she was on standby and Kevin had just called her.

"I'll talk to her." She crossed the room and picked up the phone. "Hello?"

"Mom, what are you doing?"

She backed up and sat suddenly on the blue, hard chair. "Talking to you."

"I mean why aren't you going back with Daddy right now? He said you were going to think about it. What do you have to think about?"

"Lucy . . ." Cindy let her head drop back until it hit the pine wall behind her. How could she communicate to this girl-woman who needed her parents and her home that Cindy was a woman as well as a mother, and that she might want something different? "I don't know if I can go back."

"*What*? What are you talking about?" The patented Lucy Instant Hysteria. "Why not? You said Dad would come back and you were right. Now he's back, what more do you want?"

Cindy had never understood when characters in books said they saw red, but she definitely couldn't see anything in front of her face at the moment, only the view was black for her. "I want me. I want *me* back. I don't want to be your slave and I don't want to be his doormat, is that so hard to understand?"

Silence on the line. Cindy put her hand to her forehead. What had she done? She'd never ever yelled at her baby before.

"Geez, Mom." A sudden sniff, the sound of tears in Lucy's words. "You don't have to bite my head off. I didn't know you were so unhappy."

"I didn't either." She gentled her voice, giving in, giving up, always the peacemaker, at the same time noting that her explosion had triggered an internal pressure release valve and given her some peace. Going forward she needed to speak the truth more often. Maybe that would be enough to make life better.

She didn't know. She didn't know what she wanted, not really, because she didn't know who this "me" was that she wanted back. How could she, who had so much trouble learning how to do anything, think that she could launch herself out into a completely new life and be successful?

She couldn't. She had no place to go and nothing to do when she got there. She had a life with Kevin, a duty to her daughter. Maybe there were ways she could make those roles more bearable. That was the most she could hope for.

So. She'd failed at being strong, just as she'd failed at everything else. One batch of rolls and one batch of cupcakes wasn't enough to set her free.

"I just need these last two days, Lucy. Then I'll go back."

Chapter 18

Ann stood on the beach, waiting for Patrick to show up and take Cabin Four out on *Stronglady*, the camp boat, to Eagle Rock Island for the day. One last bonfire tonight, and tomorrow they'd be graduates, sprung, reworked, and ready to face the rest of their lives. Right? Sure. Except she hadn't given Clive a final answer yet. Would she or wouldn't she? If she decided to stay, she'd still need to go home tomorrow, pack up what she'd need and bring it back. She had a feeling once she was back in Massachusetts, this time in Maine would recede into fantasy, and accepting the haven Clive offered would seem like a desperate attempt to avoid the tough stuff she needed to face. Being without Paul. Getting a job. Rebuilding her life.

She turned and glanced at the women of Cabin Four. Dinah, not surprisingly, was talking, Cindy listening politely, as she'd done for the past two weeks, though she didn't look as if she were processing the words. Cindy was going back to

Kevin, even after they threatened to pitch her in the ocean if she did. She was the only one going back to the same life. Martha's boyfriend had died; she had twenty years of being hidden away and nothing to show for it.

So were they all better? Maybe, but Ann didn't think so. This morning in particular the mood in the cabin had been edgy and tense. Kinsonu had been a nice break, but you couldn't cheat grief out of its full punishment.

"Hello, ladies." Patrick strode down onto the beach, looking tanned and particularly handsome in blue shorts and a blue and white striped shirt, swinging a picnic basket that must contain their lunch. Ann had a contribution to lunch all her own—two bottles of wine she'd picked up in a tiny store on Route 1 the previous evening. She figured the girls deserved to celebrate together.

Driving home from the liquor store, she'd been tempted to stop and see Clive, but realized with his before dawn schedule that he'd probably be asleep already. She then inanely went on to picture him in bed, and found herself wondering if he slept in pajamas, underwear, or nothing, and boy oh boy did danger signals start flashing then. It was one thing if she accepted his platonic invitation and spent time here relaxing and examining her life and what she wanted to do next, another if she spent the time imagining him naked. She wasn't ready for that. Look how quickly she'd backed off from Patrick after they'd been intimate. She needed to get to a clear-headed place. Nothing brought on brain clouds like lust. Of course, Patrick was Patrick, and Clive . . .

She turned to find Patrick-was-Patrick watching her with a sexy smile she couldn't help returning. What a piece of work. You couldn't help having a crush on Patrick, and you couldn't regret it either. Undoubtedly plenty of women in camp would happily have traded places with her in the mossy clearing.

"You ready for the big adventure?" He strode over, grinning, and she couldn't even keep back the girly thrill at being singled out.

"Oh sure. Me with my extensive big-game safari experience, I'm ready for anything."

He laughed and escorted her to the boathouse, where the two of them carried the skiff down to the water's edge.

Patrick rowed Martha and Ann out to the *Stronglady*, then went back for Dinah and Cindy, handling the oars competently but not as if he were born to them like Clive. Because he wasn't, and Clive was, and what the hell was she comparing for?

Female cargo aboard, he drew up the anchor, stowed it in the front of the boat, started the engine, and off they went. Fast. The boat tore over the sea, roaring, bouncing, fighting the waves, reminding Ann of the saying that the only difference between men and boys was the size and price of their toys. She would have liked a slower ride, so she could examine the islands and experience the sea, but at least this way the noise and wind were too loud to hear Dinah.

Eagle Rock Island was crescent-shaped, the last barrier between the bay and the Atlantic. On the bay side, the air was warm and still, little waves lapping at the pebbly beach where they disembarked and unloaded their gear. Patrick waved good-bye, winked at Ann, and promised to be back mid-afternoon to bring them home to camp.

A quick trip through long marshy grass carrying their gear—with Dinah commenting on every plant and animal she saw, and curse her Kinsonu flora and fauna class—across to a spot Patrick recommended on the ocean side. There was a drop in temperature there, a steady wind and rolling breakers that crashed and splashed into the ledges lining the coast, sending up fountains of white foaming spray.

The women from Cabin Four stood in a line facing open sea. The wind blew their hair straight back—okay, well it only ruffled Dinah's—and made Ann's eyes water. Ducks—no, not ducks. Too small for ducks, but Ann didn't care enough to ask what they were—floated, perilously close to the rocks, doomed in seconds to be broken by the ledges. Somehow they managed to avoid being smashed. Up and down, riding out life calmly, right on the edge. She could take lessons from a duck . . . type . . . thing. Soon enough she'd be back with them, riding waves, in danger of being smashed.

"Who wants to explore?" She pulled hair out of her mouth, which the wind had whipped there when she turned. She wasn't eager to ride the waves anymore. The calm bay side of the island looked more and more appealing. Was this a substantial change? Or more depressive grief fallout? She kept hearing Patrick's voice, saying she hadn't been herself married to Paul.

"I was thinking of lying out. I brought a towel." Dinah looked dubiously at the jagged ledges and the stony spread of beach.

"I'll explore with you." Cindy sounded about as excited as if Ann had suggested a stroll through radioactive thorn bushes.

Martha said nothing.

Well, this day would be super duper fun.

She broke formation and started off to her right, where

what she'd spontaneously dubbed the Stoned Beach ended in a steep slope up a forested hill. Halfway, she looked back, saw the others straggling after her, and was surprised to find herself glad she'd have their company. Well. Don't tell us Ann had actually become human?

They made it all the way around the island, pushing through scratchy branches, negotiating tricky rocks. Along the way, many discoveries. Raspberry bushes, heavy with ripe berries, wild blueberries that seemed dusted with powdered sugar, hill cranberries, a beautiful ripe red against their green shiny leaves. A cave with a tidal pool lined with barnacles pushing out tiny feathery hands from the tops of their shell castles to catch whatever meal floated by. Brine shrimp wiggled across the bottom and a sea anemone that only Dinah could see for the first several minutes, which caused her to be smug and the rest of them to think she'd been making it up, stood pink bloblike at the back near the cave wall. Across from the cave, beds of mussels exposed by the low tide, so densely packed that you couldn't step between them. And everywhere, fresh sea air and sunshine and unspoiled beauty. Ann was starting to think that her favorite color combination would always be dark green evergreens against a vivid blue sky.

And she wanted to leave here why? What was new to explore and discover in Framingham, where she'd grown up? A new flavor at Dunkin' Donuts?

But this wasn't life, her sane self argued. This was vacation. Adventure.

So . . . what, then, her new self argued back, life was supposed to be high-stress routine? Ugly? Unremarkable? She wasn't allowed to have beauty and richness and a sense of curiosity and peace and wonder in her daily life?

She thought of Clive, transfixed with her at the sight of the heron. He'd grown up here. This was his Framingham, and he'd come back to gaze and wonder and marvel all over again. The simple life.

But she wasn't Clive. A few months gazing and wondering and marveling, and it would all be familiar here too, not to mention in winter the isolation would be horrendous. Plus she'd be creating a big black hole in her résumé.

"I'm starving." Dinah paused breathlessly, teetered on her wedge espadrilles and had to grab at a nearby branch. "Feels like forever since I ate breakfast. Or maybe it was the sight of all those raspberries and mussels. I also saw several seaside growing plants that were edible. One of them tastes like—"

"Luckily we brought a picnic." Ann lifted the hair off the back of her neck. She was looking forward to getting back to a resting point herself. A couple of glasses of wine and a nice nap in the sun, and she'd count this a pretty good day. Easy living, in fact.

"Lunch sounds good. I think I'm getting a blister." Cindy gazed so mournfully at her pink tennis shoes that Ann actually missed her ditzy happiness.

"There must be Band-Aids in the first aid kit." Martha sighed one of her vast sighs and ambled through a stand of birches, trunks glowing papery white in the sunlight.

The women followed silently—apart from Dinah's usual mumbled conversation with herself—until they came to the spot where they'd set down their gear.

Ann grinned and moved forward, eager to unveil her

secret. Wine would get their moods up, relax them, get some fun silly chatter going, and maybe they could all forget their troubles for a little while.

"Look what I brought." She dragged the bottles out of her bag and out of the towel she'd wrapped them in, held them up triumphantly. "Are we going to have fun, or what?"

"Is that a chardonnay from California? That was my husband Tom's favorite wine. I could barely buy it fast enough. But I don't drink wine. Now if it was gin, I'd dive right in, though any drinking at lunch makes me gassy."

Ann rolled her eyes. Fine. Just as well. They certainly didn't need Dinah to get any more talkative. "Martha? Cindy? How about it?"

"Oh. Um. I don't really drink that much." Cindy smiled apologetically. "It will just put me to sleep."

Martha shook her head. "No thank you."

For crying out loud. Her last day here, and she was stuck with a bunch of party poopers. She'd hoped after all they'd been through they could at least have some fun now. But maybe she was being sentimental. These weren't really her friends, they'd all just been stuck together by chance.

Her friends back home would drink with her. Except they all had jobs and husbands or lovers—sometimes both—or kids, and they'd brag or complain about them the whole time. Back home she'd be Unemployed Ann Without Paul.

God how depressing.

To Clive, she was just Ann. She could share the afternoon wine with him after he got back from fishing. Or she could go lobstering with him, and they could share the bottle when they returned, or skip it and drink coffee, sitting in the lean-to, watching the sea. They could talk about their day, he could tease her when she got self-righteous, they could figure out together what they wanted and where they were going. A simpler life. A new Ann. Forgoing the wind and waves for sun and steady warmth.

She'd only be running away from life if she defined life the way she always had—the way Paul had, a grueling pace chasing financial success. Beauty and relaxation didn't have to belong only to snatched expensive vacations. If she took what Clive offered, she could have it all.

Ann put the wine back in the bag. She was going to stay.

Martha glanced at the other three women, waiting with her to be picked up on the bay side of the island where Patrick had dropped them off. They'd spent the rest of the afternoon lying in the sun, throwing rocks in the water, and watching the tide creeping in. Now, in various states of the fidgets, they waited. Patrick was nearly an hour late, and they were sunburned, tired and ready to go back to Kinsonu—and tomorrow, home. Cindy would go back to her cheating, neglectful husband; Dinah would doubtless sign up on Match.com the second she walked in her door; Ann would restart her sophisticated life and high-powered career. And Martha would go back to sitting in her apartment, only with nothing to wait for now, nothing even to dream about.

"We were supposed to talk today about what camp had done for us, and how we've changed. We didn't do that." Cindy sounded anxious, afraid of disappointing the teacher.

"Who cares." Predictably, this came from Ann.

"Well, I feel I've really changed. Very deeply. Spiritually."

Dinah jiggled pebbles in her hand so they clacked together appealingly. "After I get back, I'm going to enter a convent and take a vow of silence."

If the ocean weren't sending waves rolling over the stones, a pin could have been heard dropping.

"I'm kidding, for heaven's sake." Dinah shook her head. "Honestly. Don't you have a sense of humor? Me, in a place with no men?"

Three bursts of relieved laughter, then Dinah's cackle overall.

"But seriously, I don't know that I learned anything, really, but I did have a wonderful time, and it was great to meet you three and so many other nice women. I took a lot of great classes, I improved my tennis, got divine massages . . . Really, it was so relaxing. I feel ready to go home and dive right back into the man pool."

"Wow. Lucky guys."

"Oh, you're just a sweetie, Ann." Dinah smacked Ann's leg playfully, as usual not registering her sarcasm. "I'll always be grateful to this place. And who knows, maybe I'll be back here at camp again someday if my next marriage tanks."

Ann groaned and even Cindy rolled her eyes. Martha thought it was pretty ironic that Dinah would probably always be the happiest of the three of them. Maybe loving deeply made happiness harder to achieve. What would her own life have been like without Eldon to love, to hope and wait for? Would she have married someone else? Would that have made her happier?

She had so much love stored up to give that Eldon never had the chance to get.

A boat motor made all four of their necks crane to the north, until she came into sight from around the edge of the island. Not Kinsonu's *Stronglady*. A lobster boat.

Three necks relaxed. Ann stared a few beats longer, hand up to shield her eyes from the sun, then hers relaxed too.

Cindy tossed a pebble, which clattered down a slight incline toward the water, hit an obstacle and stopped. The waves swished in and out, in farther, out less, tide rising toward them. No breeze on the side of the island. The warmth was uncomfortable.

Waiting . . . Waiting . . .

"I'm glad to be going back home. I guess." Cindy rested her head on her hand, elbow propped on her knee, looking despondent. "I mean I really liked it here, and I did change, but a lot of the adventures turned out differently than I thought. At least home is exactly what I know it is."

"What if a different life could be much better?"

Cindy glanced at Ann in a way Martha was pretty sure she wouldn't have two weeks ago. "How are *you* planning to change your life, Ann? Going back to your parents and trying to find the same kind of job?"

"Actually . . . " Ann picked up a pebble and threw it hard. It traveled impressively far and landed with a soft thunk in the green water. "I'm staying here."

"At camp?"

"With the guy I went lobstering with. He's asked me to stay with him for a while." She held up a hand to stop the obvious questions, but Martha noticed her blushing. "Platonically. We're both drifting at the moment, so it made sense to join forces."

Martha was pretty sure also that two weeks ago Ann would not have even considered such an offer, nor admitted that she was drifting.

"What about you, Martha?" Cindy turned to her, and Martha couldn't help thinking of how her eyes sparkled with energy and friendly warmth on the first day they met, and how dull they were now. "What's going to be different for you?"

Ann cleared her throat, and Cindy clapped her hand over her mouth. "I'm sorry. I wasn't thinking. I know how much he meant to you."

"It's okay." Martha's breath came faster. She felt sweat beading on her temple. "I think . . . I'd made him into a fantasy. A little. Maybe."

Two weeks ago she definitely wouldn't have said that. Or even admitted it to herself.

"What will you do now? You want to come manhunting with me?" Dinah rubbed her hands together. "Looks like we're the only swinging singles left."

"I don't think I need a man. Not for a while." Martha wiped her forehead with a tissue she had stuffed in her pocket in case she broke down over Eldon while they were on the island. She was embarrassed to be the only one sweating so obviously.

"So what will you do?" Cindy's brow was wrinkled in concern.

Martha waited for the answer to come to her, waited for something to make sense while they all sat here and waited for Patrick.

And then Martha was damn sick and tired of waiting. So many weeks now she'd been waiting for Eldon to wake up and start living, when it was *she* who had needed to wake up and start living, for far longer than that.

No more. When she got back to Vermont, she was going to call libraries and volunteer to tell stories to kids, call nursing homes and volunteer to tell stories to the elderly. Maybe enroll at the University of Vermont for courses in creative writing. She'd even go see the shrink Betsy recommended. She didn't have erotomania, but it couldn't hurt to work a few things out.

Mostly, she was not going to spend any more time waiting. She was going to start her life all by herself. Right now. "We need to think what to do if Patrick doesn't come."

"They're not going to leave us here." Ann scoffed. "If he can't come, they'll send someone else."

"What if the boat broke down, it could be hours before they find another one." Cindy bit her lip anxiously.

Dinah patted her round belly. "I hope they hurry. I'm getting hungry."

"Well, what would you suggest, Martha?" Ann gestured in exasperation toward the bay. "Swimming for it?"

"I'm pretty sure we'd never make it in this water. Have you felt it? It's cold as anything. I remember once I went swimming during the winter after I'd been in a sauna with Frank, my second husband, and I thought I was going to have a heart attack. You wouldn't believe how—"

"Dinah, I was being sarcastic."

"Oh." She shrugged amiably. "I didn't get that."

"Did you have a plan in mind, Martha?" Cindy asked.

Martha stood up. Her breathing was coming fast, but she didn't even try to slow it down. Bianca had no power over her anymore. Eldon was gone.

"Yes. I have a plan."

"Well?"

"Dinah." Martha pointed at her. "You know what to eat here. We all saw the berries and the mussels."

"Which we would cook how?" Ann. Challenging as usual.

Cindy stood up. "We can make a fire between two of those ledges. I saw charcoal there, someone's done it before. And there's that metal bowl our lunch salad came in."

"There is a lot of driftwood on the beach. It would burn quickly and hot. I went camping with Stanley all the time in our RV, and I'm pretty good with a fire."

"The second we start, Patrick will show up, you know." In spite of her objection, Ann was standing too.

"So? We'll ask him to join us." Martha took a few steps toward the ocean side of the island, energy rising, powerful energy, the kind she usually felt only during meditation or yoga or when she told her fantasy stories. "Oh, and Ann?"

Ann and the rest of the women waited expectantly. Martha liked the feeling of someone waiting for her.

She smiled. "I think this is a good time for that wine."

Cindy finished her third paper cup of wine. My my, it tasted awfully good. The first sip was a bit strange, but it just got better and better, didn't it. Yup.

She kept thinking Patrick would show up and rescue them, but he hadn't, and by now she wasn't sure she cared, though she didn't want to spend the night there. They'd all had a really fun time, gathering berries, gathering mussels, which they washed in a deep tide pool and cooked over the driftwood fire in the metal pot. They had a few packages of butter left from lunch to dip the sweet fresh meat in, and some leftover rolls. Dinah made a fairly weird salad out of plants growing along the shore, one slightly bitter and salty, one with a distinct mustard/horseradish taste, one crisp but bland. She even found beach peas growing, though at this time of year they were way past their prime.

A feast by any standards.

They'd laughed together, even Martha and Ann had laughed some, and talked. Now they were getting slowly hammered—all except Dinah, who finally gave into wine, but only one cup—while the sun started thinking about putting itself to bed for the night. They'd missed the final bonfire at camp, but maybe this was better. In fact, yes, she was glad Patrick hadn't come on time. Everything this week had been so complicated and emotional and intense, and doubtless the final bonfire would be also. It felt wonderful to kick back with girlfriends and talk.

"Okay, who wants to play Truth or Dare? I played it with Tom, my first husband, on our first date, and let me tell you, things got pretty crazy." Dinah shook her head and made *mm-mm* noises that had Cindy imagining scenarios she didn't want to be imagining.

"Truth or Dare?" Ann snorted. "You have got to be kidding me."

"What? It's fun."

"Forget it."

"Okay, okay. Then . . . " She scooched closer into the circle. "If you promise not to let anybody else hear this, I will tell you a fabulous secret."

Cindy leaned closer in spite of herself. Even Martha looked interested. Ann rolled her eyes.

"You all promise?"

"Yes, we promise. What is it?" Even though Cindy figured it was probably something embarrassing about one of Dinah's husbands, she couldn't help being curious.

"I promise." Martha held her glass of wine as if it was fine champagne, delicately, with her pinky sticking out. The alcohol had made her features flushed, and she looked almost pretty.

Cindy felt a rush of unexpected affection. Maybe it was just the wine, but she hoped Martha could be happy now that her cheating man had died. She hoped Martha could find someone who treated her better.

Ann was lucky to have found a guy already, though Cindy wouldn't have expected her to hook up with a fisherman. She figured Ann would need the high-powered type. Cindy didn't believe for a second that it was platonic. They'd probably be having wild sex all over the place. Dinah would find someone new too, probably in less than a week.

And Cindy would go back to Kevin.

"Yes, yes, okay, I promise, cross my heart and hope to die, stick a needle in my eye, etcetera. Now tell us." Ann made a sound of disgust, obviously wanting this over as soon as possible.

"Well . . . " Dinah pushed her cup in among the pebbles and clapped her hands. "Guess what?"

"Dinah."

"Okay, okay, okay." She slapped both hands palm down onto her thighs. "You know how Patrick said he was gay? Well he's not."

All of a sudden things got much quieter around the fire.

"You know how I know?"

Oh God, please no. The wine started to pound unpleasantly in Cindy's head. She was about to go back to her husband. This was the last thing she needed. Who had found out? Who had told? Not Patrick, surely. Had someone seen her go into his cabin? Or come out? Or seen the two of them holding hands down on the rocks in that awful fog?

"How?" Martha asked sadly in a gentle voice that would have made Betsy proud of her.

"I slept with him."

Cindy gasped. Ann put her hand over her mouth, so she probably gasped too, but Cindy didn't hear it because her own was so loud. Martha looked resigned.

"*You* slept with him?" The words came out of her mouth without thinking. She felt as if she were back on the bed at home, clutching Patty's panties, missing Max and waiting for the emotions to hit, like someone tied to the rails listening to the train whistle blow.

"Uh-huh. He was incredible too." Dinah was obviously delighted at the sensation she was causing in her listeners. She just, as usual, had no idea what the sensations were.

Cindy drained the rest of her wine. "Oh my God."

"What? Why does everyone looks so upset? What is it?"

Cindy looked at Ann, and found Ann looking at Cindy with a very odd expression on her face. Then, as if she'd figured something out, her eyes widened. Her mouth dropped. "No way."

"Yes, I did. I told you," Dinah spluttered. "Why are you looking at Cindy?"

Ann finished her cup of wine and reached for the bottle. "Me too."

"Oh my God." Cindy held her cup out and let Ann fill it after hers. "Oh my God."

294 Isabel Sharpe

"Me too what? Oh my God what? Would someone tell me what the heck is going on here? You can't possibly be that shocked. There is nothing wrong with consenting adults."

"Dinah." Ann held her cup out like a toast. "Patrick and I consented too."

Dinah's turn to gasp.

"And me." Cindy took a big gulp of wine and realized it was a bad idea to drink right now. "We consented."

This time Dinah's gasp nearly choked her, and Cindy pounded her on the back to get her to stop coughing. "*All* of you?"

The three women turn to look at Martha.

Martha raised an eyebrow. "Do I look like an idiot?"

Ann spit out her wine in a burst of laughter that seemed to pour out of her like sickness. Dinah looked utterly bewildered. Cindy did not find any of this funny. How many times would she give herself to a man believing in something as rare and beautiful as love, and find out he'd just been getting his rocks off as often as he could with as many women as possible? Was that all they were good for?

"I don't think this is funny." She got up on her feet, and realized that loose pebbles were not terrific for balancing. "I don't think this is funny at all. I hate men. I'm not sleeping with Patrick ever again. I'm not even going back to Kevin. I'm going to become a nun with Dinah, like in *The Sound of Music*."

Ann laughed harder, and Cindy found herself struggling with giggles, even as her own passion and strength frightened her. "Except that when a rich handsome widower shows up needing a governess for his seven kids, I'm going to tell him to do his own work for a change, and then I'm going to kick him where it counts."

Ann toppled over, clutching her stomach, gasping for air. Cindy understood how Ann's laughter could have come out like sickness, because she couldn't stop laughing either, and at the same time she felt as if she were throwing up every angry feeling she'd ever had.

And there had been a lot of them.

"Are you serious about Kevin?" Martha wiped a tear away from her eye, and Cindy realized she'd been laughing too, and was sorry she missed it, because she didn't think Martha laughed very often. "You're not going back?"

Cindy raised her glass unsteadily. "No. I'm not going back. Screw them all."

She hadn't been serious, not really, but when she said the words, they suddenly rang something deep and true inside her. Not go back? Not go back to the shame and the boredom and the humiliation, waiting for Kevin to do this to her again? He would. He couldn't help himself any more than Patrick probably could. But where else was there to go?

Her cabin-mates cheered, and Cindy laughed again, while tears ran down her cheeks, but not from being happy. If she didn't go, her daughter would hate her. Kevin would hate her. She'd be single-handedly disappointing everyone. Again.

But maybe this time she wouldn't be disappointing herself.

"Getting serious now, ladies, I don't see how Betsy could have allowed this to go on." Dinah planted her hands on her hips. "She saw through everyone else in the whole place. She worked with Patrick closely every day."

"Everyone has a blind spot. Everyone sees what they want to see sometimes." Martha finished her wine and put the cup back in the basket. "I bet Patrick reminded her of her son."

Even Ann's laughter had died. "I bet that's it."

Cindy's heart turned over. Poor Betsy. She'd be horrified when she found out Patrick had—

The faint noise of a motor, growing gradually louder. The women turned, exchanged glances. Cindy ran down to the water's edge, peered out into the bay until the boat came into view.

Patrick.

She ran back to the women, shaking, out of breath. "It's him. What do we do?"

For once, confident in-control Ann looked blank. "We could . . . God, I don't know."

"Maybe see what he has to say?" Martha did not look as if she thought this was a good idea, even though it was her suggestion.

"Maybe pretend we didn't find out . . . " Cindy knew that wouldn't fly, but it would certainly be easier on everyone.

"Well, I don't know about you three, but I'm going to bust his skinny gay ass." Dinah got up, brushed pebbles and sand off her lemon yellow jogging suit, pushed up her sleeves, and walked down to the shore to meet Patrick.

Of course the rest of them followed her. Cindy wasn't sure she wanted to see, but then who could resist watching a professional ball buster in action?

"Ahoy there, ladies." Patrick waved over his head, grinning his charming grin. "Sorry about being late. Had a little issue back at camp."

"Probably six or eight other women found out they had something in common," Ann murmured.

Cindy winced, but it didn't hurt as badly as when she first found out. Still, as she watched Patrick striding toward them, then stopping to tie up the boat at a large metal ring submerged on the beach, her heart still gave a little flip. Maybe that was her problem, she had so much trouble letting go of what she wanted to believe about people. Maybe this was where expecting the positive got her in trouble.

"It's okay. We found things to eat, and . . . well, we were okay." Cindy didn't know why she was trying to make it better for him. Why did she always do that? He didn't deserve it.

"Good. Good for you." Patrick beamed at the four of them. "That's what I like to see, your resourcefulness in action. No helpless females here."

He was standing in front of them now, looking from face to face. His confident smile slipped a little. "So. Ready to go back?"

"You have a lot to answer for, Mr. Homosexual." Dinah lunged forward and poked him viciously in the chest.

Patrick stepped back and held his hand out to the side. He stepped back again, starting to look wary. "What do you mean?"

"You know exactly what the hell we mean. You had your dick in so many of us, you probably can't remember which is which."

"Whoa. Hey. *Dinah*. I certainly do know who is who."

"How could you do this, you bastard?" Ann stepped up next to Dinah, the two of them reminding Cindy of the girl bullies at her junior high. Cindy stepped up next to them.

"You knew we were all vulnerable." She tried to sound as angry and tough as Dinah and Ann, but she just sounded hurt and bewildered. There was only so much she could change.

"Look." Patrick pointed his finger angrily at each of them. "I gave each of you something you desperately needed. So don't start acting as if I damaged you somehow. Ann, I helped you see how your marriage wasn't what you thought. Martha, I encouraged your spiritual power and showed you love was never a mistake. Cindy, I urged you to leave your husband and follow your heart. Dinah, I told you—"

"You *slept* with *all* of us." Dinah gave him a look that put him on a level with dead amoebas.

"Not Martha. She—"

"Wouldn't let you," Martha finished for him.

"I have . . . " He touched his heart. " . . . an infinite capacity for love."

Ann's famous snort resonated. "You have a sexual addiction."

"I bet you never even went to Thailand!" Dinah shouted.

"Or Paris," Ann added. "Croissants? The Eiffel Tower? Please."

Cindy gasped. This was getting really low. Except that instead of defiant, Patrick started to look panicked, then angry. Oh God. He hadn't been to Thailand. Or Paris.

"I bet the gay lover never happened either."

The women were starting to remind Cindy of wolves circling their prey before they moved in for the kill. She wasn't sure if she would defend Patrick or not.

"University of Minnesota?" Even Martha managed to sound scornful. "Bet you're not even in their books."

"Listen, you self-righteous bitches, you think you have

the world's only problems? You come here to this pampered little camp and expect everyone to cater to you? Well I did my best, I offered each of you friendship. And I helped each of you. Right now, I have had one hell of a crappy day, and I don't need you riding my ass on top of it. So just get in the boat and shut the hell up, or I'll leave you here. Get it?"

Dinah scoffed loudly. Ann tossed her head and stuck her hands on her hips. Martha jerked as if he'd struck her, but when Cindy looked at her face, she was smiling a tiny secret smile. "We get it. Let's get into the boat, ladies."

"I'm not letting that horny bastard—"

Martha took Dinah's arm. "Into the boat. How else will we get back?"

Ann and Dinah spluttered, but knew they were beat. Obviously, spending the night on the island was as appealing to them as it was to Cindy.

The women climbed into *Stronglady*. The horny bastard started to move up the beach to untie the boat.

"Wait, Patrick." Martha grabbed Cindy's arm and squeezed hard. "Cindy, weren't you carrying a sweater when we arrived here?"

Cindy opened her mouth to say no, but caught the look on Martha's face and understood what she wanted, even if she had no idea why. "Yes. I did. My yellow one. Uh, sorry."

"It's on the other side, where we ate." Martha looked expectantly at Patrick, who rolled his eyes and threw up his hands.

"Christ. Fine. I'll get it. Wait here." He turned and stalked up the beach.

Cindy frowned at Martha. "Why did I need to leave a sweater on the ocean side?"

"Dinah." Martha smiled, eyes alight, magnetic and power-ful. "Didn't I hear you say that one of your husbands owned a speedboat?"

"That's right. My third husband, Stanley. *Stanley's Dinah*, he called her. He and I used to—"

"Get up there and drive us home."

Dinah stared, probably equally as surprised by Martha's tone as by what she was saying. "But Patrick is—"

"We know." Ann laughed, gave Martha the thumbs-up and scrambled onto the bow. "Start her up. I'll untie the rope."

"Ha! I'm with you." Dinah chuckled, shot out her arms, so her bracelets jangled, sat in the driver's seat, turned on the boat, making the motor roar. "Ready?"

Behind them Patrick shouted. Cindy turned and saw him running toward the shore.

Ann finished untying the line and tossed it into the sea. "Go. Now."

"*Hasta la vista*, baby." Dinah slammed the boat into gear and reversed hard. The boat backed up, Dinah turned ex-pertly, and they roared away from Eagle Rock Island, away from Patrick, wading into the water after them, shouting and flipping them off with both hands.

Dinah let out a warrior whoop, which Ann echoed, fist raised into the wind, hair streaming back. Martha bellowed triumphant laughter. Cindy turned back from watching Patrick and worrying how he was going to make it back to camp. Ahead of them, the ocean was wide and free, the land toward which they were racing glowed in the sun, peaceful and welcoming.

She pumped her fist in the air, then both fists. When she got home to Milwaukee, she would have to make an extra effort to cultivate girlfriends, maybe join a group that had more of a social conscience than the country club, maybe work at a women's shelter or . . . well, she didn't know, but something that would let her feel part of something bigger than her marriage and her house and her husband's world. To give her a better sense of herself without him, and find that thing she might be really good at.

Her excitement rose. Maybe she could work in a bookstore, or a coffee shop. Or a coffee shop in a bookstore. She could buy a cabin like Betsy's up north in Wisconsin. Get a dog, a new Max, to love her unfailingly until death did them part. Start slowly, take baby steps toward independence until she was ready to be out on her own.

No matter what, she wasn't going back to the way things were. None of them was.

Ann started to sing first, off key and thinly, but with spirit. Dinah joined in, then Martha. Cindy stood to get closer to her cabin-mates and joined in as well, opening her throat and letting the song pour out.

I am woman!

A+
AUTHOR
INSIGHTS,
EXTRAS, &
MORE...

FROM
**ISABEL
SHARPE**
AND
AVON A

Interview with Author Isabel Sharpe

Why did you set *As Good As It Got* on the coast of Maine?

First, because I've had a lifelong love affair with the state. In the 1950s my grandfather bought twenty-two acres of forest with a house right on the ocean for $1,000. I've gone there every summer of my life, including when I was four months old, except three: one when my family was in Europe, one when I got married, and one when my first son was born in late July.

Second, I'm not into woo-woo psychology much, but I really do believe the place has a healing quality. I know I'm at my most serene when I'm there, and because that part of the coast is still so unspoiled (knocking all the wood I can reach), the b.s. of life is cut away, and you feel somehow that you can't be anyone but who you really are. The lack of the usual distractions (computer games or e-mail, depending on which member of my family you're talking to) means you have plenty of time to focus on what's important. All that natural beauty is very uplifting too.

The first few days I'm there, I'm always still in "accomplish" mode, scheduling and planning my time, but it isn't long before spending a couple of hours sitting on a rock watching the water seems like plenty to do. Maybe I'm overromanticizing it, but I've been all over the world and I've never found anywhere like it. Plenty of places with more dramatic beauty, plenty of places more exotic and luxurious, but its rugged charm is unmatched. Obviously I'm biased, but that's what I think!

Besides the natural beauty, what makes the place special?

The natural beauty is the obvious answer. But there's also a clarity and lightness of air I've never known anywhere else, especially not in New Jersey where I grew up. I certainly talk about that a good deal in the book. It's so remarkable. When I arrive every year, the first thing I do when I step out of the car is take a huge long breath. The smells are like a good wine, layered and changing all the time.

In addition, we don't have electricity or phone service down at the end of our peninsula. Cell phones have changed that, but we use them only to call out, and only rarely. Without electricity you can't disappear into electronic games or television. We spend evenings sitting out on the screened porch watching the sunset, then watching the darkness gather and the bats flap around, and we talk and talk and talk. My kids play board games and card games and old-fashioned games like pickup sticks. We all get more exercise without even trying, and a lot more togetherness than we manage at home.

Not to mention there's kayaking and hiking, and if it's really hot (which it rarely is, another thing I love about it), we go "swimming," which consists of wading in thigh-deep, while you shiver and complain, then dipping yourself to the shoulders and coming up as fast as possible, squealing. I think the most I've ever really swum is five or six doggy paddle strokes. But the cold water is what makes the lobster so good. I won't eat it anywhere else. It doesn't come close.

You had a fun scene with Ann in a lobster boat. Have you been on one?

Not since I was a girl. I researched the process to refresh my memory and find out what had changed since then, and a wonderful man from the Maine Department of Natural Resources,

Keith Fougere, answered questions about lobster fishing and licensing. He was incredibly patient and helpful and I'm very grateful to him. Maine has done fabulous things to conserve the lobster supply, and the government and fishermen all participate willingly because they know they have to keep the population healthy. All conservation efforts should work that well.

Have you set other books in Maine?

The first book I ever wrote (which deservedly won't ever be published) was set in Maine, a romance with mild suspense. I also wrote a romantic comedy for Harlequin called *Tryst of Fate* which came out in July 2001. I'm sure I'll write more. I have such an emotional connection to the place. And did I mention the air?

Why don't you live there?

Good question. I am in Milwaukee now because that's how life turned out. But I hope to move to southern Maine when my kids leave home, maybe Portland, so I'll be closer to our property. The house there isn't insulated and the location is too isolated for this city girl to manage year-round, but I'd love to be able to escape there more often than once a year. The idea of spending a whole summer writing a book with a view of the ocean is tremendously appealing.

On to the characters. I have to ask, did Martha have a relationship with the senator or was it all in her mind?

I left that deliberately vague, because the whole book is about the fact that the quality of relationships exists mostly in our minds. There are very few facts involved, and a whole lot of interpretation. All three women come to see the romantic relationships they've spent their adult lives viewing in one way, in quite another. Martha's "What really happened?" relationship with Eldon symbolizes that. But for people who love concrete answers, in my mind their relationship before Eldon met Bianca and started a political career was real. And he probably "visited" her, shall we say, discreetly, a few times. But for him, their interactions had nothing like the import she projected onto them. I see him as a pretty selfish user, though no doubt he had a tender spot for Martha. His wife was undoubtedly not as bad as Martha saw her, but no sweetheart either.

Most of the men come off pretty badly in this book.

I'm fascinated with relationships. I love writing love stories, but I'm also interested in the darker, more dysfunctional ties as well, and you can't explore those much in the romance genre where I got my start in this business. I also love telling stories of people overcoming obstacles (which when you think about it, is what every book is about, right?). And I feel more comfortable writing women than men. So in order for women to have obstacles to overcome, given that I'm an author who loves writing about relationships, it makes sense I'd have my female characters emerging from bad ones. I don't have it in for men. Look at Clive! He's wonderful.

Tell us more about Patrick.

Patrick is modeled on a man I knew who was a compulsive liar. A charming, energetic, articulate, incredibly compelling person. Took me a while to catch on because I tend to be trusting, but once I did, I was equally fascinated and repulsed. When I challenged him, he turned on me the way Patrick does when the women challenge him.

He has a relatively minor role in this book, but someday I'd like to focus harder on a character like that because it's an interesting though disturbing phenomenon. Very eerie and disorienting when you start realizing you've been shoveled many loadfuls of prime quality b.s. from someone who appeared to have the world on a string.

What about erotomania?

That is a syndrome that actually exists, and boy, talk about disturbing. These people are absolutely convinced that celebrities of one type or another are madly in love with them, and nothing anyone says can convince them otherwise. Apparently they can make life truly miserable for their targets. Luckily it's often a symptom of some underlying treatable condition and medication can help. That research was really interesting.

Do Ann and Clive get together after the book ends?

Of course! They get married and live happily ever after, don't you think? I'm sure they have successful careers in a big city, probably Boston, but visit Maine often. How about they buy an island together? I also imagine that Cindy leaves her husband and works at a bookstore that she eventually takes over and manages if not owns outright. She also marries someone wonderful who adores her forever. And Martha must become a famous storyteller, performing all over the country for devoted fans. I think she should meet Mr. Really Right someday too.

I'm a sucker for happy endings, in case you didn't notice.

Isabel

www.IsabelSharpe.com

ISABEL SHARPE was not born pen-in-hand like so many of her fellow authors. After she quit work in 1994 to stay home with her first-born son and nearly went out of her mind, she started writing. Yes, she was the clichéd bored housewife writing romance, but it was either that cliché or seduce the mailman, and her mailman was unattractive. After more than twenty novels for Harlequin and the exciting new direction of women-focused stories for Avon Books, Isabel admits her new mailman is gorgeous, but she's still happy with her choice.